The

Book 2 of Enchena

K. S. Marsden

K. S. M

Printed by CreateSpace, an Amazon.com Company

Cover art by Jatin775

Available from Amazon.com and other book stores

ISBN-13: 978-1540691842
ISBN-10: 1540691845
ASIN: B01NBE62P1

I would like to thank everyone who has contributed to the Enchena series. To my editor, Lesley, who continues to make sense of my random scribblings.

To my beta readers, Wilmar Luna (author of Silver Ninja); Matthew R. Bell (author of Fear of God); and Jeni. You guys continue to be my source of common sense, and make Enchena real for everyone else.

To all my readers that have contacted me, your support and kind words have been priceless!

And now onto the concluding part of the story of
The Lost Soul.

One

A shadow flew overhead, blocking the sun. She looked up, her eyes fixed on the creature; her limbs locked in fear.

The creature flew across the valley, only banking to turn as it reached the wall of trees, its scales glinting in the sunlight. It beat its huge red wings to balance as it lowered its enormous body to the ground.

On land the beast started to walk, ungainly, compared to how sleek it had glided in the sky. It turned towards the only other living thing in the valley, its awkward gait covering the gap in no time. As it loomed closer, she staggered back, fully aware that she could never outrun this creature.

Something broke underfoot and she felt an excruciating pain pierce her ankle. She finally tore her gaze away from the monster and looked to the ground. It was littered with arrows, amongst the burnt remains of shelters. Smouldering wooden poles and ash fell away to leave the bare bones of the buildings.

Further on, there were glints of metal, scattered on a field of blackness. It almost looked like a slew of scorched bodies littering the valley.

Her back was becoming uncomfortably warm, and she turned to see the creature standing beside her, so tall that its chest hovered by her head like a rumbling furnace, fixing its fierce gaze on her. A guttural sound started in its chest and reverberated up its throat, until she realised that it was growling at her.

"It wasn't my fault, I couldn't do anything!" She pleaded, tilting her head back until her neck hurt, to try and meet the creature's eye.

Her words did nothing to calm the beast, as it opened its jaw to roar, a sound emerged that made her cower and cover her ears.

Panicking, she ran, not caring where, as long as it was away. She could hear the creature moving behind her, its leathery wings giving a deafening crack as they opened.

Her foot caught in a half-burnt belt and she fell to the ash-covered ground. "It wasn't my fault." She pleaded, as the creature stepped slowly and purposefully towards her.

It took a deep breath, and hot air radiated from its open mouth, ready to unleash the furnace within.

"Minaeri, forgive me."

Fire, hot flames engulfed her-

Jemma woke with a start. Sweat was pouring off her skin as she struggled to breathe. Despite being in the middle of a heatwave, she had managed to wrap her duvet around herself in her sleep.

She tossed it away and lay, star-fished on her bed for a few moments, before checking the time. Not even 10am, and the hot sun was already beating against the blinds.

"No wonder I'm dreaming about dragons and fire." She muttered.

Unable to stand the stifling heat any longer, she grabbed her towel and headed to the bathroom, keen for a nice, cold shower. Showers always helped her wake up, and remove the last traces of a dream.

Jemma sighed as the cold water sluiced over her, weird dreams were nothing new to her, and it wasn't the first to veer towards violence and death. She did wonder what that said about her poor subconscious.

Finally, as she cooled down, she shut off the shower. The dragon was definitely new, she hoped that it wouldn't reappear in any future dreams, it had been... terrifying.

Jemma towel dried her ginger hair, glancing in the bathroom mirror as one question plagued her. "Who is Minaeri?" She muttered to herself again. Jemma was convinced that it was a person, one that was mentioned in many of her dreams over the last six months. In a fit of frustration, Jemma had tried to Google the name, to try and find out who it was and why they were featuring in her dreams. There was nothing in the wide expanse of the internet that offered an answer. Jemma was just going to have to mark it down to her own wonderful imagination. She snorted at the idea and finished getting ready for the day.

When she made her way downstairs, Jemma ignored her mum's pointed look at her watch. Sure, it was after ten o'clock, but what did that matter – it was the summer holidays, time lost all meaning. She was pretty sure that she wasn't the only fifteen-year-old enjoying the lie-ins summer promised. After the six-week holidays, it would be back to early mornings and the stress of the final year of school.

"You look tired, you weren't on Facebook all night again, were you?" Her mum asked, taking in the tell-tale dark eyes.

Jemma yawned and pushed back a lock of ginger hair that threatened to fall into her cereal bowl. "No, just didn't sleep well."

"More dreams?" Her mum asked with a vague interest, turning back to her newspaper.

With a mouthful of cornflakes, Jemma grunted.

"Y'know, you should write them down." Her mum said for the umpteenth time. "What happened to that dream diary Nora got you, anyway? They might mean something."

Jemma rolled her eyes. Most of her dreams seemed pretty violent and obvious. Except the one where David Tennant was a pirate pillaging Venice – that one she was still working out.

The rest of the morning dragged by and Jemma checked her phone again, but there were no new messages. The only people that were likely to text her were her best friends, Nora and Amanda. Unfortunately, they were in Florida, and were probably still in bed, Jemma had to admit as she worked out the time difference.

A trip to Disney World had been Nora's parents' idea, and they'd kindly invited Amanda and Jemma, so it was hard for her to be totally jealous. Jemma knew her mum regretted not being able to afford the trip, so she tried to keep her grumbling to a minimum. Most of the time.

As the afternoon rolled in, her mum was in the main room, ironing work uniforms, the telly blaring in the background.

"…the teenagers have been missing for over a year with no trace…"

Jemma hovered, watching as the local news showed the same old CCTV clip of two kids leaving school, followed by their photos. They had both gone to Jemma's high school, although they'd been a couple of years above her. She couldn't remember the girl, but she'd seen the boy – David had been the school's star rugby player, and all the girls agreed that he was very lookable.

Jemma remembered when they had first disappeared, everyone had been uneasy, not knowing what to think. The police had turned up occasionally, their presence giving no firm answers, as they drifted between investigating the possible absconding teens; abduction; or even murder.

As the days turned into months, optimism at finding them faded. The people closest to them became depressed about not knowing whether to grieve for them or not, but the atmosphere of the school moved on and carried on with life. It sounded a little bit cruel, but they had to put the bad things behind them.

It didn't stop a shiver running up Jemma's spine as she saw their faces on the TV.

Jemma sighed and dropped down on the sofa, claiming the remote and changing the channel.

"Hey, I was watching that." Her mum protested as she adjusted the shirt on her ironing board.

"Why, it's not like you can help." Jemma replied, continuing to flick through the channels. So many channels, all full of rubbish. She left it on a daytime property programme and gave up.

Her mum frowned at her daughter's attitude, but let it slide. "Jemma, it's a gorgeous, sunny day. Why the hell aren't you outside?"

Jemma sighed, "Because I'll burn to a crisp."

9

It was a sorry fact that Jemma had inherited two things from her very absent dad – red hair and pale skin. Because of that jerk, she was cursed to never have a tan. No, she just got more freckles and went lobster red, before going white again. Luckily, they didn't have too many sunny days in Leeds – overcast or raining was the norm, even in summer.

Jemma often wished her dad had been olive-skinned and dark-haired. Oh, and that he hadn't been a cheating toe rag that had run off with one of her mum's best friends when Jemma was a toddler.

"Then keep to the bloody shadows." Her mum replied, tutting. "Fresh air will do you good. Surely you've got more friends than Nora and Amanda to hang out with?"

Jemma made a non-committal sound. There were people that she knew, but no one that she wanted to make the effort to meet up with. She fidgeted with her mobile, trying to ignore how much she was missing her best friends. Eventually Jemma sighed and stood up – her mum would only keep nagging until she got her way.

"Make sure you're home by half-five, I'm doing dinner early tonight."

Jemma looked at her mum and the half-ironed uniform, and the reason clicked. Her mum was doing her first night shift at the hospital tonight. As a nurse, she had always done day shifts, but the night shift paid better, and Jemma was old enough to stay home alone now.

Nothing had been said, but Jemma knew that her mum felt guilty about their financially-limited lives. Not to mention that the extra expense of college and university hovered in the future.

"Are you sure you'll be alright?" Her mum asked for the umpteenth time. "I can ask your Auntie Rose if you can stay at hers."

Jemma rolled her eyes. She could just imagine the boost of confidence her babysitting clients would feel, if they found out that Jemma couldn't be left alone at night. "I'll be fine."

"OK, just make sure you call Rose if you need her." Her mum compromised, then pointed the iron at her. "Now scoot."

Jemma ducked the spray of water and laughed at the immature attack. "I'm going, I'm going." She said, throwing her hands up in defeat.

Two

As soon as she opened the front door of the terraced house her mum rented, Jemma felt the hot air envelop her. It was so stifling she struggled to breathe. Even in her trendy short-shorts and vest top, Jemma could feel sweat start to prickle her skin. Great, she could wander around as the sweaty loser with no friends.

Jemma put on her fake Dior sunglasses and locked the front door. She jogged down the steps from the row of grey-brick houses, and headed across to the nearest park. For some reason, she had an intense desire to be around something green, which had nothing to do with her dreams of valleys and forests, and all to do with proving that she wasn't in a desert right now. Right?

Before she even reached the park, the sound of kids playing drifted by. The green field; the playground; and most importantly the ice cream van, were irresistible, drawing young children in from all over the surrounding area.

Jemma didn't mind kids all that much, they could be fun to hang out with, and they were why she enjoyed her babysitting jobs so much.

But en masse, they got pretty annoying. There would always be that one spoilt kid that ruined the harmony of the communal playground; or the one obnoxious parent that wasn't happy unless they were interfering with everything.

Jemma walked past the flattest part of the field that had been turned into a makeshift football pitch. She glanced at the boys curiously, but carried on walking when she realised that the oldest was no more than thirteen years old.

There was nobody her age in the park. Jemma wondered what the big secret was – how often had she gone to school on a Monday and heard her classmates' stories of adventures and parties? She was clearly missing some sort of memo that went round to all the other fifteen year olds.

She sighed and traipsed up the hill towards the one thing that could cheer her up. Ice-cream.

After queueing for what felt like an hour, while mums juggled toddlers to find the right change, and children struggled to make the important choice of what colour ice pop they wanted; Jemma walked away with her prize. She unwrapped her cornetto, trying not to be too annoyed at the redness that was already spreading across her arms and shoulders, thanks to queueing in the sun for so long. She should try and get some cover for a while, to let her pale skin rest.

Jemma supposed the cool thing to do would be to jump on a bus to the Trinity Shopping Centre, but she couldn't really face the hot and stuffy bus ride, and crowded shops. Jemma had her kindle in her bag and wanted nothing more than to curl up somewhere quiet and cool with it. Jemma licked her ice cream and knew exactly where to go.

*****

St Jude's Way had been marked for demolition months ago, but the project had been delayed multiple times. Jemma assumed it was legalities and council screw-ups that meant the street of old pit housing was still standing. Some of the more imaginative kids said that the project was cursed by the witch that still lived there. Others had heard rumours that DIY SOS had first refusal at regenerating the area, and the BBC was dragging its heels.

Whatever the reason, the street of derelict houses lay empty and silent. Jemma's friends refused to go anywhere near the road; both Nora and Amanda said that it gave them a bad vibe. It wasn't just them either, everybody else seemed to steer clear. It seemed like the ideal location for squatters or druggies, but Jemma had never seen any evidence of them.

Whatever was scaring the rest of the population obviously wasn't bothering Jemma. She never felt anything except safe, and a strange sense of belonging. Further proof that her subconscious must be wonky.

Jemma glanced towards the one occupied house. An old woman had lived there for as long as Jemma could remember; she had refused to move out, ignoring the money offered for her little house. There were lots of rumours about the old woman – some called her a witch; others treated her as the monster in the shadows, something to scare the young kids.

Jemma knew that it was all nonsense, but years of ingrained fear made her wary. She stayed at the far end of the street, as far from the old woman's house as possible.

She made her way up to one of the shady porches, and sat down on the cracked step. Jemma pulled out her kindle and opened the book she was currently reading. She always liked to read fantasy stories; the magic and the adventure so different to life here. It was something Jemma could immerse herself in and be distracted for a few hours.

Jemma finished her ice-cream, and her attention locked onto the digital page.

Seated in the pleasant shade of the porch, time drifted by, and Jemma hardly noticed the shadows shift as the sun moved across the sky.

A flutter of wings broke Jemma's concentration. Jemma looked up to see a bird, no bigger than a pigeon, but brightly coloured. It had a red breast and delicate blue-grey wings. It…

Jemma rubbed her eyes… she wasn't too familiar with birds, but she'd seen enough David Attenborough programmes to know that it was a bird of prey; and that it was definitely out of place here.

The bird turned its beady eye onto Jemma, and bobbed its head expectantly.

"You alright, little guy?" Jemma asked softly, trying not to scare it. She winced as she moved, her bottom felt numb from sitting on the hard step.

The little bird gave out a sharp chirruping squawk and shifted on the fence. Jemma noticed a small brown pouch tied to its leg. It didn't look big, or heavy enough to be a burden. If Jemma didn't know any better, it looked as if it could carry a message; but surely nobody had used messenger birds for fifty years or more.

"But that means you must belong to someone." Jemma said out loud. If it was a tame pet, that would explain why the bird wasn't scared of her. Jemma stood up and moved towards it.

With a flutter of wings it moved out of reach, and Jemma berated herself for chasing it off… only it stopped at the gate and perched again, looking back at Jemma expectantly.

Jemma eyed it warily, before taking a step closer. The bird took flight again and stopped at the fence next door.

"Seriously, if you want me to help, then staying still would be good right now." She said, knowing how daft she must appear for chiding a bird. She walked towards it, for the bird to fly a little further down the street. Jemma stopped and put her hands on her hips; it reminded her of the game over-excited dogs sometimes play. Either that or it wanted her to follow.

Jemma shrugged, giving up. "Fine, let's pretend this is totally normal. I'm following a bird. Lead on, feather brain."

The bird snapped its very sharp-looking bill at Jemma, then continued to fly in short spurts down St Jude's Way.

The bird stopped at another gate, its talons scraping loose the flaking paint. It looked back at Jemma with meaningful eyes, then flew through an open door.

Jemma halted in her stride. In a street full of boarded and vacant houses, the bird had to fly into the one building that was still a home. Not that you could tell from the neglected front yard. The small patch of grass was overgrown and shrivelled from the prolonged heat.

Jemma stood, her hand gripping tightly onto the wooden gatepost. The door had been left open, perhaps by mistake, or to let some air in. Jemma could only guess the reason, but as she eyed the dark hall within, her heart began to race and sweat rand down the back of her neck.

Trespassing was not on Jemma's agenda today, and not even her crazy delusions that the bright-coloured bird was leading her, would make her go inside. She should go home, she could help her mum with dinner; then have a quiet night watching movies and forgetting all about this odd episode. But even as the thoughts ran through Jemma's mind, she couldn't turn away. And when her feet moved, they took her closer to the house.

Jemma had a flash of déjà vu. She had been here before, she was sure of it. She knew this front yard, but it had been raining last time. Goosebumps ran up her arms as her skin remembered the cold, lashing rain that she had been running through, running into this house...

Jemma blinked and tried to snap out of it. That was weird. As real as it felt, Jemma was positive that it wasn't one of her actual memories. Perhaps it was from an unremembered dream; it seemed a rather random thing to dream of, but not odd compared to Jemma's usual dreams.

Jemma took a deep breath and stepped towards the familiar doorway. She hesitated at the threshold, before a powerful pull at her core made her trip into the hallway.

Jemma thought her heart was about to burst, her pulse thudded in her ears, the only sound in this silent house. Her eyes took a minute to adapt to the poor light. The sunlight behind her made the small hall look dark and dingy, making shadows of the corners. Heavy curtains had been pulled across every window, with only trickles of light seeping through to illuminate the dust that floated idly about. Ahead of her, Jemma could see a dark staircase leading to an equally dark landing. The brief thought that nothing would make her go up there crossed her mind, as she turned instead to a door that was slightly ajar. She

17

reached out for the handle and pressed firmly on the cool metal, the door slid open slowly across an old, thick carpet.

Jemma held her breath as she stepped into another dark room, all the curtains were pulled shut with very little light escaping into the house. Her eyes strained and she could make out the shape of an overstuffed armchair and settee. The air was hot and heavy with a stale smell that reminded her of old tea and cigarettes. With the need to see, to stop the feeling of suffocation that threatened her; Jemma flicked open a heavy curtain and bright sunlight streamed through the dirty laces into the living room. Jemma took a deep breath, trying to calm her racing pulse. What was she doing here, trespassing? Where was the old woman?

The room looked like it had been frozen in time, with wallpaper suited for the sixties. There was an old-fashioned gas fire, with a rickety fireguard in front of it. On the mantelpiece above the fireplace, there were old photos. A snapshot of a person's life, with a black-and-white wedding picture; a grainy colour photo of an old man; and a slightly worn photo of a handsome man in a soldier's uniform.

Jemma turned to the sofa, to see a pale and very still old woman. Her first thought was that the old woman must be dead, sending a spike of fear through her heart. Jemma stepped closer, suddenly struggling to remember a single piece of First Aid her mother had trained her in.

"Hello." Jemma's voice came out as in a strangled whisper; she coughed and tried again. "Hello, can you hear me?"

The old woman gave a snort, her eyes rolled beneath her blue-veined lids, before slowly cracking open to look at Jemma with an accusing gaze.

Jemma was so relieved that the woman was alive that it took Jemma a few moments to realise that she was trespassing.

"Who are you? What are you doing in my house?" The old woman snapped, shifting her aching bones to sit more upright. Her gnarled fingers grabbed the walking stick propped up against the seat, tilting it up at the stranger.

"Sorry, I didn't mean to barge in. The door was open, and… and this is going to sound strange, but I was following…" She broke off, biting her lip. "There was a bird that flew in. I'm sorry, I shouldn't have…"

The old woman reluctantly lowered her stick, her grey eyes wary and more than a little confused. "You came into this house?"

Jemma hesitated, a little thrown that her first questions hadn't been about the bird. "Yes, I'm sorry."

The old woman broke into a coughing fit, and leant forward, reaching for a glass on the low table. Jemma stepped closer and picked the glass up, quickly handing it over. The old woman patted her hand in thanks, taking a sip of the water.

"You came into this house…" The old woman repeated, musing over the idea. At Jemma's confused look, she waved a hand to dismiss it. "Most people avoid it, like the plague. Anyone would think this place is cursed."

Jemma didn't understand the ghost of a smile that crossed the old woman's lips, but didn't have time to think about it when a familiar feathered friend flew in and perched on the sofa.

"Aye, it's you." The old woman said, eyeing the bird, hardly surprised that it was there.

"Is he yours?" Jemma asked, as the bird squawked and tilted its head.

"Humph, no, though he likes to make himself at home. He's from… well, another place." The old woman turned her head and saw the pouch strapped to his leg. "Danu's got you playing messenger again?"

Jemma watched as the woman untied the little leather pouch; she didn't recognise the name – Danu? The mystery owner of the bird?

The old woman pulled out a piece of paper that was folded numerous times. Her eyes scanned it, then she stopped and looked up to Jemma. "The bird brought you? Did he bring you?"

Jemma was taken aback by the harshness of her voice. "Yes, I already told you."

"And you came into my house." The old woman repeated. "If you have any sense, girl, you will go home now and forget all that has happened."

"I… I don't understand." Jemma murmured.

"Now why doesn't that surprise me." The old woman turned to the bird. "She can't be the right one, she hasn't an inkling of insight."

The bird ruffled its feathers, and turned its huge eyes towards Jemma expectantly.

"I'm sorry, I think I'm missing something." Jemma replied, starting to feel frustrated by the old woman's nonsense. Was she not all there?

The old woman held out the piece of paper, and when Jemma didn't immediately take it, she shook it impatiently.

20

Jemma took the paper reluctantly. It was rough to the touch and discoloured. It had an elegant script on it that was a little worse for wear after the incessant folding.

Danu, Erudite of Enchena and priest of Minaeri.
To the honourable portal guard,
Salutations.
The war between the Gardyn and the crown will soon start again, the time for the return of the Gardyn Lady is nigh. By my art, I have yet seen this war turn against the Gardyn in disastrous fashion. It is time to bring another of your noble kind to play a part in guiding the future of Enchena.
Enclosed is a necklace containing the 'Initiatus' crystal.
My trust is with you, Elisabeth.

Jemma read the letter twice, not being able to make any sense of the thing. Someone – the Gardyn – was in trouble, and they were going to be helped by an old woman and a cute little bird?

The word Enchena struck a chord with her, though. Jemma was sure that she knew it, a place, but her memory was hazy. Had she gone there as a child? And Minaeri, written on the paper, was surely the same name that had haunted her dreams of late.

She slowly returned her gaze to the old woman. "Are you Elisabeth? The portal guard? Is that code for something?"

"You can call me Gran, like the last one." The old woman said, with a hint of bitterness in her voice. "What is your name, child?"

"Jemma McKinley. What other one?" Jemma asked. "What does all this actually mean, Gran?"

21

"It means that people need help." Gran answered, taking another sip of water. "Jemma, do you believe in other worlds?"

Jemma shrugged, "Maybe: in books, and films. But those aren't real."

"Why shouldn't they be real?" Gran asked, a hard edge to her voice. "Stories always come from somewhere. Other worlds exist, and they inspire so much around us; but people are too clever, they tell themselves that it is only fiction."

Jemma sighed, quickly going back to the idea that Gran wasn't all there. Should she humour her, until she got the chance to leave this house?

Gran could see the doubt cross the girl's face and tutted. People these days seemed to have lost all ability to believe; they all seemed to need proof. Gran pushed herself to her feet, and after a moment correcting her balance, she shuffled past the table and towards the door that led to the dining room and kitchen. "Come with me, girl."

Jemma glanced over her shoulder; she could leave right now, she could just about see the front door. She'd leave and… oh, who was she kidding? She was going to follow Gran into the kitchen. Once she had humoured the old woman, she could pacify her with a nice cup of tea and be on her way, feeling very much the Good Samaritan. Jemma stepped through the doorway and stopped in her stride.

Something very large and unusual caught her eye. Jemma moved forward, sure she must be hallucinating. What other reason could there be for the dense purple and black smoke that took up half the kitchen?

Gran watched her patiently, waiting for the young girl to tear her eyes away from the anomaly. After a few minutes, her patience began to wear thin, and she spoke to snap her out of it. "Is everything alright, dear?"

"W-what is that, Gran?"

"It is the portal I guard." Gran said matter-of-factly. "But you don't believe in that, do you? Not even now, with the evidence in front of your very eyes?"

"It's…" Jemma licked her dry lips. "How can that be real?"

Gran felt a wave of fatigue hit her; she shuffled over to the stool and sat, looking up at Jemma with her tired grey eyes. "It is what it is. A door to the land of Enchena, a world governed by the goddess Minaeri."

Minaeri was a goddess? The nugget of information slowly sunk in. How could Jemma have been dreaming about a goddess from a land she didn't know existed?

Jemma finally looked away from the purple and black portal, and frowned as she noticed the ashen pallor of Gran's skin. "Are you alright?"

"It's just old age; nothing to be done." Gran replied with a bitter smile. "For hundreds of years my family have guarded this portal, it's a little sad to think that it will all end with me."

"Don't you have any family?" Jemma asked quietly.

"I did, once. A husband and a son." Gran answered, wistfully. "My only son, Johnny, was only twenty-six when he died, which is a much worse thing than old age. He'd just been made a lieutenant, and he'd been sent to Ireland to help with the Troubles… It seems that there is no world without war, no existence without strife. My Johnny was always standing up to defend others, he would have had no regrets. Afterwards, there was such

23

a hole in our life... I always said that my husband died of a broken heart. I've had to go on without them for so long now; but I will join them, soon enough."

Jemma felt a twist of discomfort, it seemed wrong that Gran was speaking of her death so calmly. Wanting to change the subject, she asked, "So what is the other place like?"

"Beautiful. Enchena is beautiful, but dangerous. It has been ruled by a long line of tyrants, with the power to raise the dead. Their immortal armies have kept the world in a state of submission." Gran closed her eyes, visualising the world that she had served for so many years. "Minaeri's representative stepped up to save the last rebels from being crushed. She took the Gardyn to a safe haven, but as my esteemed colleague Danu writes, it is time for them to return and overthrow the violent kings."

Jemma paused, trying to make sense of the strange words littered through her answer, "What is going to happen?"

"Well, with any hope, Lady Samantha will lead the Gardyn to victory. She is the only one who can defeat King Hrafn."

Jemma looked back to the portal; now that the shock had worn off, it was actually quite soothing and hypnotic, as the smoke surface swirled and receded. It all sounded very familiar to Jemma, as though she'd read the story somewhere before. Jemma wondered when she had stopped humouring Gran, and had started believing her. "Why are you telling me all this?"

"Lady Samantha cannot do it alone, the Gardyn need all the help they can get." Gran answered, looking pointedly at Jemma.

24

"Me?" Jemma asked, shaking her head. "Um, no, I don't think so. They must be bloody desperate if they need someone like me; I can't fight in a war."

"Watch your language." Gran warned.

"Sorry."

"There are more ways to help than to pick up a sword and fight." Gran countered.

"They fight with swords? Seriously?" Jemma asked, eyes widening.

Gran sighed, feeling that they were getting off topic. "Enchena is not as advanced as our world. They have always been quick to enforce their laws – including one that sentences to death anyone who possesses magic. It has halted the development of any technology that could appear magical."

"Still, why me?" Jemma asked with a shrug. "I'm not special."

"You came into my house."

Jemma sighed at the old woman's repetition. "Great, so you've just been waiting for the first person to walk through the door, and you're going to throw them into some battle? Lucky me."

Gran frowned, her lips growing thinner as she observed the girl. "Are you really so dense to truly think that? This has been decided by fate, by the gods themselves. I wasn't joking when I said the house was cursed, girl. It is spelled to repel people that have no involvement with Enchena; which means you must have felt the call."

"I didn't feel…" Jemma broke off, thinking of the way she had entered against all logic. "I was following your friend's bird." She finished lamely.

"Fine." Gran replied dismissively. "It's not as though you've been having the dreams…"

"You know about my dreams?" Jemma piped up, before she could stop herself.

The old woman smiled, a soft expression that Jemma had not been expecting. "If I may give you some advice, Jemma: trust your dreams. The gods have given them to you for a reason."

"But they don't make sense."

"Not yet." Gran replied, knowingly. "You need to be on Enchenian soil before they will flourish."

Jemma turned and stared at the portal again. "This is insane." She muttered.

"Not to rush you, my dear, but there's a whole world waiting for you." Gran said, tapping her stick on the kitchen floor with a note of impatience.

Jemma took a deep breath, "What do I do?"

Gran held up the little leather pouch and pulled out a necklace. At the end of a thick silver cord, a single small jewel hung, glinting with all the colours under the sun. "This is for you."

Jemma reached out, her fingers brushing the jewel. She took the chain, the necklace heavy in her hand. "Thank you?" Her voice went higher, betraying her question.

"It is an initiatus crystal, although I have no idea how Danu came to possess it. It is very rare, so never take it off." Gran instructed. "It is the only known item that will allow a mortal to pass through the portal unaccompanied by a god."

What do you mean?" Jemma asked, looking at the jewel warily.

"If you were to pass through the portal without the aid of godly powers, your soul would be torn from your body and lost to the void. The initiatus crystal allows the traveller to retain their soul."

"It won't hurt, will it?" Jemma asked nervously.

Gran's silence didn't fill Jemma with confidence. The old woman turned her head and gave a sparse whistle. There was a flash of wings, and the colourful bird flew into the kitchen and landed on the sink drainer.

"Time to go home, my friend." Gran said to the bird, who simply looked calmly back at her. "Jemma, you can follow him through."

"He doesn't need an inis... int... crystal to get through?"

Gran shook her head. "Birds are the messengers of the gods, and their servants. They travel freely. Now, when you get to Enchena, speak to none but Lord Siabhor. Tell him that you are of Lady Samantha's homeland, and that the time for her return has come."

Jemma lifted the silver chain over her head, as she committed Gran's words to memory, the jewel hung low enough to tuck into her vest top. "Is that all? I mean, I only have to pass on that message?" Jemma looked suspiciously towards Gran: she was to be a messenger? Surely crossing the barriers between worlds and getting embroiled in a foreign war was pretty extreme, when the message could simply be tied on the bird's leg just as easily.

"That is the first step. You will work out what to do when you are there. For now, finding Siabhor will be enough of a task." Gran gazed at Jemma, her grey eyes softening. "Your path may be difficult, just remember that you were chosen for this. You were born for something more."

Jemma fiddled with the necklace, and stepped closer to the portal. There was nothing different in the air around the swirling smoke, it was as warm and stale as the rest of the house. "What have I got to lose? Come on, birdbrain."

With a sharp squawk, the bird jumped from its perch and flew into the smoke. Jemma closed her eyes and, taking a deep breath, she stepped...

Three

Jemma felt pain beyond anything she had ever known. A strong wind tore and buffeted her, and a fire ripped through every inch of her body. Jemma's screams were torn from her lips, lost in the void. Her hand tightly grasped the initiatus crystal as though her life depended on it. It could not have lasted more than a few minutes, when Jemma found herself on her hands and knees on rough ground.

Her head span and she felt violently sick, Jemma screwed her eyes shut and took a few careful breaths, trying to keep from herself retching. Had Gran known that it was going to be such a horrible experience? Jemma thought for a moment that taking part in this foreign war couldn't be half as bad as trying to repeat that journey home.

Jemma sat up, finally taking in her surroundings. She was in the middle of a small clearing, surrounded by large trees that limited her view. The sun pierced the leaves, dappling the grassy ground with pools of warmth. Jemma took a deep breath of fresh woodland scent the most refreshing thing she had ever experienced.

"It's all real, I can't believe it!" Jemma said to herself, part of her had been expecting the portal to be an elaborate prank; or that her psychosis would break as she stepped face-first into a wall, instead of a magical doorway.

Jemma pushed herself to her feet, and looked behind her – there was nothing but trees. A wave of panic swept over her; her way home had vanished! A sharp crack sounded across the clearing, claiming Jemma's attention. She turned, her eyes trying to catch any movement.

"Hello?" Her voice came out, barely above a whisper. Jemma cleared her throat and tried again. "Hello, is somebody there?"

"State your name and whether you are Gardyn, or no." A man's voice demanded.

Jemma took a step towards the voice. "My name is Jemma, a friend of the Gardyn. I'm looking for a Lord Siabhor."

There was a rustle as branches parted and two men stepped into the clearing, with arrows on strings, bows taut and ready to let fly. One man looked to be in his mid-thirties, whilst the other was barely twenty years old. They both wore grey-green tunics and trousers that blended well with the wooded area.

The older man lowered the tip of his arrow, pointing it away from the girl. He looked surprised by her presence, slowly taking in her appearance with wide eyes.

"Saxton," the younger man hissed, not lowering his weapon, "she could be lying. She could be a spy."

"She's too young."

"They could be copying the Lady Jillis." The young man argued, not taking his eyes off Jemma. "Don't you think it's suspicious, that we should find a young girl, alone in the middle of the Great Forest?"

The older man sighed, and turned to Jemma. "Where did you come from, Miss? Who sent you?"

"Yeah, because she'll tell the truth." The younger man snorted.

"Angrud, hold your tongue." Saxton snapped.

"You can't believe-"

"I said be quiet." Saxton repeated, holding a hand up and listening intently. "I hear horses. Get to cover, now."

Jemma looked in the same direction as Saxton, but couldn't hear anything above the rich birdsong. She felt someone grab her arm and drag her towards the trees. Jemma fought back, trying to twist her arm free, glaring up at the younger man that dared to manhandle her. There was pressure behind her knee and Jemma lost her balance, falling behind a thick bush.

He lifted a very sharp knife to her face. "Get down now."

"Both of you be quiet." The older man hissed, crouching down next to Jemma and Angrud.

Jemma held her breath, she could hear the thud thud of trotting hooves on the dirt track; and when the riders drew closer she could hear the creak of leather tack.

The horses were drawn to a halt, and some of them snorted and stamped with impatience. Jemma, keeping an eye on Angrud and his knife, leant to one side where a small gap in the foliage allowed her a glimpse of the newcomers. There must have been twenty horses crowding into the clearing; their riders wore black and red uniforms, each wearing a sword at their hip, and many with bows strapped to their saddles.

Some of the riders dismounted, and quickly scouted the area on foot.

"No sign of the Gardyn, Captain Losan." One soldier reported to the man that was in charge.

"Very well, lieutenant. I want men guarding this gate at all times, until I come to relieve you."

Jemma tried in vain to see the Captain, but the shrub blocked him from view. His voice was deep and direct, and it sent a shiver of caution up her spine.

"This is the first time the gate has been active since the Lost Soul's arrival." The Captain continued, and Jemma couldn't miss the stark warning in his voice, aimed at his men. "The Gardyn will probably be drawn to it in their desperation. They must not get control of the gate. Kill anyone who come near, I have no need for prisoners."

Having said his piece, and having no doubt that his men would obey him, the stern Captain moved his horse forward. He circled the gathered men and, with two soldiers for company, he rode back down the forest track at speed.

Jemma eyed the remaining soldiers, who all dismounted and quietly proceeded to set up camp in the clearing. She didn't want to find out if they really would kill her on sight.

Jemma felt someone pinch her elbow, and she turned to see Saxton's gentle brown eyes silently pleading for her to come. At a loss to what else she could possibly do, Jemma nodded, then followed on her hands and knees, crawling after Saxton.

He led away from the soldiers for quite a distance, stopping regularly to check for danger. Eventually he felt that they were far enough away to get back to their feet.

He pressed his fingers to his lips and motioned for Jemma to follow him.

When she glanced behind her, Angrud scowled and waved her on, his knife still firmly fixed to his hand.

Jemma hurried after Saxton, finding the older guy the safer companion. Soon, amidst the woodland sounds, running water could be heard. Jemma realised how thirsty she was, as a stream came into view. She knelt down at the waters' edge and scooped up the cool, fresh water. Her hands were stinging, and Jemma looked at the red scratches on her palms. Her knees were a similar mess, covered with beads of blood.

"Here, let me look at that." Saxton said, holding his hand out to hers, "I am sorry I made you crawl, Miss Jemma."

Jemma was hesitant to give her injured hand over to a stranger, so she curled it back up, trying not to wince. "It's fine. I'll deal with it later."

Saxton tutted, finding her reaction amusing. "You remind me of my son. He never admits when he's hurt. Come on, drink up, then we must go."

"No. I'm not going anywhere with a knife pointed at my back." Jemma stated, looking purposefully at the sullen Angrud. "Who are you guys?"

"None of y'business." Angrud growled.

"It is my business if you want me to walk into the forest with you." Jemma snapped back.

"Fine, if you'd rather tackle the Great Forest and all its dangers alone, we won't waste our time helping."

"Help-"

"Enough." Saxton interrupted, as loudly as he dared. "By Minaeri, we have enough things to worry about without this. Jemma, my name is Saxton Marsh, this is Angrud Iveston. We are a scouting team for the Gardyn."

"Do you want to tell her anything else while you're at it, Saxton? Perhaps a few Gardyn secrets and passcodes? I know, let's draw her a map to the hidden safe places." Angrud offered drily.

"How do I know that you're really Gardyn?" Jemma asked hesitantly. Despite her briefing from Gran, she didn't know what she was doing, or who she was looking for, beyond a name. Jemma highly doubted that the Gardyn would have it tattooed onto their foreheads.

"You just have to trust us, Miss Jemma." Saxton replied, meeting her eye calmly.

"How do we know that you're not a spy for the King?" Angrud blurted out.

"King Raven?" Jemma asked, trying to recall the odd name Gran had used.

"Hrafn." Saxton corrected, somewhat confused that Jemma could get it wrong. "King of Enchena, and High Lord over all lands? The most infamous tyrant of our times?"

"That's what I meant. Hrafn." Jemma repeated, trying to get her tongue around the strange name. "I'm not a spy, so I guess you have to trust me, too. Which means no more waving around sharp knives, unless it's absolutely necessary."

"Define necessary?" Angrud countered, but he returned his knife to the leather sheath on his belt. "Are you contented?"

"For now." Jemma replied, forcing a smile towards the unlikeable man.

Saxton sighed at their bickering and stood up. "We need to leave now, and put as much distance as we can between ourselves and the King's soldiers. I imagine Captain Rian will be very interested to hear they're guarding Saviour's Gate again. Angrud, can you scout ahead?"

The younger man nodded, "Treefort?"

With Saxton's agreement, the younger man moved in front and quickly disappeared from sight.

"Miss Jemma, we had better start walking." Saxton said, offering to help her up.

Jemma hesitantly took the man's hand and let him pull her to her feet. "Is it far?"

"It is... a reasonable distance." Saxton replied vaguely. "I'm sorry we can't provide horses."

"Um, that's alright, I don't ride." Jemma said quickly.

She looked up, movement catching her eye. Angrud had returned, and with an impatient gesture, he motioned for them to follow.

Saxton gave Jemma an apologetic smile. "He's not the easiest person to get along with, but he's an excellent scout and tracker. He's one of the best in the Gardyn – just don't tell him I said that. He's just young, ambitious; wants to be the next Rian."

Jemma had no idea who Rian was, so she just concentrated on walking. A tricky enough challenge with the rough terrain, the ground's inclination changing sharply and without warning. Jemma was glad that she had opted for trainers, rather than her flip-flops when leaving the house today.

"So where do you come from?" Saxton asked, walking beside her with ease. He glanced at her bright hair and clothes. "You're definitely not local."

Jemma trudged along, acutely aware of the effort it took. "I'm not sure if I'm allowed to say, until I've spoken to Lord Siabhor."

Saxton looked at her curiously. "Not many people want to speak to him, even amongst the Gardyn. you're braver than I am."

"Why?" Jemma asked, suddenly nervous that Gran's task was harder than she had initially hoped. "What is he like?"

"Well, you know what he is." Saxton replied, with a shrug. "It intimidates most people; and scares the hell out of the rest."

Jemma bit her lip. What had this Lord done to inspire such fear? Was he just some awkward noble bastard, or was the man violent? Jemma couldn't imagine how to deal with either option. There was no point getting worked up about it now, she told herself, she had this trek to think about how she would introduce herself; how she would make the Lord Siabhor take her seriously.

"So, where are you from?" Jemma asked, turning Saxton's question back on himself, in an attempt to distract herself from worrying.

"One of the small, outlying villages just south of Reisguard. I have a small farm." Saxton grimaced. "Had. It was burnt down after the Riots."

"The riots?" Jemma echoed.

Saxton glanced at Jemma with suspicion that she didn't know of them. "The Winter Riots? That spread across Enchena only six months ago? Left hundreds dead and wounded?"

Jemma shook her head, "No, I'm sorry, doesn't ring a bell."

Saxton shook his head in disbelief, but humoured the girl, "After the last battle with the Gardyn, the King was incapable of properly bringing his soldiers back from the dead. This greatly depleted his numbers. There was a decree that it was now compulsory for all young men to enlist in the King's army; and they have dropped the age limit. It used to be that, at the age of thirteen, you could choose to train in the arts of war; or stay and train in the family business. My son, Russit, is only eleven years old. They wanted to take him away, put a sword in his hand, and make him a pawn in a King's war."

Jemma stared at Saxton, trying to take in what he had said. She couldn't imagine being forced to fight at only eleven; she couldn't imagine fighting now, at fifteen, but that was a different matter.

"It was only a matter of time before things erupted. For countless years, they had overtaxed the villages. Yet, they were no longer content by taking the food from our mouths to feed their army; they wanted the blood of our children, too.

"I was not a Gardyn, back then, but the rebels' victories helped embolden us all; to awaken a pride that has not existed in the people of Enchena for generations. They proved that the King was not invincible; and servants of the King had false authority over our lives. For a brief and beautiful moment, the common people stood up to defend their families, and to demand more for their lives. Until the army came. Pride and hope can only go so far, when you have farmers with pitchforks, fighting against cavalry and swords. Not to mention their leader, Captain Losan. I'll wager that you've heard of him..."

Jemma shook her head again, blushing at her own ignorance. Couldn't Gran have given her more than a few sketchy details and names to go on? Jemma doubted her smart phone could hop onto the local internet for a Google search.

"Really?" Saxton asked, with a defeated sigh. "The King's closest ally and advisor; the leader of the once-invincible army; and undefeated warrior?"

Jemma gave an apologetic smile and ducked beneath a low branch, trying to half-pay attention to where Angrud was leading.

"Captain Losan is a terrifying power in his own right. He does not need the King to intimidate. No man, no force has ever gone up against him and lived. He is a master of death and no amount of begging or bribery will help. He only had to show up to the riots, and whole villages laid down their arms. He came to our village; I saw Captain Losan with my own eyes. The fighting stopped immediately, but it wasn't enough. The soldiers hadn't had their violent release – they came back later and set fire to the houses and barns. They killed anyone within reach, men, women and children alike; then ran back to their master. Those of us that survived the fire and the slaughter were left with nothing. Our homes and our hard-earned stores for winter were gone. Burnt to the ground. If we stayed, we were sentenced to a slow and cold starvation. After we had buried our dead, we travelled north to the Great Forest, for we had heard many tales of the Gardyn and the forest.

"They took us in, gave us food and shelter. We were not the only people to seek the help of the Gardyn – other survivors of the Riots came over the following months, and none were turned away. We have quite the thriving community, hidden in the forest, away from the King's reach. I had not realised that I was so unhappy with life, until I came here and learnt what could happen, what should happen."

Jemma mulled over it all. "Would you really send thirteen year olds into war?"

Saxton shook his head. "No, they started training. They might go on a few patrols, but they weren't expected to fight until they were sixteen. But now... King Hrafn is impatient to fill his ranks, especially with the Gardyn threat hanging over his head. After the death of his own son and heir last year, he thinks nothing of sacrificing the sons of his country."

"I'm so sorry," Jemma said quietly. "It all sounds awful."

"You know, I can hear you two chattering half a mile away." Angrud stomped back towards them, pushing branches out of his way. "You need to take care."

Saxton frowned at his fellow Gardyn, "Any problems?"

Angrud nodded, "Listen."

As they fell silent, Jemma tried to work out what she was supposed to be listening to. She couldn't hear anything out of place – no more horses; no more soldiers. In fact, she couldn't hear anything.

"It's so quiet." She murmured, afraid to break the silence, now she had realised it was there.

Where was the birdsong? The rustling of animals? Everything was suddenly eerily still. Jemma could only hear her own thudding heartbeat after the unplanned hike; or at least she thought that was what she could hear.

Something distantly tapped in time, becoming louder with every passing second. The rhythmic clacking of nails on wood set a shiver down Jemma's spine.

Her growing sense of panic wasn't helped by Saxton and Angrud suddenly jumping to attention.

"Mallus." Angrud confirmed, the word making no sense to young Jemma.

"I didn't think Siabhor's pack was due in this area today." Saxton replied, his voice low.

Angrud gave him a long look. "They're not." The young man fitted an arrow to his bow, in readiness.

Saxton copied him, looking up into the trees. "Miss Jemma, whatever happens, keep behind us. Hopefully they'll pass us by."

"What is...?" Jemma's voice trailed off as she saw a dark shadow moving through the boughs of the trees. The shadow was joined by another, and another. The sound of clicking and clacking came from them, as they moved through the canopy. As they drew closer, Jemma could make out the dirty-brown fur that offered the creatures camouflage.

"Hold until we know they're not ours." Saxton said quietly to Angrud, the younger man shooting a look that conveyed his lack of optimism.

Jemma shrieked when one of the shadows leapt from the trees and landed on the grassy ground in front of them. The creature was a mass of spindly limbs, crouching on all fours, as it padded towards the humans, its long and lethal-looking claws digging into the turf. Its bulky chest and strong shoulders were as high as Jemma's waist. The creature turned its head, yellow teeth and yellower eyes gave it a grotesque appearance.

It paused, a mere ten feet from where the humans huddled, and sniffed the air. A hiss of disgust escaping through its foul teeth.

"You smell of traitors."

Jemma was startled at the gruff, rumbling voice. The creature could talk? There was an almost human element in its frame, but Jemma was still surprised that it had the ability to speak. Yet it was pure animal, as it crouched and looked ready to pounce.

"Not on our side, then." Angrud remarked, letting his arrow loose.

It zipped through the air and hit the oncoming monster dead in the eye. Jemma watched in horror as the creature fell limply to the ground, without a sound.

A moment later, chaos broke loose, as three others jumped down from the trees and attacked in a mass of stinking hide, teeth and claws.

Saxton's arrow caught one beast in the shoulder, making it snarl in pain.

The threat pressed too close, and Angrud threw down his bow, drawing his long knife instead.

Both men held their ground, too focussed on survival to feel any fear. They didn't hesitate, and fought with a strength and confidence that only comes with training.

Poor Jemma panicked at the charging monsters, and the blood that was spilt; she curled into a protective ball, praying for it to stop. Something grabbed her arm, and Jemma screamed and lashed out.

"Miss Jemma, it's over." Saxton's voice called out.

Jemma cautiously raised her head, and saw Saxton hovering over her. The girl forced her frozen limbs to unravel, embarrassed that she should appear so weak.

Looking around in disbelief, she saw two of the monsters lying dead on the forest floor. She felt a stab of fear, wondering where the other two were. "W-where...?"

Saxton offered her a hand, helping her back to her feet. "The other two scarpered. Typical of wild mallus, they flee as soon as the odds are against them."

"Cowards." Angrud spat, inspecting his bloody arm, shreds of fabric hanging from it. "Have you seen what the bast-"

"It's their nature to be opportunistic. You'd get your head bitten off, calling the mallus cowards." Saxton argued.

"Fine," Angrud grumbled, "have you seen what those opportunistic, flea-bitten-"

"How badly are you hurt?" Saxton asked, serious.

"Oh, it's only a scratch; but this is a new tunic!"

"What were those things?" Jemma interrupted, her eyes fixed on the strange animals.

"Mallus, in the flesh. I always thought they were a myth, before I moved to the forest." Saxton answered. "You look very pale, Miss Jemma, do you need to sit down?"

Jemma looked at the dark, bloody heaps. She couldn't think of anything worse than staying around them a moment longer than necessary. "Let's get out of here."

Four

Far away, in the capital of Enchena, the royal palace stood stark against the sky. Its tall towers cast a shadow over the city, a constant reminder of the unquestionable power of the King.

A young man stood by the window on the top floor, his eyes fixed on the dark green blur of the forest that stretched away to the horizon.

David had grown taller over the last year, and even though he'd always been physically fit, his frame and muscles had taken on a more mature set. A breeze from the open window ruffled his hair, which had grown longer than he'd ever worn it at home, it was now a shaggy mess of golden blond.

He was still handsome, but his once-gentle blue eyes glinted with ice and hatred.

David gripped the windowsill so firmly his hand turned white. He was full of restless energy, every nerve heightened and on fire. For two days he had felt it, a thrumming call through every fibre of his body. The gate was open, his world was calling him home.

Home. David hadn't given it a single thought for months. He had a good thing here, and had no intention of ever returning to England. Why would he? He had been so proud of his life, without knowing how little it was.

David couldn't imagine returning to it now. He had blood on his hands and he had changed so much from that doe-eyed boy, he could never go back to the rules and restrictions of home.

"Your highness-"

David jumped at the unexpected voice at his shoulder, he turned, instinctively grabbing the person by the throat and throwing them against the wall.

The servant's eyes widened with panic and he gasped, stuttering an apology.

"What do you want?" David snapped, towering over the weak-looking man.

"Your…" the servant trembled and tried to force the words out. "The Princess Helena sent me… she bid me… she would like the company of her husband."

David glowered, he had better things to do than visit his wife. It had only been a few weeks since she birthed him a daughter, and Helena was still fat and even less appealing than she had been when they had first met. Besides, her hormones left her emotional and impossible to talk to.

He hated having to pander to her every need, coddling that silly girl. But it was only temporary, soon he would secure his place as Hrafn's heir. Then once Hrafn and his wilting queen were out of the way, there would be no protection for Helena's nonsense.

As he thought of his wife, David didn't notice his hand tightening around the servant's neck, the man's fingers clawing desperately at the prince's hand, silently begging for release.

"David."

David snapped out of his daze and glared towards the person who dared to stop him.

Captain Losan looked thoroughly unimpressed by the young prince. "Let the servant go, David. Killing the last one was an accident, but this is getting to be a habit."

David grunted; trust Losan to bring up the last one: a chambermaid that had fallen down the stairs last winter.

Between his disdain for following orders, and the fact that he didn't care if his servant lived or died, it was with reluctance that David released him.

The man fell to the floor, choking and gasping for air.

"I have a title, Captain. You would do well to remember it."

Losan crossed his arms, his cold eyes fixed on David, his scarred face sneering in his direction. "I have a title too, Prince. And I had to do more than sleep with a princess to earn it."

The servant got unsteadily to his feet and backed away from the two men in the room.

"Now, if you're done posturing, your King requires your presence."

After a moment's thought, David turned to the fearful servant, patting the man amiably on the shoulder. "You may tell my dear wife that her father has demanded my time, but I will attend her as soon as I possibly can."

David turned and strode away, letting Captain Losan follow in his wake. He led down several flights of stairs to the throne room.

No matter how trivial the meeting, or how few men were to attend, King Hrafn always insisted on using the throne room. There was a confirmation of power, when Hrafn sat in the hall of his ancestors. The dais raising him above the others, a not-so-subtle reminder of his place.

David mused over the transparency of it all. But Hrafn grew weaker as his doubts grew stronger.

"Your majesty." Losan bowed, showing his King all due reverence.

David followed suit, a simple gesture to humour a simple man.

Hrafn motioned for them to rise. He had aged in the last few months; he was still an intimidating figure, but his raven-black hair was streaked with grey. His once-clear and focused eyes now moved incessantly, unable to calm.

"Captain Losan, anything to report?"

"I have set men at the location of the gate. There was no sign of activity, or of Gardyn presence, but my men will handle anything that arises." Losan replied.

"Yes, well excuse me for not having much faith in that after last time." David drawled. "Your men were trained for everything except two foreign teenagers, it seemed."

Captain Losan grit his teeth, his hand tightening around the hilt of his sword.

"David, do not antagonise the Captain, otherwise I will drop you into his arena and see how long you survive." The King warned. "Losan, my friend, he has a point. David thwarted your attempts last year, and he seems to have a preternatural link to that gate when it is active. Tomorrow he will ride out with you; see if he can sense something you can't."

David and the Captain shared a look of mutual distrust, but bit their tongues before the King.

"You are dismissed."

Five

They marched on, with no further breaks. Over the duration of the trip, Jemma's many questions were answered, to an extent. Not by Angrud, who continued to look darkly at the girl every time he rejoined them, but by Saxton who willingly offered his time, answering what he could. Eventually, Jemma's questions tailed off, replaced by a concerted effort to keep one foot moving in front of the other. Her energy had been sapped by fear during the mallus attack, and it was only stubbornness that pushed her on. Trainers or not, Jemma was going to have some wicked blisters at the end of this.

Her stomach rumbled with hunger. The ice-cream seemed like a distant memory, and had hardly set her up for a serious cross-country march. Although it was cooler here, and the canopy blocked most of the bright sun, Jemma was still hot. She kept wiping beads of sweat from her brow, and twisted her thick hair away from her neck, trying to get cool air to her skin. What she wouldn't give for a cold drink right now; a nice, ice cold Sprite. Her mouth watered as she imagined such luxuries were at hand.

47

Lost in thought, Jemma collided with Angrud's back, not noticing that the young man had stopped. He grunted and turned, clearly displeased with her.

"Sorry," Jemma muttered, her voice a rough whisper after the long journey.

"Well take her through," Saxton said, smirking at Angrud's discomfort.

Angrud hesitated, rubbing his sore arm. "What if they don't know the difference between one person and two?"

Jemma frowned, trying to work out what on earth they were talking about. Through where? Which 'they' worried Angrud? She looked around and saw only more trees and grass; if this was their destination, it was definitely an anti-climax.

"Jemma's on our side, they won't hurt you." Saxton reasoned.

"She says that she's on our side, but a spy would say the same thing!" Angrud argued.

Saxton sighed, giving up on the younger man. When he turned to Jemma, the amusement still lingered in his gentle eyes. "Now, Miss Jemma, what is about to happen may be... unusual, but I need you to keep walking beside me. Can you do that?"

Jemma smiled, after everything that had happened today, she was pretty sure nothing could be 'unusual' by comparison. "Of course, no problem."

Saxton gave a knowing smile, and directed her towards their right, firmly holding her arm. Jemma saw that the forest was subtly different; the trees weren't just close, they were tightly packed, without a glimmer of light getting through.

Saxton started to walk towards the natural wall, pulling Jemma along with him. Before she had a chance to compose a sarcastic comment, Jemma froze, she couldn't believe her eyes.

The ground began to rumble, and the trees shuddered. With an agonising creak, they began to move. A space started to form in front of them, splinters and leaves drifting through the air. The space widened enough for two people to pass through.

Jemma looked up at Saxton, her eyes bulging with fear.

"Trust me." Saxton asked.

Jemma nodded, swallowing her nervousness. She grabbed onto Saxton's arm and shuffled next to him, and he moved towards the gap. The ground was churned up, and Jemma struggled to keep her balance. As she stepped into the space, she looked up at the massive trees that stretched up to the sky. The trunks seemed scarily close, and was it only in her imagination that they quivered eerily?

At last, they were through. Angrud jogged through after them, and the trees shifted and closed, knitting the gap with living wood. Jemma stared at it, barely grasping what had happened.

"W-what...?" Jemma coughed uncertainly. "Is this... normal in Enchena?"

"No," Saxton replied, "It was a gift from Lady Samantha, before she left. She promised that the Gardyn families would be safe. The trees obey her. It is said that, if anyone who tries to enter Treefort and wishes the Gardyn harm tries to enter Treefort, the trees will crush them. Hence Angrud's reluctance."

"Can't be too careful," Angrud's voice came from behind her. "Minaeri knows how the trees distinguish who is on our side."

Saxton shook his head at his companion's grumbling. "Anyway, Jemma, welcome to Treefort."

Jemma had been so preoccupied by the trees that she had failed to notice the first signs of civilisation she had seen in Enchena. Tents and huts made from hides and wood, spread out across a half-mile space. Every few metres, small fires were already lit and anyone not on duty was helping with the organisation of a feast that was to be held for visiting Gardyn captains later that evening. Jemma glanced up, the sun warm on her face, beaming down on the valley, filling it with warmth and light. The trees, nothing more than a dark fringe.

Jemma brought her gaze down to the make-shift village, and started. The idyllic camp suddenly tore apart to reveal hellish devastation. The tents were broken and many were burning bright, smoke curling up into the choking air. Bodies lay strewn across the ground, wild-eyed and bloody. The survivors ran as another ball of fire flew out of a deep smoky sky, crashing to the ground, not a metre from Jemma. The impact knocked her backwards, she felt her heart constricting.

"Miss Jemma, are you alright?" Saxton was kneeling beside her, a strong arm supporting her.

Jemma's focus shifted from his worried face, daring to look at the camp again. All had reverted to the pleasant scene.

"Did you see...?" Jemma paused, as she noticed the confusion on Saxton's face. Perhaps it had been her imagination, even though the scene remained vivid in her mind. Could she trust herself? Thrown into another world, into a strange war with unknown forces, that was questionable enough. Suddenly Jemma felt all alone, perhaps it would be better not to stand out in any way; at least until she figured out who to trust.

"I'm sorry," she finished lamely, struggling to get back to her feet. "I've just had a tiring day and felt faint."

"You had best rest at my camp until we find out what to do with you. My wife will take care of you." Saxton said, helping her up.

"What!" Angrud exclaimed. "She's a prisoner. We should shackle her to a tree or something."

"A tree or something?" Saxton repeated, drily. "She's just a kid, Angrud. Don't worry, I'll take any blame that comes our way. Go get that arm checked out by the healer, and I'll meet you shortly."

Saxton led past the first row of tents. People gave him the briefest glance as he passed; but their gaze lingered on Jemma. Jemma felt a warm blush creep up her neck as she realised the attention of so many strangers was fixed on her. Men, women and children alike, watched her with surprise. Was it so obvious that she was a stranger? Surely they couldn't tell she was from another world by her looks – they all looked normal to her. Did that make her an alien, to come from another world? The thought made her skin crawl.

Jemma increased her pace until she was walking beside Saxton. "What are they all looking at?"

Saxton hesitated, and reluctantly answered. "You're clothing is somewhat unusual, and... they are not used to seeing someone with your colour of hair..."

"What?" Jemma looked back at the staring faces, nobody else wore shorts or a strappy top, nobody wore bright white. There were trousers and skirts, and comfortable tops with muted colours. As for their hair, it ranged quite boringly from brown to black; no blondes, and definitely no redheads. Jemma had thought it bad when some of the meaner kids bullied her at school, seeing her hair as a weakness; but now she felt like she might as well have a beacon on her head. "Great, that's just... fantastic."

Saxton glanced at her, but refused to comment. He walked directly towards a small group of women. They looked round at his approach, and one of the women smiled and moved towards him, her oval face and big brown eyes emanated a warmth and kindness that immediately put Jemma at ease. A young girl grasped her hand and looked in innocent wonder at the stranger.

"Saxton, I wasn't expecting you back until later."

Saxton swooped down on the little girl, scooping her up in his arms. He then kissed his wife gently on the cheek.

"Jemma, meet my wife Siarla, and my youngest daughter, Betony." Saxton smiled to Jemma, then spoke to his wife, "You don't mind Jemma staying with us until Captain Rian gets here, do you? It's just she's young and..."

"And you have a soft spot for strays." Siarla teased. "That's perfectly fine, Saxton."

"I have to go report to my superior, before Angrud says something he shouldn't." Saxton lowered his daughter back to the ground. "I'll be back within an hour, I promise."

Siarla's smile faltered as she realised that her husband was leaving her with Jemma, but she shrugged her worry away.

Jemma stood very self-consciously, a nervous blush colouring her cheeks, she had never felt more out of place.

"Well, my little flower," Siarla was kneeling down and tapped Betony lightly on her nose. "Shall we find your brother and sister?"

Betony giggled and wriggled away from her mother, her big brown eyes staring up at the girl with the orange hair.

"The other two are in our tent." Siarla said, standing up. She gave a friendly smile and led the short distance to a large, patched canvas; big enough for the family of five to sleep comfortably.

Siarla entered the tent, the flaps thrown wide open. A young girl jumped nervously and looked up, biting her lip guiltily.

"Jemma, this is my other daughter, Kiya. Kiya, Jemma is staying with us for the evening, can you make up another bed?" Siarla looked about the tent, before slowly turning back to her daughter. "Kiya, where is your brother?"

Kiya's attention was elsewhere, and she stared open-mouthed at the strange girl with the flaming hair. A sharp cough from her mother brought back her manners.

"He went out, mama. He said he wanted to see the mallus."

"Did he now?" Siarla said, thin-lipped. "Jemma, stay here with the girls, I just have to go and get my wandering son."

When Siarla promptly left the tent, Jemma stood uneasily, the two sisters staring up at her.

"So, er... you're Kiya, and you're... Betony?" Jemma asked weakly, at a loss of what to say. The girls nodded silently, wide eyes fixed on Jemma. "They're nice names."

"Thank you, I think Jemma is a pretty name too." Kiya replied quietly. The girl bit her lip, then blurted out, "Why do you have orange hair?"

"What? Oh, my dad had ginger hair, so it's his fault." Jemma reached up and gently twisted a lock of hair. "I guess not many people have this colour here."

Betony giggled again and Jemma's thoughts returned to the tent. "So, how old are you two?"

"I'm seven already." Kiya said proudly, holding her head high.

Betony looked down at her hands, counting on her little fingers. She grinned and held up her right hand with three digits pointing up.

"Three? Wow." Jemma replied, finding her quite adorable.

"No Betony, you're four years old now." Kiya corrected.

"...how many times have I told you to stay away from those creatures?" Siarla's exasperated voice grew louder as she returned to the tent, a boy in tow. She looked to Jemma apologetically, "And finally, this is my son, Russit."

Russit was a little older than his sisters and had the gangly look of someone that had just gone through a growth spurt. Apart from the surly expression, he looked so much like his father.

"Hi, I'm Jemma."

Russit sighed, and fidgeted where he stood. "Fine, I've met her, can I go back outside now? Dylan says-"

"You are not seeing Dylan again. Every time you go chasing after him, you end up outside the walls; or pestering the mallus." Siarla snapped, "You will stay with your sisters for the rest of the day, or Minaeri help me, I will-"

"Alright, alright." Russit replied mardily, reading the warning signs in his mother he plonked down on the nearest bed.

Siarla turned away from her son and tried to mask her annoyance. "Now, Miss Jemma, is there anything we can do to make you more comfortable? You look exhausted; a wash? Fresh clothes?"

"That... that sounds really good," Jemma replied, surprised by the honest hospitality.

"Kiya, can you show Jemma to the bathing area? Betony, come help me pick out some clothes." Siarla said to her daughters, before fixing on her son. "Russit, stay right where you are."

Before Jemma could feel too sorry for Russit, she felt a small hand slide into hers and pull her out of the tent. Carrying a towel, Kiya led with purpose towards an area set up with individual stalls, next to a well.

"Pick one." The young girl suggested, before sitting on the stone wall that surrounded the well.

Jemma kicked off her trainers and sweaty socks, and stepped onto the reed matting. There was a wooden door that she pushed shut for privacy. A bucket of water sat in one corner of the stall, and there was a somewhat scratchy sponge with it. Oh well, better than nothing.

Jemma stripped off, listening intently for trouble; but nobody approached her here. She sponged some of the cool water over her back, and gasped with the shock and how lovely it felt.

"Why is your skin so red?" Kiya's curious voice drifted in. "Is it supposed to match your hair?"

Jemma paused, twisting her neck so she could see her shoulders. Damn, they were bright red; she dreaded to think what state her face was in. "Um, no. I was out in the sun for too long and burnt. Badly, it seems."

"Oh, but that's normal, that happens to me." Kiya said, sounding somewhat disappointed. "I thought you were a red and orange person."

Jemma snorted. "No, I'm very normal, I just have ginger hair," she replied quickly, out of habit, before realising that actually, she was very much an alien.

Feeling very awkward, Jemma rushed her bath and pulled her dirty, sweaty clothes back on. When she opened the door she paused. The sun had dropped low to the horizon, filling the campsite with shadows. Every new angle she saw seemed more beautiful than the last.

A fire was being built in an open area towards the middle, and people began to migrate that way. Kiya seemed keen to get back to her family, driven by the need for dinner; she practically dragged Jemma back to the tent.

Upon returning, Siarla pushed a pile of clothes into her arms. "Here, you can borrow some of mine. Although you'll need a belt – you're nothing but skin and bones! Didn't they feed you at home?"

Jemma made a somewhat positive noise. She worked so hard to stay slim – it was difficult when her best friends were naturally so beautiful and skinny.

"Everybody ready for dinner?" Saxton asked, ducking back into the tent. Kiya ran and grabbed his hand; Russit shuffled up behind his father.

Outside, there was the pinkish glow of sunset to the west; elsewhere in the heavens stars were already pricking through a quickly darkening sky.

The open area within Treefort was dotted with lamps, and a fire which the families gathered around. They all sat in casual groups, waiting for their neighbours to arrive before they started on the evening meal which was a shared labour and a shared occasion.

In the crowd of strangers, Jemma recognised Angrud, who currently dithered about a group of men who sat apart from the families. Jemma found it amusing that, even at a distance, Angrud managed to look arrogant.

Saxton's family quickly sat down, along with the entire population of Treefort, some two hundred people or more. Nobody could pass without staring towards Jemma, some discreetly glancing sideways, others not bothering to hide their interest. Jemma found the attention unnerving; she might be dressed like an Enchenian now, in her borrowed clothes, but nothing would hide her flamboyant hair, made all the more noticeable by the red firelight.

Gradually everyone settled down to the feast. There was a wide variety of fruits, vegetables and meats, most of which Jemma thought she recognised from home. There were many girls, a similar age to Jemma, that carried platters between the families, before returning to their own. These girls passed to and fro, and Jemma had a strange suspicion that they were lingering near the group of men she had noticed earlier. Jemma was amused by the obvious show, Enchenian girls weren't that different to British girls. Jemma looked up again, and started to feel uncomfortable when she realised how many stares were aimed at her.

Her attention was caught by a familiar flash of wings, and Jemma was less than surprised to see the small and colourful falcon hopping on the grass beside her knee. "Oh, you decided to come back, did you?"

The bird tilted its head to look up at her, and squawked importantly.

"Wow, he's pretty!" Kiya exclaimed.

"Is he yours?" Russit asked, as he inched closer to the bird.

"Mine? No, he belongs to..." Jemma broke off. How could she begin to explain Danu and Gran to these children? "He belongs to a friend."

Suddenly Betony was crawling into Jemma's lap, her chubby little hands digging into her leg, and her face lowered towards the bird. "What's his name?"

"I don't know. I don't even know if he has one." Jemma confessed. "Why don't you guys pick one?"

"He should be called Betony." The little girl stated, making her brother and sister laugh.

"Betony's a girl's name, silly." Kiya cooed. "How about Feathers?"

Russit stuck his tongue out at the idea. "I think he should be called Bern."

"Bern?"

"Yeah, after the famous Gardyn, Bern." Russit answered.

"I don't think I know that one." Jemma admitted.

"Mum tells the best stories about Bern," Russit said, not taking his eyes off the bird, "he lived in the old days and did loads for the Gardyn."

It was when most of the food had been picked off that Angrud came striding up importantly.

58

"You and the girl have to report to Captain Rian immediately." Angrud announced, not bothering to keep his voice down.

Saxton merely nodded and stood up, "Come, Jemma."

Jemma scrambled to her feet, her nerves returning. Everyone spoke in awe of Captain Rian, and she was suddenly afraid to say the wrong thing. Or would they not listen, and throw her out to the wild woods?

The small falcon flapped his wings and found a place to perch on her shoulder. His sharp claws dug through the rough material of her borrowed top, but his presence helped to calm her pulse. "You're not a bloody parrot." Jemma commented, out of habit.

When he simply clacked his very sharp-looking beak, Jemma hurried to catch up with Saxton and Angrud, who were already striding towards the group of men.

Saxton and Angrud bowed their heads in humble salute. Now that she was closer, Jemma scanned the faces of those in front of her, and understood the previous behaviour of the serving girls. The men were reasonably good-looking; but more importantly, they had an air of command about them. Even though they dressed like everyone else, and sat on the ground casually, they stood apart.

One in particular drew Jemma's attention. He looked a little younger than Saxton, his face was hard, and his brown eyes were sharp. His black hair was long and unruly, and... Jemma had never seen such an attractive man...

The man caught Jemma's analytical stare, and the girl dropped her eyes, missing the frown that crossed his handsome face.

"So, this is the girl you found wandering the forest?" The man asked.

"Yes, Captain Rian." Saxton answered. "She was by Saviour's Gate, sir."

"Yes, your patrol partner explained that to me," Rian countered, with a pained expression, "in great detail."

Captain Rian looked back at Jemma, trying to take in the red hair and the... bird on her shoulder. "Angrud told me all about you, Miss Jemma, that you will only speak to Siabhor and that you have been putting on a very believable act of ignorance. I don't suppose you can talk to me? Tell me where you're from? Who sent you? Give us a reason to trust you?"

Jemma shook her head, finding it somewhat difficult to put words in the right order around Rian. She was somewhat grateful for the sunburn on her cheeks that would hide the fact that she was blushing. "I-I'm sorry, sir. I've been told to tell no other but Lord Siabhor. But I am here to help the Gardyn, I promise. If it were otherwise, the trees wouldn't have let me into Treefort."

"Lord Siabhor." Rian sneered. "I'm afraid Siabhor is out with his pack, hunting. We expect him to return tomorrow. Saxton, can you and your family make room for this girl tonight?"

"Yes, sir."

Captain Rian nodded gently, and they were dismissed.

Six

That night, Jemma's mind travelled far in her dreams. It started off innocently enough, as she dreamt of an endless forest, and Saxton and his family riding unicorns, always out of reach. But soon it morphed, the green disappearing into grey as Jemma came out at the foot of a great mountain. She felt that she was being watched, and searched until she found a glassy eye fixed on her. The eye blinked, and the bluish-grey rocks around it began to move, extending long limbs and clawing its way up.

Jemma held her breath as the creature became entirely visible against the mountainside.

Dragon.

This blue monster was easily as large as the red one she had dreamt of before, and looking at its bared teeth and cruel eyes, Jemma guessed it was just as dangerous.

She scrambled back to try and get to safety, but the dragon flicked her into the air with its wing. Jemma screamed as she fell, landing on the creature's broad, scaly back.

Without warning, it cracked its wings and leapt into the air. Jemma clung onto the icy-cold spines on its back for dear life, watching the ground get further and further away.

All she wanted was to close her eyes, but they were frozen open, having to take in every detail of this traumatic flight. The dragon's body jerked with each stroke of its wings, as it propelled forwards.

The mountain soon fell behind, and new hills came into view. On top of the largest, Jemma could just make out a stone building, half in ruin.

"Now." A loud, rumbling voice came from the beast that carried her, the sound enough to deafen her. "Now."

The dragon banked sharply, and Jemma felt her flimsy hold slip. She scrabbled against the rock-hard scales, but slid across the creature's back. Jemma felt her foot touch air, and soon she was falling, falling...

Jemma jerked awake, feeling very disorientated. She opened her eyes to see a canvas wall, the unfamiliarity confused her, and her thoughts were slow to catch up.

She heard the whimpering of a young girl, then a woman's voice speaking quietly, fearfully, "Stay with me, my darlings, and he won't hurt you."

Siarla. Jemma suddenly remembered all that had happened yesterday, and exhausted from her journey, she had fallen asleep as soon as she'd returned to the Marsh family tent last night.

She felt the hairs on the back of her neck prickle and heard a hissing sound behind her. Jemma rolled over and her eyes widened with fear as she was confronted with a monster that was terrifyingly familiar. The first thing she noticed were the slanted yellow eyes glaring out of a hairy face, and pincer teeth through which foul breath rasped.

With thoughts of yesterday still painfully fresh, Jemma tried to scramble backwards, but fear froze her to the spot and robbed her of her voice.

"Humans be waste of time."

Jemma shuddered as the living nightmare spoke in rough, grating tones. How had this thing gotten into camp?

The creature shifted its long, spindly limbs to move back and sit down. "They says you want to speak to me."

Jemma didn't reply as she tried to take everything in, from the murky brown coat that seemed tinged with green; the strong, skeletal frame that looked like a cross between man and wolf; the spindly limbs that ended in hand-like claws, with nails several inches long and covered with what Jemma feared was dried blood. Then the face, covered with grubby hair, its features flattened. She had already witnessed that these mallus were hunters, nightmare prowlers.

"No." She finally replied, shakily. "I need to talk to Lord Siabhor."

The monster gave a bark of dissatisfaction, "I be Siabhor."

"What!" Jemma's surprise overtook her nerves. If this creature was important to the Gardyn, perhaps she was joining the wrong side. "I thought you'd be human."

"I am mallus." Siabhor hissed, his chest puffing out with pride. "Now, what you be wanting to say?"

Jemma lowered her gaze, no longer able to look at the terrifying creature. She was just a messenger, she could give her message, then work on getting home. "My name is Jemma, I am of Lady Samantha's home. The time for her return has come."

The mallus' expression softened, then he got up and loped out of the tent, looking rather ungainly with his spindly limbs.

Betony quickly stopped crying once the mallus had left, and Siarla loosened her grip on her children. The woman looked over at Jemma, her usually friendly expression turning cold. "How could you bring that thing to our tent?"

"I'm so sorry, Siarla. I had no idea-"

Siarla stood up, grabbing Kiya's and Betony's hands. "After an announcement like that, I imagine you will be summoned to the council shortly. You had best stay in the tent, so they know where to find you." Without another word, Siarla dragged her daughters out into the sunlight.

A few paces back, Russit followed his mother, pausing to grin at Jemma. The strange redhead had found respect from one of them, at least.

Feeling guilty about scaring Siarla and the girls, Jemma spent the next half hour alone in the tent, fretting and nervously tidying. It helped to distract her, folding the blankets and straightening the beds. She felt a shiver of amusement, what would her mum say if she found Jemma making other people's beds when she never made an effort with her own? The humour was quickly replaced by a pang of homesickness. Was her mum back from her night shift? Did she even go to work when Jemma didn't return home yesterday? Jemma hated to think of her mum stewing alone at home, with no idea where her daughter was.

Jemma felt a lead weight sink into her gut. She'd never given her mum a second thought when she'd followed Gran's instructions – perhaps because she still didn't believe that she would end up in another world. Now the shock of being in Enchena was starting to wear off, Jemma realised that it might have been a mistake.

The tent flap was flung open, a fresh breeze and bright light breaking through Jemma's thoughts. Angrud stood in the doorway, his cold eyes finding Jemma's.

"I am to take you to the council immediately." He said, his tone short, and evidently annoyed.

Jemma could only guess what was irritating Angrud today. Surely it wasn't her fault this time, she hadn't had time to say or do anything foolish yet this morning. "Lead the way."

Jemma thought briefly about pulling on her trainers, but her blisters protested. Going barefoot seemed weird, but frankly, Jemma didn't care if they considered her more weird than she was yesterday, with her funny hair and general sense of not-belonging-here. She jogged out to catch up with Angrud, who marched through the camp with no concern for Jemma's shorter legs.

Treefort was mainly for the Gardyn families, so the council was gathering beyond the camp, at the far end of the valley. There were seven men that Jemma recognised from the evening meal, including Captain Rian, who looked even more handsome in daylight. Crouching low to the ground, initially mistaken as a shadow, Jemma saw Siabhor. There was also a woman that Siarla had pointed out was the head of Treefort, and there to represent the families.

"Ah, Miss Jemma," one of the men greeted, "now that you are here, you can explain your message to Siabhor."

"What do you mean?"

"I mean, where did you get your information from? How did you know we were planning to retrieve the Lady Samantha?"

"I think everyone in Enchena can guess at our desire to have Samantha back, Rinar." Captain Rian interrupted, drily. He turned his attention back to the strange girl. "But why now? What do you know, that we don't?"

Jemma felt a blush spread across her sun-burnt cheeks and she stumbled over her words. "Um."

Beside her, Angrud chuckled, obviously amused by the effect Rian was having on her. Jemma's embarrassment was replaced by annoyance, couldn't he give her a break for five minutes?

Rian must have had a similar thought, and looked up to Angrud. "Soldier Angrud, I hardly think you have anything to add to this council. I would hate to delay you in today's duties, you may return to them. Now."

It was Jemma's turn to smile, as Angrud looked a little hurt. But the soldier bowed his head to his superiors, and quickly made himself scarce.

"Miss Jemma?" A male voice brought her attention back to the questions.

What could she say, but the truth? "Honestly, Gran told me. She had received a letter from a Danu, saying that it was time for Lady Samantha to return. She charged me to deliver the message."

The council looked unimpressed with what she had to say. Obviously Gran and Danu had no bearing amongst these Gardyn. Only Rian looked thoughtful.

"Danu... the same Danu that helped Lady Samantha last year?" Rian asked. "She disappeared for over a week, and when she returned she spoke of visions and of another world that would offer us refuge..."

Jemma stood silently, feeling more than a little useless; all she had seen was a name on a letter.

"Do you have any proof to confirm your story?" One of the men asked.

Jemma scrambled for some sort of answer. Proof? If she said that she was from another world, they might accuse her of madness. All she could do to prove that was ramble on about things they didn't know, of cars and planes... and likely to be considered fanciful and mad. She pulled at her collar nervously, and paused as she felt the chain against her fingertips.

"Gran gave me this." She said, pulling the necklace out of her blouse, so that the jewel sparkled in the bright morning sun. "She said that it was an inta... initiatus crystal."

"Let me see that."

A low voice made Jemma jump. She span round to see a tall cloaked figure, dark and imposing; his face hidden by the shadow of his hood, only for a further mask over his nose and mouth. His approach had been so silent, that none had noticed his presence until now.

"Oh, so now the great cloaked ally has arrived." Rian remarked, looking disapprovingly up at the man. "It seems too much of a coincidence that you should appear so soon after this girl."

The man ignored him, and held his hand out to Jemma.

Jemma took off the necklace and handed it to the newcomer. As soon as she passed it over, she felt anxious to have it back. She had sworn not to remove it, and she felt vulnerable without it.

The stranger lifted it to his eye-level. "She speaks the truth." The man announced, handing the necklace back.

Jemma accepted it, her fingers brushing the coarse skin of his hands, and she looked up. The stranger had his oversized hood and a dark cloth concealing most of his face, but his intense green eyes could be seen, rimmed with traces of age and worry.

Jemma stared into those eyes and felt a familiar, weightless sensation. She felt torn between two realities, in one she saw the aged eyes suspended in time, in another she saw the same eyes belonging to a lad, no older than herself.

Jemma went through the motions of another person, whose sight she had borrowed. As she watched the lad she felt a mixture of anger, pride and love wash over her. They both stood outside a grand house, the boy holding his horse, packs already positioned behind the saddle.

"Orion, don't be so damned foolhardy." Jemma spoke with a man's voice. "Accept who you are. You have responsibilities to your station, why throw that all away?"

The lad smiled and grabbed her hand, forcibly shaking it. Jemma snatched her hand back and folded her arms, furious that he was being so damn stubborn.

"Sorry father," the lad replied, "but I don't want to live on the family name. If I'm going to be somebody, it'll be because I deserve it."

The lad turned and led his horse into the open to mount, swinging easily into the saddle.

"Goodbye father. Minaeri's blessings." He called from the saddle, then picked up a trot.

"Orion! Get back here!"

"Orion! Get back here!" The faint words died from Jemma's parched mouth.

She lay on the ground. Siarla had been called for when Jemma collapsed, and now cradled her while she stirred and muttered words that all the council members strained to hear.

68

Jemma started to wake and Siarla held her steady, soothing her as the girl's pale blue eyes rolled wildly.

"Where am I? Where's Orion?" Jemma cried hoarsely, finding it difficult to let go of her vision.

"Hush, you're with us again, Siarla's here." Siarla Marsh said softly, as she did with her own children when they were plagued with nightmares after the Riots. She felt the girl relax in her arms.

Jemma sighed and forced herself to sit up, feeling a headache threatening. She glanced around, noticing that the council were staring at her with worry and curiosity.

"I'm sorry." She mumbled.

"Don't be sorry," Rian said softly, kneeling down beside her. "Does this happen often?"

Jemma thought for a moment, "It's only happened since I came here. Twice. The first time I saw the destruction of Treefort. The second, just now, I saw that man's past." Jemma spoke quietly, afraid of being declared mad, but desperate to finally tell of these visions.

"Why didn't you tell anyone?" Rian asked, then stopped her, "Never mind, just describe these visions fully."

Jemma started hesitantly at first, but grew stronger. No one interrupted her and after she finished, everyone remained silent.

Captain Rian stood up suddenly, an air of authority about him. "Rinar, I want fifteen of your fastest riders, we're going to the Temple of Gates."

"So… you would go on a wild goose chase because some girl with strange dreams says Lady Samantha will return?" One of the other council members asked, incredulous.

"Stranger things have happened, these past few years." Rian stated. "And as for Orion, it is about time you told us who you really are."

Rian turned to face the cloaked man, to find that he had disappeared.

"I didn't mean for Siabhor to scare your family earlier." Jemma said apologetically, as she walked with Siarla back to the Marsh tent.

"It's ok, Jemma." Siarla replied, without looking at her. "I'm sorry that you thought I blamed you. You clearly didn't know who Siabhor was when you requested to speak to him. If you don't mind me saying, you don't seem to know much about anything."

Jemma sighed, the older woman's comment had no malice behind it, she was simply stating her observations. Clearly Siarla was much sharper than Jemma had originally thought, with her gentle warmth and motherliness.

"I'm... not from Enchena." Jemma replied quietly, watching Siarla closely for her reaction.

Siarla merely nodded, "That would explain it. Why are you here?"

"I was sent to pass on a message. Now that's done..." Jemma shrugged, "I don't know, I guess I should find a way home."

"Are you sure that's all you've come for? It's a rather meagre role to set an oracle."

"Yes, I'm sur- a what?"

"An oracle. I'm guessing that's the correct term, forgive me if it's wrong, it's been so long since we last had one." Siarla answered.

"Why would you call me an oracle?" Jemma asked, her pulse starting to race.

"Because of your visions; because you came to foretell the return of our heroes." Siarla replied. "Do they have a different name for it where you come from?"

"It's not..." Jemma stopped in her tracks. She'd never had a vision in her old life, she'd had vivid dreams, but none of them had come true. It had all been a bit of nonsense, to joke with her mum and friends what her imagination had come up with. It was a little crazy, but nothing out of the ordinary, lots of people had strange dreams. But then, Gran had mentioned them... and Minaeri had haunted her sleep for months...

Siarla turned when she noticed that Jemma was no longer walking beside her. She saw the girl, lost in her thoughts, a pained expression on her face, and realised the truth...

"Oh, Jemma, this is all new for you, isn't it?"

A shiver ran up Jemma's spine, and she gave a hurried nod.

Siarla came and wrapped an arm around her shoulders. "Come on, let's get back to the tent, and I'll see about making you some tea."

Jemma felt a wave of gratitude towards Siarla, along with the pain of missing her own mother's warm hugs and hot drinks whenever she was sad.

Back inside the cool tent, Jemma sat on her bed, hugging her knees, tucking them up to her chin.

"Siarla... would you...? Can you tell me about the Gardyn? About Enchena?" Jemma asked. "I'm tired of not knowing."

Siarla set some tea to brew on some burning coals outside, then came to sit beside Jemma.

"That's a lot to tell, Jemma. I'm not sure where to begin... Well, I suppose it all starts with the first King of Enchena, Ragoul. He was a strong king, who created invincible armies that demanded respect. He was a tyrant though, and he would have sold his soul to have more power. You see, Ragoul was not only murderously ambitious, he also had the power to create floods and drought; to bring fallen soldiers back to life, so he could never be defeated. It is also said that he created the mallus to scare the people of Enchena into submission." Siarla paused, checking that Jemma understood all that she had said. "As the needs of the common people were being ignored, many opposed Ragoul being king, but if anyone made their views heard, or caused suspicion of treason, whether it was true or not, they were killed. He also relentlessly hunted down and killed any person accused of magic, paranoid that they would prove a threat to him.

"This disregard for his subjects drove the rebels into hiding, and they formed the Gardyn, to protect the oppressed.

"Over a thousand years have passed since the days of Ragoul, and the Gardyn work tirelessly against his descendants, who inherited his powers and his evil. They infiltrate the courts and councils, to help reduce the monarchy's damage. There have been small attacks to stop slaughters and work to bring the towns and villages some sense of freedom. When I was a girl, I remember there were times when the families of my village would wilt from hunger and submission to the King's demands; only for a wagon of food and crops to come from an anonymous donation. It was just enough to keep our bodies going; and you can't imagine the hope it instilled in many a soul.

"The Gardyn have always been a thorn in the crown's side, an irritant that could never be eradicated. But the Gardyn were never strong enough to make war and overthrow the king; that was until Lady Samantha came. She lit a fire in our hearts, a hope that was too powerful to ignore. Minaeri sent her into our lives, riding astride a silver unicorn, to free us all. Lady Samantha united the unicorns and the mallus as our allies; and her own powers make King Hrafn as mortal and vulnerable as any man."

Jemma sat silently, taking in all that Siarla shared. Surely she wouldn't play a significant part in such an immense story. "So where is Lady Samantha now?" Jemma eventually asked.

"She opened a gate to another world and took as many as she could through to freedom. That was almost a year ago. The Gardyn are always looking for signs that she will return and lead us to victory." Siarla answered. "Now, if you don't have any more questions, I have to collect Betony and Kiya."

Seven

Jemma was on top of the hill, a gentle breeze murmuring over long grasses. In front of her, crumbling stonework showed the remains of a once-great temple. Jemma stepped into it, unafraid. She looked up to the clear blue sky, the temple roof having fallen long ago.

In the derelict building, walls had gaping holes, and tiled floors had been reclaimed by wild grass. In fact, there were only two objects that had withstood the test of time: two life-sized statues of kings or great warriors. Jemma stared at their stone faces, perfectly wrought. From this angle, the sun formed a halo behind the figure on the right, and behind the left figure was the faint glow of an early-risen full moon.

The statues were designed so the figures held out their swords to form an arch to walk underneath.

Jemma waited. Beneath the extended swords, the air thickened and shone. The ground began to rumble and the remaining stone walls crumbled, yet Jemma waited fearlessly.

Finally the moment came, surprising even Jemma, who thought she only waited for Lady Samantha's return. Colour and softness washed over the two statues, sending life into the stone, and two living men stepped down from their...

74

"Jemma, how are you feeling?"

Jemma groaned slightly as the voice woke her. "Damn, twice in one day," she muttered to herself. She squinted against the sun, attempting to see who was silhouetted against the entrance of the tent.

Saxton looked down at the strange girl, "I've just finished duty and thought I'd ask. It seems that you've had quite a day."

"Well, it's not over yet." Jemma replied, almost bitterly. "I need to talk to Captain Rian; there's something I need to warn him about."

"It will have to wait until he gets back, he's gone to the Temple of Gates."

"Already?" Jemma exclaimed, jumping to her feet. "Can we catch up?"

Saxton frowned, looking questioningly at the girl, "what is so urgent that it cannot wait?"

"I think I just had... a, um..." Jemma broke off, she'd had a dream, nothing more, nothing that would make a sensible grown man race after Rian.

"A vision? Siarla told me you were a fledgling oracle." Saxton sighed and looked away, calculating the distance. "We're about an hour behind them already, and they will be riding hard and fast; but if it's important, we can try. You, ah, can ride?"

"What, a horse?" Apart from pony rides at the beach and at fairs when she was younger, Jemma had only sat on a horse once. "I know how to hang on," she replied unconvincingly.

"That will have to do, come on."

Saxton led over to the horse paddock that Jemma had seen earlier. A small figure ducked out of view, scared to be seen out of bounds by his father, but Saxton was too quick.

"Russit! Get over here." Saxton demanded.

The boy slinked out, ready to be scolded.

"Get a horse tacked for Jemma." Saxton ordered. "I need to find Angrud."

Saxton was right about Rian and his troop riding as fast as possible. They had not stopped travelling until it was too dark to see, and their horses were exhausted.

Angrud had come along with them; Saxton argued that they might need his expertise, and that Rian would put him in the stocks if he found out that Saxton had tried to make the journey with their new oracle alone.

Jemma felt some discomfort that she was now a person that required protection. She didn't know how she felt about it, to be honest. There was a vague pleasure at realising that she was needed; which was countered by the fact that they only wanted her because of her weird dreams. Dreams that she could not control.

Angrud's company made travelling awkward, but at least on horseback it was easier to cling onto the saddle and just ignore him. It was only when they stopped to camp for the night that they all had to sit around and play nice.

Angrud took the first watch, and Saxton lay down, his snores soon reverberating across their campsite. Jemma was exhausted, but her limbs were hurting so much, she couldn't get comfortable on the hard ground.

Angrud snorted with derision as she turned again.

"What?" Jemma snapped.

"You can't ride for sh-"

"So? Normal people don't ride horses back home. We have cars, and trains, and even stinking buses. There are cushioned seats, and you can sit reading while someone else drives you where you need to go." Jemma whined. "And now I'm sore, bruised, and I stink of horses. I don't need your snotty comments."

Angrud smiled darkly, "Fine, you're giving it everything you got. Seems like a lot of effort, chasing Rian after meeting him twice. I can't blame you, there's a lot of women that wish they could do the same, but don't have the gumption to presume they are important enough."

Jemma twisted in her bedroll, to look up at him, "Seriously, you did not just say that? This is about returning heroes, and the bigger picture. It has nothing to do with Captain Rian."

Angrud chuckled, "Oh, I know, but it's funny how much of a fool you act around him. I have to entertain myself somehow."

"So you've never done anything embarrassing, of course." Jemma spat.

"I'm not weak enough, I'd never make a fool of myself over a girl." Angrud replied knowingly.

"No, you're such an arrogant git, I bet only a good mirror would get you excited." Jemma snapped, then rolled over, blocking his further comments.

It took another whole day of hard riding for the temple to come into view. Saxton had given rough directions, to head north; but as they went on, Jemma realised that she already knew the land and where to go. The grassy hills were so familiar, she soon kicked her horse on, taking the lead.

Even nightfall didn't stop them, trusting their horses to find a safe path, while their eyes were locked on a small fire on top of the highest hill.

"Who's there?" One man cried out, jumping up from the ground as the trio got close enough to be heard, yet unseen on this dark night.

All the men were on their feet immediately, ready to fight.

Jemma and her two companions rode into the circle of firelight.

"Saxton Marsh? What are you doing here?"

Rian came running out of the temple ruins, to see what the disturbance was, he hesitated as he saw the newcomers. "Miss Jemma, what is going on? Marsh; Iveston? You do not have permission to leave Treefort."

"Captain Rian, sir." Saxton dismounted his horse and saluted, "Jemma had another vision pertaining to this mission. We thought it best to come."

There was a pause as Jemma was helped down from her horse; she staggered slightly as her numb legs hit the ground painfully. She leant against the horse that had carried her so far and tried to meet the Captain's gaze, aware that Angrud would be judging her, as she did so.

"Yes, sir." She replied quietly, "I saw that it is not only Samantha that will return."

"Yes, we know." Rian interrupted. "We're expecting the Deorwines, Lord Mgair, and hopefully a small army of Gardyn."

Jemma ignored the strange names, shaking her head slightly. "No, I mean – ah, there are two statues in the temple. When the portal thing opens, they come to life."

Jemma heard the mutters and even a laugh from one of Rian's group. Nobody believed her. After the exertion of the long ride, Jemma felt close to tears, that all of her two-day journey was for nothing. What was the point of having visions if people pick and choose which ones they believe?

"I appreciate you riding out to tell us this, but...well, we don't know how accurate your visions are." Rian finally said in a low voice. "They may just be metaphorical. We'll see tomorrow. First watch, you're on. The rest of you, get some sleep."

The Captain turned and walked away alone to the ruins, knowing that he would not sleep.

Jemma slept fitfully, flashes of her visions returning in her dreams, and the ground made no more comfortable by a couple of thin blankets and her aching limbs from riding.

She woke early, a familiar musky smell disturbed her, and a rasping muttering reaching her ears.

"These cureta humans, thinking I not be here..."

Jemma sat up and span round to see what she now recognised as a mallus, sitting on a boulder like a big, grotesque dog.

"Siabhor?" Jemma mumbled.

The mallus snapped his head towards the girl, hissing.

"I didn't know you'd be here." Jemma shrunk back, looking for help. He might be an ally, but he was still a monster.

"Where else would Siabhor be?" The mallus spat, "I only be helping humans because of Samantha, and humans think they leave Siabhor behind when they be bringing her back. Filthy cureta." Siabhor swore and hissed at the end of his rant, his yellow eyes flitting angrily over the assembled soldiers.

"Hey, something's happening!"

A shout rang out across the hilltop. There was a shocked pause, then everyone moved towards the temple. The mallus loped away to the ruins and Jemma, hesitant at first, got up and followed.

The temple was just as her visions had shown, a large, airy chamber in which two statues were erected, their swords drawn. Between them, the air seemed to thicken and take on a silver sheen.

"This is it," Saxton said excitedly, standing at Jemma's shoulder, "we get to see some real Enchenian heroes."

Everyone fell silent as the portal grew larger and more solid, then the anticipated moment came.

A tall, proud figure stepped through, a smile on her face as she took in everything about her. She was a few years older than Jemma, and humbly dressed, yet carried herself as if she owned the world. Her plain look could not be called beautiful or striking, but there was something noble about her.

Lady Samantha led her warhorse, a handsome pale cream stallion. He was currently doubling as a packhorse, carrying her things.

Rian and his soldiers moved forward to greet and help her, but the Lady held up a hand and ordered them all outside the temple. Everyone obeyed immediately, surrendering to her authority. Her reasoning soon became clear when two more figures appeared. A young lady, extraordinarily beautiful, with dark hair and eyes; and a young man who was subtly handsome and similar in looks to the girl for them to be related.

They made their way out to stand beside Lady Samantha on the sunny hilltop, but they were not the last to emerge from the portal. Jemma watched with disbelief as two mythical creatures stepped out, their frames akin to the daintiest of horses, but protruding from their foreheads a single pearly horn. Unicorns. A palomino with a golden coat that shone like a second sun; and a silver-grey that was made for the stars.

The palomino threw up its head and took off, past where the humans gathered, and with flashing speed he galloped across the plains, heading to the Great Forest. The taller grey unicorn snorted and remained.

Everyone's attention returned to the temple, as people were coming steadily in twos and threes, some leading packhorses, others carrying their own belongings. Jemma lost count, as several hundred individuals amassed on the hill in ordered lines, both men and women aged from fifteen to over fifty, all armed with a sword, or spear and a quiver of arrows.

"Rian, your army." Lady Samantha explained, bowing her head.

The captain was speechless, looking about the ranks, that were as fit and well-trained as any King's soldiers.

"You are full of surprises, Lady Samantha." Rian eventually said breathlessly. "But, ah, women warriors?"

"I have fought." The lady replied sharply. "The women have trained as hard as the men, and are just as deadly."

Jemma couldn't help staring at the famous Lady Samantha. After all the stories that she had heard, it was hard to believe that the young woman was standing in front of her, flesh and bone. It was almost wrong for her to look so normal, with her light brown hair and summer-tanned skin.

She must have noticed Jemma's scrutiny because Lady Samantha looked through the crowd, directly at the strange girl. Jemma dropped her gaze, missing the lady's frown.

Suddenly there was a rumble and the ground began to shake. People shouted out in fear and pushed away from the temple, as the stonework split and the remaining pillars collapsed.

All became still again and the Gardyn soldiers glanced about with confusion, praising Minaeri that none were hurt. The dust from the fallen rubble began to settle and two final figures stepped out from what remained of the Temple of Gates.

"The princes... alive... Lugal, Cristan..."

Everything happened so fast, Jemma felt exhausted trying to understand. When the two statues had come to life, Lady Samantha seemed unfazed, as though she had been expecting it, but murmuring went through the army.

When Captain Rian came out of his daze, he quickly organised those assembled, starting the southward march back to the Great Forest. As for Jemma, Saxton and Angrud, he had arranged them a small escort and ordered them speedily back to Treefort with instructions to prepare for their increased numbers.

It was nearly three full days since the portal had opened and Jemma was working alongside Siarla and the other families of Treefort as they prepared sleeping quarters and food enough for the celebrated return of the Lady and her army.

82

Jemma was more than happy to participate in the chores, she hadn't even been asked to ride on with Saxton, Angrud and the others to the Valley and Woodvale. As curious as she was about the other Gardyn strongholds, Jemma's aching backside and leg muscles didn't regret it.

"It was a long time ago, no one knows how much of the story is true, how much is fabricated." Siarla talked as she worked, making the time pass quicker and informing Jemma on another part of Gardyn history. "Two hundred years ago, King Gearalt had three sons – his heir, Brandon; and the twins Lugal and Cristan. Back in those days, there was a lot of superstition, and twins were considered an ill-omen.

"Gearalt couldn't keep the twins in the capital; but he couldn't bring himself to kill them. He knew that if his first heir failed him, he would need a second son. So, while they were still babies, King Gearalt sent the twins to his country castle, to be raised away from the many eyes of court.

"Anyway, when Gearalt died, soon after the birth of Brandon's son, Brandon became king. The story is that he hated and mistrusted his brothers, knowing they had a strong claim on the throne. It has happened before – a second son, murderously envious of the crown, and unwilling to fade into the shadows of history. Not that Lugal and Cristan would ever feel this way; they had grown up away from the poisonous court, they had all the benefits of a noble upbringing, with the freedom to follow their own moral compass.

"King Brandon was not going to take any chances, and he sent an assassin, in the guise of a messenger, to tell his brothers that their great father had passed on. But what Brandon didn't know, was that the Gardyn had replaced the assassin with one of their own men – the famous Bern.

"Bern went to the Princes Lugal and Cristan, and warned them of their brother's plan to kill them. He smuggled them out of their own castle, under the noses of Brandon's spies, and away to the north.

"For a year, Lugal and Cristan lived with the Gardyn, doing their duty to relieve the suffering that their brother forced on the peasants, and any that opposed him. Then, one not-very-special day an oracle sought them out. She told the princes that they were fated to take the innocents away to a place where the king could not reach them. That only they could find the long-abandoned Temple of Gates, only they could open a gateway. She warned that they would have a choice to make – to open a doorway to another world would not only take their pure hearts and faith in Minaeri; it would take their lives.

"Soon after this revelation, King Brandon ramped up his persecution of the Gardyn. He had discovered that his brothers had not died, as planned, and he was going to punish any and every person capable of helping them.

"Knowing that the increased death and pain was directly connected to them, Lugal and Cristan started to search for the Temple of Gates. It was with Bern's help that it was discovered, and the Gardyn and innocents travelled in mass, in the hope of peace and freedom. The princes stood in the centre of the Temple, and when they drew their swords, a gate between worlds was formed. Their people passed through, to a land named Caelum; but the price had to be paid, and when the last person had stepped through, the princes turned to stone where they stood." Siarla broke off, and smiled, "I always thought that part was made up, and that the statues had been erected in their honour, or for someone else completely forgotten in history. I always thought that, at least until now..."

Eight

That evening Treefort was packed; the soldiers would soon welcome their beds for a few hours of refreshing sleep before they continued marching south to join the camp in the Valley. But for one night, everyone rejoiced, singing and dancing into the early hours. There were wild stories told, of the famous Lady Samantha, but the remarkable young woman herself was nowhere to be seen.

Jemma had attached herself to the Marsh family at the gathering, and was thoroughly enjoying the evening. She did not even wonder where the lady was until a young man approached her with summons.

"When you are presented before the Lady Samantha, you must curtsey. And do not speak unless you are spoken to." The messenger informed Jemma, as they hurried to a newly-erected tent.

Jemma nodded nervously, taking little jogging steps to keep up.

A guard outside the door nodded them through, lifting the canvas back. Inside, the wide tent was dim, having only a single flickering oil lamp for light.

Jemma was left in the tent by the messenger and she clasped her hands behind her back to stop herself fidgeting further. A movement caught her eye and she started slightly as a young woman got up from a bench and walked towards her.

Jemma remembered her instructions and made a clumsy effort at a curtsey, when she stood up again, she kept her eyes lowered to the ground and failed to see the lady's faint smile.

"I have been told that you are the oracle that foretold our return. For that, I thank you." The lady said quietly, "I was also told that you claimed to be of my homeland. That is impossible. What is your name?"

"Jemma McKinley," she replied, then added quickly, "miss. Forgive me, I only repeated the message that I was given."

"Jemma. Do you know who I am?" Her calm, almost sad tones continued.

"Yes, miss. The Lady Samantha, miss." Jemma's glance flicked up as she finally dared look into the lady's face. A jolt of recognition made her gasp. "You're Sammy Garrett!"

"Where did you hear that name?" The Lady Samantha asked, with a mix of fear, surprise and even anger.

Jemma just blinked and continued, "Gran said that I was from your home, but I didn't understand until now."

Lady Samantha seemed to grow faint and sat down on a near bench, her expression fixed. "You know Gran. I never told anyone about her, except the Deorwines. Then you truly are from back there, back home?"

Jemma looked down at Samantha, and she began to see something other than an untouchable lady; a girl only a few years older than herself, someone she must surely have something in common with. Jemma hesitated, as shocked as Samantha, and unable to completely ignore the hero figure that the lady had already become in her eyes, since meeting the Gardyn and their amazing stories. Slowly, Jemma lowered herself onto the bench next to Samantha.

"For the past year you've been classed as a missing person. There's been searches, appeals, everything. Everyone assumed that you'd run away with your boyfriend, because David Jones disappeared at the same time."

"David?" Samantha grunted, "He was never my boyfriend, and now he's nothing but a curse to us."

"David is here as well?" Jemma asked with sudden surprise.

Samantha nodded slowly, "King Hrafn, the one we are at war with, went to Earth to bring me back. It would have been physically impossible for him to drag me through the portal, so he made sure that I saw him kidnapping another student and played on the hope that I would be stupidly heroic and follow." Samantha paused and sighed, "It was just bad luck that David was chosen. So it is my fault what happened to him."

Jemma plainly saw the misery that Samantha felt, but her curiosity was brimming. Jemma let the silence linger for a while, then asked in what she hoped were consoling tones, "What happened?"

Samantha hesitated, she had only spoken of this once before, when she confessed all her woes to Jillis Deorwine, when she was a prisoner in the royal palace. Now she was considering telling a girl she had known five minutes. What right did she have to know, just because she was from home?

"He died." Samantha began, suddenly feeling very detached from the words that tumbled out. "We had just found out we couldn't return home. We were in the forest and didn't notice the soldiers creeping up on us. David was killed by a single arrow to the chest and I was taken to the King, unconscious. When I awoke, I found out that Hrafn had used his powers to bring David back to life, with the intention of tempting me to willingly help him." Samantha paused and shook her head. "A person cannot retain their soul after death. David came back as an evil reminder of a once good person. None of that would've happened, none of this would've happened without me."

"Don't say that." Jemma said, once Samantha had finished. "Because of you, an oppressed world has hope and courage enough to fight for freedom. David, and many others, have died because of Hrafn; we will fight to avenge that."

Samantha looked at Jemma, the thin line of her lips betraying how unimpressed she was with Jemma's unasked for advice. "How old are you, Jemma?"

"Fifteen, miss," Jemma replied, puzzled by the question.

"Fifteen? You must be very wise to be giving me advice at your age. You've only been in Enchena for a few days; do not dare pretend to understand what I've been through." Samantha paused, knowing that she was being unfair, but unable to stop the outburst. She sighed heavily, "Forgive me. No matter how many people tell me those exact words, it never helps. Don't worry yourself with my problems, I would not wish them on anyone. If I keep them solely for myself, only I can be hurt."

Jemma felt uncomfortable, sitting next to this young woman who had obviously been through so much already. The errant thought arose that Samantha was only half-way through her journey, and there was a lot more pain to come.

"Where are you staying, anyway?" Samantha asked, changing the topic.

"Here at Treefort, with the Marsh family."

The name was unfamiliar to Samantha, so she assumed they must have joined the Gardyn army after she had gone to Caelum. "You had best go back to them, if they will have you. Until we decide what is to become of you."

Jemma frowned at Samantha's choice of words, "I don't understand? What's to be decided?"

"How we are to get you home; or if the portal is sealed, how to keep you safe. My return will mean war. By Minaeri, why did Gran send you?"

"B-but..." Jemma stuttered, then spoke again before her confidence drained, "but I don't want sending away, can you consider that? Sammy, I have been sent to help with this war."

Samantha stood up suddenly. "Please refer to me by my title, Miss Jemma. War is not a game, you have no idea what it means to fight, to kill, and by Minaeri I will not let you learn."

"I'm sorry, Lady Samantha," Jemma corrected, impatiently, "What if you need me? I am an oracle."

"Yes, so Rian tells me..." Samantha replied, clearly unimpressed with the term. "The Gardyn do not need you, we have other methods of receiving messages from Minaeri. Danu-"

"Danu sent me." Jemma snapped, then looked away, "I'm sorry, I just... if there is something that I can do to help, I would do it. I might not have been in Enchena long, but I would do anything to make sure that Saxton and Siarla don't have to suffer from King Hrafn anymore; hell, I'd even help Angrud, although that's a close one. They matter to me."

Samantha gazed coolly at the girl for a long moment. "I will take your wishes into consideration. But now I have a council meeting to attend, so forgive me for cutting this meeting short."

She walked over to the entrance and pulled back the flap, holding it back for Jemma. Samantha watched the girl walk away, her expression tense. She had noticed the redhead when they gathered around the Temple of Gates, and on the ride home, Rian had filled her in on the part Jemma had played. It had been easier to believe that the girl was getting visions; than it was to believe she was from home.

Home. It was a thought that had haunted Samantha for the past year. Of course she missed her family and often longed for the simplicity of that life again, but that was lost to her. A different life, a different Samantha; would they even recognise her now? She had worked out such thoughts and frustrations on the training grounds, whenever it got too much. She turned her energy into training herself and the army that had gathered to her in Caelum.

Samantha hesitated in the dim refuge of the tent. She could hear the celebrations and longed to join them, but she knew that she was expected in council. Tobias and Jillis were probably already there, wondering why she tarried. She smiled as she thought of the brother and sister, they had all grown so close and were now the nearest thing she had to family.

Samantha set off across Treefort, heading to the crowd of people gathering towards the horse paddocks, to gain some privacy from the masses. She detoured to where her cream stallion was penned, taking the time to give him a stolen apple, before she turned her attention to more serious matters.

The council had the usual group of captains and the woman nominated as the head of Treefort; but tonight there were those that had not joined the council for a year: the Deorwines and, more noticeably, a silver-grey unicorn who lay comfortably in the grass. Samantha felt soothed by the unicorn's presence, Alina was of the noble line of Praede and a dear friend.

"Samantha, we were just filling their highnesses in on the past couple of hundred years." Rian announced with his trademark smile as Samantha sat down next to the Deorwines.

"There's a bit of recent history we'd like to know about." Tobias spoke out.

"You mean what happened after you went to Caelum." Rian didn't even bother making it a question. "Well, Hrafn had encircled us at the Temple of Gates and it seemed like that'd be the end of all of us; our rescue came just in time. The unicorn leader, Autumn, must have noticed Hrafn following us as he was making his way back to the Great Forest. Now, Autumn may dislike us for all the problems we bring, but he's a decent fellow and did the right thing. He gathered as many of his kind as he could and came to our aid.

"There must have been fifty unicorns, I've never seen anything like it. They spirited us away to the safety of the forest; Hrafn could not hope to keep up with their speed." Rian paused and shrugged, glancing at Alina, "We haven't seen the unicorns since. I think they're finally done with us.

"Throughout autumn, we split into several divisions and kept moving to spread the word to our allies and to avoid confrontation with the King's army. We had thought of going overseas and taking over Drake Island as a base, but Hrafn must have heard something – he caught the Gilded Rose ferrying near a hundred Gardyn – he killed them all, crew too."

The Gardyn captain paused again, letting the rest of the council share their disgust. Samantha sat quietly, her memories overwhelming her thoughts. As much as she hated the loss of life, she found it difficult to pity the crew of that ship.

Rian continued again, "When winter set in, we came back to the Great Forest. Winter was heavy and made it impossible for the King to attack us and although it was difficult, we could survive. We also had help from Siabhor and his pack sharing their hunting kills.

"Hrafn turned his anger on the villages and towns. We heard of the Winter Riots as everything boiled over between the peasants and soldiers. We did our best to protect them; we brought as many as we could into the safety of the forest. The harsh winter gave us some defence, the heavy drifts staying well into spring." Rian looked about the gathered council, "Since then, there have been a few small skirmishes. More and more of the King's patrols have been sent into the forest of late, anticipating... your return, or some intervention by Minaeri."

There was a murmuring between the council members when Rian finished. The first to speak aloud was one of Rian's captains.

"What happened in the other world?"

Jillis took her turn to speak, "We all arrived safely in Caelum. It was a world much like our own - it was hard to believe that it was an alien sky above our heads. Despite overpopulation and the fact that their lands were fit to burst, the people of Caelum were kind and welcomed us warmly.

"Their world was full of advancements that we can only dream of, and I admit that some people were somewhat... condescending in their treatment of our backward existence. We were very welcome in their homes, but were curiosities to most civilians.

"By Minaeri's blessing, there were still descendants from the last Gardyn to cross over from Enchena. They had blended with the Caelum folk, but still kept their history alive, their tales written in books and ledgers that were kept in this magnificent library... They told us about the part that Prince Lugal and Cristan had to play; they are revered as Saints, the sons of the Gardyn's enemy, giving their lives to save the innocent."

"Is this true?" One of the princes asked in disbelief.

"Aye," Jillis replied with a smile, "They never forgot you. In fact, it may have inspired many to return with us. They heard that they could come and finish the war that plagued their ancestors, forcing them to cross worlds to find peace. Many were keen to embrace the adventure and would not be dissuaded. For months we lived and trained together, waiting for the time we would return. Those brave souls never could have dreamt that

Prince Lugal and Cristan would return, they have been abuzz with excitement since."

There was a pause as those gathered took in all Jillis had to say.

"There is one missing from this council. Where is Lord Mgair?" Rian eventually spoke up.

Those that had returned from Caelum exchanged looks. Samantha supplied the answer, relishing the moment. "Mgair has deserted us. Once we got to Caelum he forgot about his desire for a glorious death, he gave a big speech about Minaeri sparing us, then settled down. He made no effort with the army and turned a deaf ear when we said we had found a way back to Enchena."

"We all know what Mgair was like, we are better off without him." Tobias added. It was no secret that the young man had a deep-seated dislike of Lord Mgair.

"Yes, but it throws our plans into chaos somewhat. When we overthrow King Hrafn, Lord Mgair was going to head a parliament," Rian explained, glancing about excited, "It's this wonderful idea of a democracy where we rule in accordance with the common people."

Everyone at the council seemed to approve of this idea, their faces brightening at the thought. All but one.

"No."

The single word was spoken so quietly that it could have been missed. Everyone turned to the speaker. Samantha sighed, feeling a headache coming on at the mere thought of politics.

"True, it will begin honourably enough, but those in parliament will be raised above the commoner. Greed will set in, corruption; they will use words instead of swords to suit their own purposes. Lord Mgair would have been a terrible choice for a leader." She argued.

"As a noble lord in Enchenian court, and a leading voice in the Gardyn, Mgair was the obvious choice to bridge both sides." Rian countered, without any real conviction.

"And what of the masses that do not side with ourselves or Hrafn? They will not accept a Gardyn parliament running the empire alone." Samantha continued. "What we need are heroic figures with a strong, direct bloodline to a king, an honest claim to the throne after Hrafn is deposed."

Lady Samantha's words were heeded. All eyes turned to the silent and thoughtful princes.

"And what do you know..."

"*Lady* Samantha," Rian said curtly, "just how would you recommend going about this? By Minaeri, who is going to believe that these are the long-dead sons of Gearalt? They will accuse the Gardyn of finding twins and planting a wild story, just so we can get our puppet on the throne. No offence, your highnesses."

Samantha crossed her arms and waited for him to finish. "Well, *Captain* Rian, half of Enchena are convinced that I am a deity; and the other half know that the current heir to the throne is from another world. Not to mention, that everyone knows King Hrafn brings people back from the dead on a daily basis. So really, I think two-hundred-year-old-royal-Gardyn-sympathisers isn't much more of a stretch."

Rian leant back, observing her shrewdly. "I shouldn't even try arguing with you anymore, should I?"

"Not if you hope to win." She countered with a smile.

"If I may intercede," Prince Lugal spoke up, "My brother and I were never meant to rule, and we have assuredly never desired it. We did not come back to take over."

"We had not chosen to come back, at all." Prince Cristan said in agreement. "Also, I do not know if it has escaped your notice, but there are two of us. How do you intend to select the new king? Will the people approve of your choice?"

Samantha shrugged, "Simple, we have two kings."

There was a burst of laughter and disbelief around the circle.

"Two kings?" Tobias echoed, "What barmy country has ever been ruled over by two kings and queens?"

"It might not be the worst idea." Jillis silenced her brother, "Especially if we want the people of Enchena to adapt to the concept of several people ruling them in a council- sorry, a parliament."

The Gardyn looked towards the Lady Jillis, starting to warm to the idea.

"But we are getting ahead of ourselves, first we must win this war." Jillis said gently, looking purposefully towards Rian.

The captain nodded, taking his cue, "I have sent messages to the rest of the Gardyn. Any man capable of carrying arms is to report to the Valley. With any luck we will be at full force before the month is out."

"A month is a long time to wait." Prince Cristan sniffed.

"Most of our men are out there, in Enchena, trying to staunch the damage of the King." Rian said pointedly, "We only have the bare minimum here to protect the families."

"Surely the army that Lady Samantha brought back is enough."

Rian sighed, "Even with these brave people, King Hrafn has always had better numbers. Ever since he came up against Lady Samantha, he has realised that he is as flawed and mortal as any man. Hrafn has been recruiting, driven by fear that it will not be enough."

Nine

Captain Losan paused as he walked along the upper corridor of the training barracks. There was the unmistakable ring of metal as swords clashed together, the sound floating out of the yard and echoing around the bare buildings. The Captain grit his teeth, a cold feeling flooding through his veins. He had his suspicions of who would dare use a sharp sword in the practice arena. Losan muttered to himself as he turned towards the nearest staircase, descending to the yard where his men were encouraged to sharpen their skills.

Despite his reputation for being brutal, Captain Losan drilled his men with wooden swords. He hated the idea of good steel being broken in novice hands; and there was no point in his men getting too bloody before battles, especially now the King had lost his ability to heal and revive others.

The thought itself was treason; King Hrafn had become more desperate to seem infallible and above the mortal man. The more desperate he became, the more rumours and doubt crept into Enchena.

All his life, Losan had worked tirelessly to ensure that people respected his King, that they never questioned Hrafn's rule. But now he felt the unease of political waters shifting for the first time since Hrafn took to the throne. Powerful men and women were using the disruption to see what could be gained, and the populace as a whole, as much as they were starving and downtrodden, knew that the balance was changing.

The list of people Losan trusted was growing shorter by the day, but for the time being, he could still drive fear into the hearts of men and cow those that he did not trust.

Captain Losan rounded the last corner to the training yard, and spotted the man he trusted least.

Prince David was in the centre of the yard, wielding a sword and shield, turning slowly to keep his two opponents in sight. A third man was already on the floor, whimpering and clutching his bloody leg. At the edge of the sand arena, other soldiers stood, rapt and excited by the show.

David yelled at his opponents, goading them to attack, as he raised his own sword to strike the nearest man.

Losan watched for the briefest moment, and he had to admit that David had taken his training well. He was balanced, controlled his blade, and moved faster than the two that he fought.

"Who gave the prince real swords?" Losan demanded from the nearest soldier.

The man panicked at the sight of the feared military leader, and he struggled to get his words out. "No one, Captain. I mean... the prince... apologies, Captain."

Losan sighed and turned away from the stuttering soldier, as the men gave a cheer. David had caught one of his opponents off guard and thrust his shield up under

100

his chin with force. The man had collapsed, whether he was dazed or knocked out, Losan couldn't tell. He only hoped he wasn't dead.

In the middle of the arena, David turned to his final opponent. Losan could tell by the nervous twitch of his blade, that the man's confidence had completely drained. The prince could surely see the sign of weakness as well, but instead of calling the practice bout off, David exploited the weakness and charged at him.

The soldier's sword was knocked uselessly aside, and he cried out in pain as David sliced his side on the back stroke. The man fell to his knees, and looked up to his prince, waiting for mercy.

Fuelled by the bloodlust and electricity of the enraptured crowd, David raised his sword aloft, ready to make his final move.

"Enough!" Losan bellowed.

The soldiers jumped sharply to attention at the familiar voice. David turned his head, his defiant blue eyes meeting Losan's. After a few lingering moments, he sighed and relaxed, lowering his sword and stepping away from his victim.

"Captain Losan, how good of you to join us." He drawled.

Losan crossed his arms. "I would appreciate you leaving my men in one piece, your highness."

"I thought you'd approve of me providing extra training, Captain." David replied with a smirk. "What with the impending Gardyn threat."

"Aye, and how many Gardyn have you fought and defeated, young prince?" Losan asked mildly. "Leave the training to me."

David scoffed and turned away.

101

"You doubt my ability to teach, boy?" Losan shouted, then gestured to one of the soldiers. "Sword."

One of the men hurried forward, offering his captain a sword.

David hesitated, eyeing the Captain warily. Noticing the increasing interest from the men surrounding the arena, he knew he couldn't refuse the challenge. He shifted the sword in his hand and rebalanced his shield, and slowly turned to face Losan.

The Captain stepped down into the sand arena, and circled the prince, taking his time, waiting for the slightest weakness in David's stance.

The prince didn't wait, he took the opportunity to attack and swung his sword. Losan parried it and pushed him back. He was surprised at the strength of the blow, this was no longer the weak boy he had dragged back from the forest a year ago. Losan put the thought aside and started an attack. He settled blow after blow across David's sword and shield, making the prince hurry back and stumble. Losan pressed his advantage and threw David off balance, who landed ungracefully on his arse, his sword skittering away across the sand floor.

David tried to raise his shield, but Losan stamped it down, sending waves of pain through the prince's wrist.

"Had enough, Prince David?" Losan asked, barely out of breath. "Do you feel you have benefitted from training? Or do you need a few more cuts?"

David grimaced, he bit his tongue, not wanting to play the Captain's game any longer.

Sensing he was getting nothing out of the prince, Losan turned away, throwing his sword into the sand. "Get these weapons locked up; and get those men to the healers now."

102

As the Captain watched as the soldiers scurried to do his bidding, he wondered how much longer he would have control over his men. How long before Prince David had infected that authority too?

"I have a mission in the Great Forest. When I return, if I find anyone has used real weapons, they will wish they had ever been born." Losan growled to the commanding officer.

*****

The following morning there were a few sore heads from the previous night's festivities. But the travelling Gardyn dutifully packed up, tacked up, and got ready to venture on to the Valley.

Samantha and Jillis carried their packs toward their horses, walking amiably side by side. Samantha wondered whether she should take a few minutes to speak to that girl, Jemma. She had perhaps been a little harsh last night, whether she had good reason or not.

Before she could come to any conclusion, Samantha noticed that Jillis had been stopped. Most soldiers were intimidated by her beauty, and by the deadly fact that she could shoot a flea off a cat at a hundred paces; but occasionally one would try to speak to her. Samantha turned, wondering which hapless fool it was today. To her surprise, she saw one of the princes rising from a bow.

"Lady Jillis, I was hoping that I might... offer myself as an escort for you, today. I find myself still lost in current affairs, and I have been told that you are one of the most knowledgeable sources."

"Why thank you, prince..."

"Lugal, my lady."

Samantha was a little surprised to see a light blush cross Jillis' cheeks, and she bit back her smile as she witnessed her friend accept Lugal's offer, and quickly forget all about Samantha.

"My brother always had a fine eye for beauty."

Samantha spun round to see the spitting image of Lugal, with a somewhat tired expression. "Prince... Cristan?"

"In the flesh." He replied, with a bow of his head. "Although I am still getting used to that fact after centuries in stone."

Samantha regarded him for a moment, she hadn't thought that the princes might be as out-of-place as she had been when she first came to Enchena.

"Might I carry your bag for you, Lady Samantha?"

Samantha scrutinised the handsome face and intelligent brown eyes of the prince. "It's alright, I can manage. But you are welcome to ride with me, if your brother has abandoned you."

Cristan gave half a smile, "My brother has always followed his head."

"Does that make you the heart?" Samantha asked, conversationally. "I would have thought the heart to be more distracted by a pretty girl, than the head."

"Perhaps; alas my brother was the first to claim Lady Jillis' attention today. Which may yet work in my favour, he is a dreadful bore and I can't imagine her wanting to speak to him twice."

Samantha chuckled as she threw her bags across her horse's back. She mounted Legan, and waited for the prince to get on his borrowed horse. "Ah well, you have the consolation prize of accompanying me."

Cristan froze, "Oh. I meant no offence, Lady Samantha, I am of course very honoured-"

Samantha waved for him to stop. "Enough, I am not offended. Jillis is as good on the inside, as she is beautiful on the outside. Not I, nor anyone else, can compare."

"I actually wanted to thank you for supporting us at the council last night." Cristan added, "My brother and I will serve the Gardyn in any way we can."

"That's alright, I-" Samantha froze, then smiled as sweet thoughts reached out to her. She was filled with excitement as she turned back to the prince. "Forgive me, Prince Cristan, but Alina has returned from Autumn. I have to find out any news from the herd."

Samantha nudged her horse into action, leaving Cristan feeling quite deserted.

"I am sorry your highness, but unless you have four legs, you won't keep her attention." Tobias remarked as he walked closer after witnessing them, "I should know."

As they walked through the forest, drifting away from the main army, Samantha and Alina were quickly joined by Siabhor.

The grey unicorn kept jogging along as she rejoiced in returning to her home forests. Alina practically hummed with joy as she tilted her head to look up at the tree boughs, looking towards the mallus. "We feared we would never see you again."

Siabhor's hairy head hung down from the canopy momentarily. The mallus was confused at his own feelings – he was the natural predator of unicorns and humans and had always lived by his hunter's instincts. Last year he had found it unnerving that he could be friends with such creatures. When they left him behind, he was surprised to find that he actually missed them, and now he appreciated their return more than he would ever admit.

"I be here because of my old pack." He said, as he set off again, his claws clacking against the wood of the trees. "No other pack would take me in, but I find mallus of old pack – Sahr's pack. The ones that live, they still be hurt from the battle and in winter would die, but for a time we all run together, they all follow Siabhor."

Samantha looked up at the fleeting shadow with surprise, "But... males never lead mallus packs!"

Siabhor gave a throaty bark of satisfaction. "They all follow Siabhor. And as winter comes, I do not be wanting them to die. Then that Rian-man come; I be trusted by both humans and mallus, so we make deal. They heal mallus, we help them hunt and wait for Samantha to return."

Siabhor shot a more than usually sly look at the glittering unicorn below him. "But Siabhor did not get to meet junior unicorn, Sundance. After all he be annoying me last year, he left fast."

Alina kept going straight on, getting her thoughts in order before she shared them with her friends. For all her effort, she couldn't keep the hint of worry from her words. "It was very hard for Sundance – coming of age in a world without unicorns. For all that the people of Caelum meant well, he was overwhelmed by the humans' curiosity and constant presence. He has long been desiring our return home. We will probably find him in the Valley, or at Wentra."

It took several hours to get to the Valley, the original Gardyn sanctuary in the forest. It was a large,

106

open area that had once been the home of Autumn and his herd of unicorns.

When they passed through the natural defence of high, impenetrable brush, Samantha noted the absence of the unicorns with some distress. She had brought the problems of the human war to their forest; and she felt that it was her fault that Autumn felt driven from his home to the hide in the unicorn sanctuary of Wentra.

Now, half the Valley was taken up by horse corrals that contained the bulk of the Gardyn cavalry and heavy horse. The rest accommodated the people, rows of tents and huts, some still being hastily erected for the army Samantha had brought from Caelum.

Alina said her goodbye to Samantha and Siabhor and trotted away to find Sundance, before returning to visit Autumn at Wentra.

As Samantha and Siabhor continued to the tents, people would stand aside to let them pass, saluting as they did so. A couple of years ago this would have startled Samantha, but she just nodded graciously and pushed her horse to keep up with her favourite monster.

From one of the larger canvasses a familiar captain emerged. "Lady Samantha, welcome home." Captain Rinar said formally.

Samantha stopped her horse and dismounted, pleased to see the Gardyn. Rinar might not have the shining career of his cousin, Rian, but Samantha found he was one of the most trustworthy allies she had.

"Thank you, Captain. I'm glad to be back" Samantha replied with a smile. Home. With a slight bitterness, Samantha acknowledged that her home was with the Gardyn in Enchena, more than it ever had been in Leeds. "How is everyone settling in?"

Rinar sighed at the dull mechanics of settling an army. "Everyone is fine. We've sorted out Lord Mgair's old accommodation for the princes to use. Everything will soon be on track for us to attack Hrafn."

"Good, an army this large won't escape notice. I'd be surprised if Hrafn doesn't already know of our return."

Samantha hesitated, looking uncertain. "I want to see it."

Rinar knew immediately what she meant. "The city? Of course, we'll go first thing tomorrow."

Samantha nodded, "I want a small party. Include the Princes Lugal and Cristan – they have the right to see it. And I want the girl Jemma, to come with us. Have her sent for immediately."

*****

"Jemma, can you come out here please?" Saxton asked from the tent entrance.

Jemma stood up obediently; she had offered to tidy the tent and was glad to step outside into a fresh breeze on the hot summer afternoon. "What is it?"

Saxton glanced at a man that Jemma didn't recognise. "You've been summoned to journey with a small party led by Lady Samantha herself."

"Oh," Jemma was surprised by the news, she was quite sure that Lady Samantha didn't like her. "But, why?"

"That's not for us to know," Saxton replied softly, "You have to go with the messenger to the Valley. I'm sure everything will be explained there."

"On my own?" Jemma asked, panicking. She had already gotten so comfortable with the Marsh family and Treefort, she couldn't imagine being stuck in the middle of the Gardyn stronghold with only the daunting Lady Samantha as company.

"Angrud and I will accompany you." Saxton replied, glancing at the messenger for any sign of argument. "The Gardyn won't want their precious oracle to go without an escort. Go pack a bag for the journey, I will get the horses ready."

Jemma managed a thank you, then ducked back into the humid tent. She immediately went to the corner that had been reserved for her few possessions since she had become a permanent guest of the Marsh family.

"What are you doing?"

Jemma glanced over her shoulder to see Russit staring at her.

"I've got to go to the Valley." Jemma replied truthfully.

"Really?" Russit's voice rose with the excitement of the idea. "That's where the main army is. Can I come too?"

"I don't think so." Jemma replied a little too quickly. She saw the sour look that preceded one of Russit's tempers and added quietly, "You're not thirteen yet, your parents are still in charge of you and I doubt they'd let you come."

"What if I asked them?" Russit asked, his face still dark.

Jemma sighed, "Even if they said yes, you weren't invited."

Russit was about to answer when the tent flap was drawn back and an impatient-looking Angrud looked in.

"Are you ready, Jemma?"

Jemma nodded and slung her bag over her shoulder. Once outside, she took the reins of the docile bay mare and accepted the offer of a leg-up.

"I'll see you when I get back, Russit." She called down to the young lad as her horse began to follow the messenger's steed; Saxton and Angrud quickly falling in behind them.

*****

Samantha strolled down to the far end of the Valley, where a handsome young palomino unicorn was pacing. Frustrated, his forelegs reared up to paw the air as he cast a spiteful glance at the forest.

"Hello, Sundance." Samantha called out, trying to sound as though nothing worried her.

Sundance suddenly turned towards her, horn lowered. Samantha was shocked by the intensely furious thoughts that seeped from the beautiful creature.

Seeing that it was Samantha that approached him, Sundance relaxed and the fury that lit his eyes faded. "Samantha, I was not expecting to see you." Sundance seemed once more the honest colt that Samantha knew, embarrassed and ashamed by his show of exuberance.

"I came to see how you are." Samantha explained, "I actually expected you to go with Alina and visit Autumn and the others."

Sundance snorted and glanced away to the looming forest. "I have no wish to see Autumn, he is only interested in my aunt."

The sorrow and confusion the young unicorn felt was suddenly expressed so strongly through his thoughts that Samantha felt suffocated.

"I want to be with my friends, but I have changed so much and they have not. Everything about them seems almost... pointless." Sundance couldn't meet Samantha's gaze. "I just wish my father was still here."

Samantha nodded sadly. She had briefly known Nmirr, a pale grey stallion who was respected throughout all unicorn herds for his wisdom and good natures; and the only unicorn that drove fear into the black hearts of the dark unicorns. It made sense that Sundance would want his guidance above all else. Unfortunately, the great Nmirr had been killed shortly after he had aided the humans.

"I know, and I'm sorry for you." Samantha replied quietly, "It would have been better if David and I had never come to Enchena. David is a plague to us all, including poor Nmirr."

"You mean, when David betrayed my father and his herd?" Sundance kept his thoughts steady to draw the truth out of the girl, but inside he was crumbling.

"If only we hadn't met your herd; Hrafn only killed them because he was afraid of Gardyn allies."

Sundance tensed, shock flooding his body. The young stallion suddenly shied away and ran to the border of the Valley and into the forest, racing away from the humans as fast as he could.

Samantha watched and the heavy realisation dawned on her: what a terrible way for Sundance to find out the truth about his father's murder.

*****

Elsewhere in the Valley, the two princes were being given a grand tour of the Gardyn camp. All that was left was the training grounds and, at the request of Prince Lugal, their guide took them first to the armoury so that they might kit up and test their reflexes after two hundred years suspended in stone.

The armoury was one of the few permanent buildings that the Gardyn had taken the time to build from the

111

abundant timber. The people were hardy and the large tents with heavy canvasses were enough for them. The store of weapons and armour that they had accumulated was important enough to deserve permanent shelter.

The store was frequently used for training and scouting purposes, so it came as no surprise as the two princes approached the large wooden hut, that they heard the voices of recently returned scouts.

"By Minaeri, I can't wait to lay down and sleep for at least a week." One man's voice moaned, punctuated with a yawn.

"I know what you mean, these shifts are murder. But what can we do, except keep looking for danger while the army sits on its fat arse-"

"Don't start that again, Teron. I've had two bloody days of your moaning." The first voice cut in, annoyed. "Rian's not going to move us just 'cause you're fed up."

"It's not about me being 'fed up'. We're here living the free life while Hrafn forces the rest of the world to live in hell."

Outside the door of the armoury, Cristan and Lugal exchanged looks, their royal blood not interfering with their eavesdropping ability.

Their guide looked sheepish overhearing his fellow Gardyn, "Um, perhaps we should..."

Cristan ignored him and opened the door, walking into the large, dimly lit building. Lugal followed closely.

"...a lot of the lads agree with me." The second man, Teron continued, oblivious to the entrance of the two princes.

"I know, you've told me, but I'm not changing my mind, nor will Captain Rian." The first man to speak hesitated as he spared a glance at those coming in. Every soldier had heard the buzz around camp about the two princes, twin sons of the ancient King Gearalt It took a while for the facts to register, it had never occurred to the man that he would actually come across them. "Y-your highnesses, sirs!"

"Please, do not let us interrupt your conversation, sirs. We merely come to find things suitable for practice." Cristan said with a slight amusement.

"It is nothing sir, your highness, sir. My friend was just speaking inconsequentially."

"I wasn't." Teron dared to speak out, ignoring the terrified glances and obvious hint from his colleague. "Your highnesses, know that I am loyal to the Gardyn and I would never go against their leaders. But we have been waiting in hiding and preparation for nearly a year with no sign that this is going to change. We are Enchena's only hope, yet we hide away waiting for nothing, while Enchena slowly dies under the tyrannical grip of Hrafn. I am a lowly soldier, but I would march into battle tomorrow, alone and unarmed, rather than wait and allow the suffering for one more day."

Teron's friend blanched as he dared to speak out, but the princes stood quietly in thought.

"The Gardyn are lucky to have a soldier as dedicated and passionate as you. Do not fear, I do not think the waiting will last much longer, now that your Lady Samantha has returned. Continue to put your trust in Captain Rian, he has not led you wrong so far." Lugal replied sincerely and carefully, trying not to upset the man's fervour. "Now, if you gentlemen would please excuse us, we have training to get to."

The two soldiers nodded, and gave clumsy bows before fleeing from the armoury.

"He has a point, brother." Cristan said quietly, after the two men had left. "From what I have heard, many of these men have been sitting around for months and are spoiled and rotten from not confronting their enemy."

Lugal shook his head, "Dear brother, he was bordering on treason. I cannot believe that this Captain Rian would sit around and wait if he had the means of destroying the current king."

"Treason or not, when a man speaks with such sense, he should be listened to." Cristan replied, irritated by Lugal's cool attitude.

"We have been part of this era's fight for a few days, what can you know? Come, Cristan, you are still compelled by our last battle. That was different, this will be different. The Gardyn have built a skilled fighting force and have the very blessing of Minaeri in Lady Samantha. Ah, brother, let us take a sword to the practising area and see if we can satisfy that fighting spirit of yours." Lugal smiled knowingly at his impulsive brother. He picked up a sword and its scabbard from the nearest shelf and handed it to Cristan.

Cristan took a deep breath and, as much as he wanted to slap that patronising look off his brother's face, he deigned to smile back. "Very well, let us see if two hundred years have improved you. By Minaeri, I can only hope it has!"

Ten

"Where is it...?" Samantha muttered as she searched the tent she was to share with the Deorwines, rummaging through more stuff than she thought she owned.

It was late in the evening and Samantha wanted to be completely prepared for tomorrow's journey, but she still couldn't find Legan's rug. Which was hardly surprising; they had only just arrived in the Valley, and all their belongings had been thrown into the tent and was yet to be organised.

"Let me guess, you chose your own horse." Tobias softly repeated chiding words from long ago, a teasing smile playing on his lips.

Samantha spun round, trying not to seem to startled and trying to calm her racing pulse that had nothing to do with fright.

Tobias seemed uncomfortable, but held up a murky-looking webbing. "Here, we borrowed it this morning."

Samantha took the rug that camouflaged her pale stallion and mumbled her thanks. She put it beside her sword and sat down on her bed. The silence stretched on between them, growing increasingly awkward. Samantha

115

always used to be comfortable around Tobias, and she wondered when that had changed. They were close, and continued to live like brother and sister in Caelum. He knew her better than almost anyone, he always tried to support her mad ideas, he knew how to stop her arguments and how to react when she was upset.

So why did it make her so nervous, when he looked at her now?

"There was-"

"I didn't-"

Samantha blushed as she blurted out at the same time as Tobias. "Sorry."

"It's alright. What were you going to say?"

Samantha shrugged, having nothing but nonsense and awkward small talk in her head. "Nothing important; just that it feels weird being back here."

Tobias sat on the bed next to her, sighing. "It's hard to believe that a few days ago we were in a different world. It already seems like some strange dream. I imagine that is how you felt about your home world."

Samantha grimaced, she didn't like thinking about England. "It was a different life. Enchena is my home now, with you. And Jillis, of course."

Tobias' eyes fixed on a loose lock of hair, and he reached out, gently pushing it out of her eyes, his hand lightly brushing the side of her face. "One day this war will be over, and we will be free to make what we wish of this life. We'll go anywhere you like; visit the foreign lands and see everything this world has to offer."

Samantha's skin seemed to burn where he touched her cheek, and Tobias' words fed the fire within her. She turned to face him, completely aware of how close he was.

She bit her lip as he leant forwards, her pulse racing and panic rising as Tobias tilted his head towards her-

"Lady Samantha, I-" Someone burst into the tent. "Oh, I'm sorry to intrude."

Samantha took a deep breath, feeling both relieved and cheated. At the entrance a messenger hovered uncertainly, looking scared at barging into the scene.

"What is it?" Samantha asked irritably.

"My Lady, the oracle Miss Jemma has arrived. You did ask to be informed."

Samantha almost groaned and stood up. "Yes, of course." She made her way out into the cool evening, but paused to look back at Tobias, "I'll... see you later, I suppose."

Tobias sat for a few minutes immobile, then sighed and looked up. "You really don't like me, do you Minaeri?" He asked through the canvas roof to the heavens.

He stood up and ran a hand through his black hair, then shook his head and stepped out of the tent.

"So, what happened?"

Tobias bumped into his sister as soon as he was outside and looked down to meet her curious gaze.

"What do you mean?"

"Really Tobias, I make myself scarce all evening so you and Samantha are alone and you ask what I mean?"

Tobias felt a stab of embarrassment. He was only just coming to the realisation that he cared for Samantha, and he didn't like the idea that Jillis knew about his feelings before he did. He looked down at his annoying little sister, "No, none of your matchmaking. Why don't you look to your own future? Have you decided which of the

117

princes has taken your fancy, or do you intend to string them both along a little longer?"

Jillis expression cooled after her brother's unusually cruel remark. "I will not be taking relationship advice from you, Tobias. And just so you know, I have been nothing but friendly towards our new allies. Nothing less, nothing more. It is not my fault that men mistake friendship for romantic intentions when a pretty face is involved."

"I'm sorry, I didn't mean that." Tobias sighed, feeling guilty. "I should be going, I want to speak with Rian and Rinar before dinner."

*****

After taking the briefest possible meeting with the oracle and her guards, Samantha strolled towards the corral, keen to stretch her legs and... honestly, to put off being in her tent with Tobias for a little while longer. She still hadn't worked out what it all meant when Alina trotted up and interrupted her thoughts.

"Samantha, have you seen Sundance?" The grey unicorn asked.

"He ran into the forest earlier today and I haven't seen him since." She glanced about and lowered her voice. "We were talking about Nmirr – Sundance didn't know the truth about David, did he?"

Alina was startled. Her slowly forming thoughts were reluctant to be shared, but eventually ashamed thoughts echoed in Samantha's mind. "There was never a right time, after all that has happened. Then in Caelum he grew so angry with the world I thought it kinder, safer, to let him think it was nothing more than a group of skilled hunters, killing for their own profit and amusement."

Samantha reached up and ran her hand down the length of Alina's smooth neck, trying to sooth the unicorn; she could almost feel the stress resonating through her. "Do you think he went to Wentra? Or perhaps your old herd grounds?"

Alina nickered, "Yes, it's possible. I worry about him being alone."

"Sundance is smart and fast even faster than you now, he'll be alright." Samantha replied, "But if you're worried, you can ask Siabhor to help you track him down."

Alina flicked her tail, the tension starting to fade. "You are right, I am over-reacting. If you see him, tell him that I wish to speak to him, to explain."

"Of course, Alina." Samantha replied, "I'll get Captain Rian to alert the scouting parties, they'll find him in no time."

*****

Sundance didn't care where he ran. As the forest darkened and chaotic thoughts ravaged his mind he surged along unknown paths. Eventually, even the adrenaline leant to him by his fury burnt out, and he came to a stop far from any place he knew. His lithe golden frame was darkened with sweat and stinging cuts from clawing branches. His head was so low that his pearly horn almost touched the ground.

A fading part of Sundance felt anxiety and a need to seek his friends, but the gloom and shadow of the overcast night told him that he was all alone. His thoughts raced and turned his anxiety to confusion and anger. All he knew for certain was that his friends were false, feeding him lies to keep him complacent and even helping those that had killed his father.

119

Dark claws seared his heart and tore at his soul. He had been betrayed. The rawness of his hatred filled his exhausted body, it came like a fever to his mind and Sundance did not attempt to dispel the feeling, but nurtured it.

A unicorn's ability to communicate with the mind is a powerful thing and the intense despair and anger that Sundance felt seeped out like tendrils into the dark forest, subtly calling forth a certain type of creature.

The black unicorn stallion emerged from the trees like a wraith, formless and silent. As he stepped out of the shadows, the only part of him clearly seen was he pearly horn that protruded from his forehead. The darkest and most dangerous of unicorns, the infamous Dark Being.

"Who are you?" The stallion's oily thoughts reached out to the young palomino, both demanding and curious of the intensity of the individual.

"Nobody." Came the shallow, dejected reply.

"That is probably true, but I asked for your name." The Dark Being lowered his horn, his muscles tensing, ready to attack.

At this point, Sundance lifted his handsome head and met the Dark Being's fiery gaze. "Then kill me, I have nothing to live for."

The two stallions stood face to face. The Dark Being was old, but he had not diminished in strength nor presence, his sharp mind had not dulled with age.

"You do not know fear. You encourage dark thoughts so strongly that it could call me forth." The black stallion bowed his head slightly, "May the night bless thee."

Up to this point, Sundance had remained detached from everything, but the Dark Being's final thought made him shiver. May the night bless thee, the formal greeting and acceptance into the herd of dark hearts.

Sundance's gaze did not waver, the Dark Being's herd was known for choosing to fight rather than flee and were famed for chasing down any wandering humans, and it was for humans that Sundance's intense hatred burnt.

"Name yourself and follow me."

Sundance felt the last of his uncertainty ebb away, being replaced by a new strength. "I am Torment."

He did not feel nervous or afraid as he followed the sure strides of the Dark Being. Torment, as he now called himself in his heart, felt a strange nothingness. His body owned no heat, his skin couldn't feel the breath of wind nor the branches that raked his sides; no thoughts disturbed the dark abyss of his mind.

As Torment and the Dark Being moved through the midnight forest, the young palomino noticed they were no longer alone. He caught fleeting glimpses of bright eyes, or pearly horns, momentarily coming together in the form of a unicorn, before dispersing into shadows. Torment would have dismissed it as his imagination, if it weren't for the thoughts that leaked out of their control; half-formed wonderings and curses that threatened to cloud the peaceful emptiness of his mind.

"Torment," The Dark Being called. The black stallion had come to a more open area and the faint moonlight gleamed against his sleek back.

The palomino stepped forward, sealing the fact that he was forever more Torment and that his title of Sundance was as dead as his father. Torment joined the Dark Being and both looked upon a gathering of unicorns. The night leeched the colour from their coats, the chestnuts, bays and black unicorns that lifted their heads at the return of their leader. It was not too different from the herd of the great Nmirr, except there was not a single individual that did not bear a scar across their beautiful hide.

Torment no longer cared enough to be curious about why.

"Answer to me alone and live free. Take whatever mare you are strong enough to keep and control."

Torment barely nodded his acknowledgement of his new leader's words. He went to step down among the herd, but was called back again before he had got too far.

"And Torment, know that in darkness and despair you found me. I alone can guide you, you belong to me now."

The Dark Being watched the young stallion move away. "Say what you will, you snivelling excuse of a beast."

The grating thought was directed to a rather small and ugly bay stallion that had shadowed him from the meeting of Torment, and now sidled out to stand beside his leader.

"My lord of night, saviour of us all." The bay unicorn's grovelling, wheedling nature dominated his thoughts, "Why do you bring a colt made for the sun to our herd of perfection? This Sundance, this Torment is not one of us. Many will not tolerate a son of Nmirr."

The Dark Being swung his entire body round in one fluid movement, his horn scythed the air to meet the flesh of the insubordinate stallion. The bay's legs buckled as he stumbled back, his throat filling with blood.

"Weasel!" The Dark Being snorted as the angry thoughts escaped him. "How dare you question me?" He ignored the fallen unicorn, not caring whether he survived or not, and instead opened his thoughts to the others that had shadowed his journey. "He is proof, that even a son of Nmirr can be… educated. Still, he is not to be trusted yet; watch him closely."

Eleven

Jemma had spent a restless night in the main camp of the Gardyn army. After arriving the evening before, Jemma had been daunted by the number of people, and how many stared at her. Their gaze was curious for the most part, attracted to her bright ginger hair. There was also a hunger in their eyes, an expectation. Did these people think that she was going to do something extraordinary, just because she came from the Lady Samantha's homeland? Just because they tagged her with the title of Oracle?

Jemma stayed inside the guest tent as much as possible. Thankfully her night was without dreams, and she was summoned in the morning, alongside Saxton.

Angrud had already gone to get the horses ready, and he was stood holding the reins of three sleepy-looking beasts. The young man hovered close to a group that was busy assembling. Jemma recognised Lady Samantha, Captain Rian and a couple of the men she thought she remembered from the council meeting at Treefort. There were also the two princes, who looked exactly as they had in her vision.

124

Amongst a few other soldiers, Jemma spotted a dark-haired young man and possibly the most beautiful girl that Jemma had ever seen. Obviously Angrud agreed with her, as he was standing mesmerised when Jemma and Saxton approached.

"Are you alright, Angrud?" Saxton asked, taking the reins of his horse.

"Yeah." He grunted.

A moment later, the black-haired girl came towards them, she looked a couple of years older than Jemma, and had large, kind brown eyes. The two men bowed at her approach.

"Lady Jillis." Saxton greeted.

"I am sorry that I didn't meet with you yesterday." Lady Jillis said warmly, "Are you all ready? Samantha and Rian are determined to get going without a moment to waste."

"Yes, ma'am." Jemma replied, "We are. I am looking forward to seeing the city."

Jillis gave a soft smile, dipped her head and carried on past them to where her own horse was waiting.

"Who was that?" Jemma asked Saxton.

Before Saxton could reply, Angrud spoke, "Lady Jillis Deorwine. She was one of the youngest and most successful Gardyn spies; and now she's a close friend to Lady Samantha. Not to mention she's one of our best archers."

Jemma was shocked that Angrud had said so many polite and useful words towards her, but had a niggling idea as to why. "So, an encyclopaedic knowledge of Lady Jillis, and being unable to speak in her presence... I wonder what that means?"

125

Angrud went bright red and refused to dignify her with an answer. He did proceed to throw her up into the saddle, perhaps a little rougher than necessary.

Jemma just chuckled as she gathered her reins. She had no idea how long today's journey would take, but it was suddenly more palatable, if she could spend those hours getting her own back, teasing Angrud about Jillis, just as he had teased her reaction to Captain Rian.

Jemma's laughter was quickly stifled as she caught the eye of Lady Samantha. The young woman was so very plain compared to her companions, but there was something fierce and confident in her air. Her green eyes were cold and detached as they fixed on Jemma. The lady frowned, and turned away, shouting to the group to move out, as she kicked her own white horse into action.

The ride went smoothly, with their scouts checking out the surrounding forest and reporting nothing of concern. The group of Gardyn still rode quietly, and on alert, not wanting to risk attracting any of the King's scouts.

Jemma jumped as a brown shadow shot past her foot and ran alongside the horses. A mallus. Jemma was still not used to the monsters, despite the time she had spent with Siabhor. She envied the horses, surprised at how relaxed they were at having a predator for company.

Jemma watched the mallus settle into an awkward walk beside Lady Samantha and her horse, towards the front. Jemma assumed that the mallus was Siabhor, but to be honest, they all looked the same to her. She marvelled again at the strange companionship between the monster and Samantha; how could anyone even think to be allies with one, never mind friends. And this was the lady that

126

Gran wanted her to help, this lady that entertained monsters and gave her the cold shoulder. How was Jemma supposed to do… anything?

"Miss Jemma, do you mind if I ride beside you?"

Jemma turned in her saddle to see Lady Jillis' brother riding his horse closer. He shared his sister's dark hair and big, brown eyes, and was subtly handsome in a pleasant way. "Of course, my lord."

He gave a tired smile, "Just Tobias, I am no lord."

Jemma's brow creased, and she looked to *Lady* Jillis.

Tobias caught her look and hurried to explain, "We are baseborn, mere commoners. Over the years, my sister has done many accomplished things and continues to win the hearts of the Gardyn. As far as they are concerned, she is their Lady Jillis, and they will not have it otherwise. Meanwhile I… I have yet to work out my role."

Jemma liked the sound of his voice, and open attitude. After this brief meeting, and that of his sister earlier, she was no longer afraid of these Gardyn 'nobles'.

"I hear you are our new oracle, Miss Jemma." Tobias continued.

Jemma shrugged, "I guess so, but I don't know what it really means. I've just had a couple of visions that… I just feel that, if I hadn't had them, everything would still have happened the same. Samantha would have still returned, likewise with the two princes. I haven't done a single thing that's… special."

Tobias smiled and sat quietly for a minute. "Minaeri would not have sent you, if she did not have a bigger plan. Perhaps this has all been a warm-up for something more… special?"

"Perhaps." Jemma replied, a little sullen. "But how am I supposed to help if… Lady Samantha… she doesn't like

127

me. I know that she'd send me home if she had half a chance."

"Samantha doesn't dislike you, Jemma." Tobias replied quickly. "She doesn't know you yet; I'm sure when she does, it will all be fine. But for now, you're the girl from home."

"Why should that be a problem?"

"Because just when she was putting all thoughts of homesickness behind her, you appear and make it all come rushing back." Tobias answered honestly, "It is also a harsh reminder of what she has been through. She has killed, and watched friends die; she was betrayed and broken; then you come as an innocent reminder of what she used to be. It is easier for her to keep you at a distance."

Jemma rode along, absorbing it all. "You know her really well, don't you?"

Tobias looked up to where Samantha rode up front, "She's become one of my closest friends, I can't imagine life without her. She's like a sister."

Jemma watched as he gave only the slightest hint that his final comment was a lie, but she said nothing, not wanting to embarrass the guy when he'd been so friendly and otherwise open with her.

The journey was an interminable scene of trees and tracks, but eventually they came to their destination.

They stayed in the perimeter of the forest, safely out of sight to any that looked out from the city.

The forest ended and the land dipped down steeply, rising again to meet a high, defensive wall that completely encircled the capital city. Above the wall, only the tops of the tallest buildings could be seen; turrets and towers for the important court of Enchena. Only the palace could be seen more clearly, sitting imposingly on top of a hill, casting its shadow over the city.

Jemma stared with amazement at her first glimpse of the city. It was beautiful, and daunting, and she suddenly wished for the safety of Treefort.

"It looks just as it did two hundred years ago," Prince Lugal said, with a note of relief in his voice, as though he was glad something in this mad world had stayed the same.

"The Kings of Enchena do not like change," Captain Rian stated.

"Let's see what we can do about that." Samantha said, quietly. Her eyes scanned the great wall, and she paused, "the main gate is closed."

"Hrafn has gone mad. The Gardyn have disrupted his authority so greatly that he withdrew to his city and closed the gates. They allow food wagons through once a week, no others may pass. The citizens are condemned to starve to death."

"There are other ways out of the city," Prince Cristan argued, "we had tunnels built for us to avoid our brother, Brandon; and so we could move freely about the city. Surely they still exist."

Rian grit his teeth, but nodded respectfully. "Forgive me, your highness, but most of your tunnels are now derelict. The only one that we know is open leads straight into the palace grounds."

Cristan frowned, not ready to admit defeat, "If the King has shut himself in the palace, let us try to draw him out. Let us attempt to take over the rest of Enchena first; get him away from the city so that we may help those trapped."

Rian shot a look to Samantha before speaking, "This has been attempted, your highness, but we found the army too well organised against our reduced numbers. We ended up losing the lives of loyal Gardyn and gaining nothing. The King may be a recluse, but the armies are being controlled most efficiently by his advisor, Captain Losan… and by his heir."

Samantha's attention was caught by this news, "David?"

"Wait a minute, David? David Jones is the heir to the throne?" Jemma spoke up, trying to comprehend what this meant. "You said he was helping the King."

"It's a long story," Samantha said dismissively, "but it does make things more difficult. We want to replace the current King with someone more sympathetic to the Gardyn. But if the great army of Enchena is already loyal to the one named as heir to the throne…"

Samantha sighed, her concentration returning to the city before her. Inside, determination welled up and the spark that made her different grew stronger.

The rest of the small party sat silently, each nurturing their own thoughts.

Jemma refused to concentrate too strongly on the city before her, because as she did so she heard phantom cries of woe from thousands and felt the odd, lightening sensation that came before a vision. The girl looked back into the forest, willing the oncoming vision to stop. Lady Samantha was here now, there was no reason for her to have these terrible experiences anymore. The sensation faded and left her completely.

"So, what do you plan then, Captain?" Cristan spoke up, his hard gaze directed towards Rian. "We cannot leave the civilians to suffer."

"I hate leaving them to starve as much as any," Rian replied, trying very hard to remain polite. "We are still waiting for the rest of the Gardyn."

Lugal was about to speak, but Cristan cut in, "Waiting? If I am not mistaken, Captain, your army just swelled by many hundreds that came from Caelum, plus a lady that is Hrafn's equal."

"Hundreds that could die in a day." Rian snapped. "It is still not enough. The rest of our forces are expected any day now. In your impatience, would you rush in before they arrive and have us slaughtered?"

Cristan seemed insulted by Rian's harsh words, as though the prince had never had to suffer such treatment.

Lugal saw trouble brewing in his brother and interrupted the argument. "Cristan, peace brother. Captain Rian, I apologise, I understand your position. Please accept our skills when the battle is finally fought."

Captain Rian inclined his head to Prince Lugal, thankful for his show of grace. Rian turned his attention away from the two princes and instead looked to Samantha. He knew better than anyone else present what would eventually have to happen.

"Have you one of your plans, Samantha?"

Samantha shrugged, "I have some thoughts. I've seen all I need to see, I want to go back to the Valley." Without waiting, she turned her horse back to the refuge of the forests.

Everyone followed her lead and started back to the west, but Rian paused. Samantha stopped and rode back to where the Gardyn captain looked serious.

"You do know," Rian said quietly, "that David may have to die."

A pained look crossed Samantha's face and without saying anything, she joined the others on the western path.

Samantha steeled herself and rode up beside Jemma. "Have you... had any visions about what... what happens next?"

Jemma was momentarily speechless that the lady would speak to her, but hurried to answer. "No, ma'am. I haven't."

Samantha chewed her lip, she still didn't believe they needed an oracle, but perhaps the others were right and she should use what was available. "How does it work?" She asked with some scepticism.

Jemma felt an embarrassed blush creep up her neck. "I don't actually know. I can't control them, I go light-headed and then they take over. I never know what they are going to be about."

They rode along in silence for so long, Jemma was starting to think that she had confirmed her lack of worth to Lady Samantha. What use was an oracle that couldn't decide what to see? How could she sit around and wait for a vision that may not come?

Eventually Samantha turned in her saddle to look directly at her, something more human in her green eyes. "I remember when I first came here, I had no idea what I could do and I couldn't even tell when I was doing it. You see, I'd convinced myself that David was the one with the powers that everyone sought – I was just the sidekick.

"It was a very confusing time, and I was more of a danger to the Gardyn than a real advantage. My friends helped me. The first step was to truly accept that the powers were mine, that they were a part of me and nothing to be afraid of. After that, I had to work out what

132

triggered them – mainly strong emotions on my part. Then it was simply practise."

Jemma was struck that Samantha was probably the only person that knew what she was going through, and she was making it all sound so simple, "I don't know if I can..."

"You owe it to yourself to try, you were sent here for a reason." Samantha insisted.

"Hmph, what reason? You're here as a goddess, and I'm a cut-price Mystic Meg."

Jemma was surprised when she heard Samantha snort and laugh, she hadn't been that funny, had she? Jemma grinned, looking away to preserve some sort of professionalism.

Samantha sighed and wiped a tear from her eye. When was the last time she had found something funny? When had she last laughed? It was a good feeling.

"The visions scare me - not the content, that's fine. But the fact that I am there, with no control over my body, I feel like a puppet." Jemma sighed, "I should be used to it, I've had crazy dreams for as long as I can remember."

"Did you ever dream of Enchena?" Samantha asked.

Jemma shook her head. "Not that I know of, but I did dream a lot about Minaeri recently. Oh, and a couple of crazy dreams about dragons, but I asked Siarla and she said dragons don't exist here. What a shame, I thought there might be a chance they did after I learnt about unicorns and mallus."

"Ah, what... did the dragons look like?" Samantha asked with forced casualness.

"The night before I came here, there was a red one, that chased me with fire. And my first night here, I had a dream about a blue one that came out of a mountain and

133

flew with me to the Temple of Gates. I can't even begin to describe how huge they both were." Jemma rattled off.

Samantha looked over her shoulder to make sure that no one was riding close enough to overhear her. "Caminus and Leukos."

"What?" Jemma frowned at the weird words.

"Caminus and Leukos," Samantha repeated. "Their names. Caminus is the red dragon and Leukos the blue."

"What?" Jemma echoed.

"They are the last of their kind, hidden beneath a mountain, but with an uncanny ability to see everything that has happened, and will happen." Samantha bit her lip, "No one except the Deorwines know they exist, I trust you will not tell anyone else. If they appear to you again, you need to know that they are real, and they are most likely your best allies."

Having said her piece, Samantha nudged her pale stallion into a trot to catch up with Captain Rian at the head of the ride.

Twelve

With permission from Captain Rian, Jemma and her companions split from the group and rode directly back to Treefort.

Jemma still held her breath as they passed through a gap in the tree barrier. Clinging to the saddle for dear life, she knew that she looked less than elegant. But as a positive, she managed to land on two feet when she dismounted this time. She was getting used to this riding lark, her legs aching less as she led her horse back to the corrals.

Saxton and Angrud had to officially report to their commanding officer, leaving Jemma alone. Having nothing better to do, Jemma dropped her bags off at the Marsh family tent and went to find Siarla.

Siarla was sitting with one of the other mothers, as their younger children played in the fresh air. She looked up and smiled at her return, "Jemma, you're back. Did you have a nice ride?"

"It was, er, unusual." Jemma replied hesitantly, her mind still on the bombshell that Samantha had dropped.

"I should say so, you were in the presence of royalty! Well, I'm glad you're back. Just to warn you, Russit has been moping around all day wanting to ask you about every tiny detail. You'll find in him the tent."

"I've just come from there, I didn't see him."

Siarla sighed, "Why does Minaeri curse me with such a son? He'll be off at the corrals again, or pestering the mallus. Don't worry, he'll be back when he's hungry."

Jemma felt a pang of unease – she hadn't seen him at the corrals either, but she trusted that Siarla knew best.

Evening came and there was still no sign of Russit. Jemma offered to look after Kiya and Betony while their parents searched Treefort and asked every family if they'd seen anything.

As night set firmly in, Jemma got the two girls to their beds, and after telling them Little Red Riding Hood twice, they finally fell asleep. Jemma moved towards the entrance of the tent, hearing the return of Saxton and Siarla.

"Did you check with Dylan's family?" Siarla asked.

"Yes, twice." Saxton confirmed, his voice level in an attempt to calm his wife. "I have to go meet Angrud and the others."

"I can't believe he's outside Treefort. Alone." Siarla murmured, "My little boy."

"There are scout parties out searching for him, and Siabhor's best trackers will be sent for. Russit is... he's a smart kid, Siarla, they'll find him."

Back in the Valley, the small party returned through the defences. They had all ridden in a much quieter mood than when they had headed out that morning.

136

It was with little effort, that a single figure broke away from the group.

Prince Cristan had been stewing for the whole ride back. To see the capital city so quiet and oppressed; to hear of the struggles of the civilians and to do nothing; to ride back as though it had been a pleasure jaunt. He had avoided his brother – he knew that Lugal would attack him with logic until Cristan was both bored and his temper doused.

Cristan nursed his anger, he would need his passion soon. If the heroes of today weren't willing to stand up and save the innocents; he would have to lead the Gardyn again.

It took quite a while for Cristan to find the one man he knew was thinking the same. Teron. He had only known the man for a few minutes, but Cristan was convinced he was the ally he needed right now.

After a few hurried enquiries, Cristan found Teron by the large tent he shared with four other soldiers.

Teron looked up, startled to see one of the princes striding towards him. He made a clumsy effort at a bow, "Your highness! Please, is there anything I can do for you?"

Cristan stood silently for a moment. "What you said, the other day, were you telling the truth when you said many men were ready to march against Hrafn?"

Teron just nodded numbly.

"As you have probably heard, I have been to the capital today," Cristan continued, "I was not aware of how bad the situation was. Do you have enough men to move immediately to free those poor souls?"

Teron struggled to speak, "Y-your highness, I believe that I can get several hundred at a moment's notice."

Cristan nodded grimly, "Well, here is your moment's notice, Teron. I intend to lead those that would do the right think within the hour towards the capital. The city could be free by dawn."

"No!" Teron blurted out suddenly.

"What, you are not a man of your word?" Cristan asked, his face darkening.

"Forgive me, sir, perhaps I was speaking too figuratively. To gather the men and calm any last fears and arguments, to get provisions and have everyone kitted. Not to mention secretly enough to avoid Captain Rian's suspicions – for we do not want him stopping us – your highness, I can have everyone ready at first light tomorrow."

Cristan wavered. He wanted to leave now. He could not imagine spending the sleepless hours of the night with the knowledge he now had of civilians suffering, but he saw sense in Teron's words. "Very well, keep me informed, and make sure the men are willing to follow me."

The prince hesitated, taking a deep breath. They were going to do this, they had to do this.

*****

Deep within the forest, Torment began to realise how much he had yet to learn. Most of the dark herd came and went without any rules or reason, and many left him alone. But there were many who sought out the young palomino stallion, often attacking without warning.

It was only natural in unicorn herds that a newcomer had to find their place in the pecking order. Whereas with other herds, most unicorns were satisfied with demonstrations of superiority, the dark herd revelled in the sadistic pleasure of violence. Or perhaps they wanted to test Torment's resolve.

A few days, and several sore cuts later, Torment was starting to find his place. Although he was young, he was holding his ground. He never instigated the fights, but Torment quickly found that many of the unicorns were weak, and far from his equal.

He wasn't here to make friends, but as time went on, there were definitely some unicorns that were becoming less hostile towards him.

There was one that he had caught sight of, but had yet to meet. A fine black mare, not much older than himself. Torment had the slightest glimpse of her that first evening, so brief that he thought he had imagined the beautiful creature.

Another evening, he caught only her scent, as she melted into the surrounding forest.

Torment was old enough to have mares of his own, and this new need was a dizzying sensation. He only knew that he had to speak with this mystery mare, he had to satisfy his swiftly-growing obsession.

One night, he was sure he sensed her near the stream that cut through the herdland, and he followed the faint promise that she was there.

The mare heard his approach and gracefully raised her fine head, her horn reflecting the glittering moonlight. Her beauty was soon marred, when she pinned her ears flat back against her skull and bared her teeth.

"Run away, spawn of Nmirr." The cold thoughts emanated out. "We have no use for little light lords here."

The insults were nothing compared to what he had suffered recently, but Torment stood uncomfortably, not sure what he was supposed to say.

The black mare's countenance softened as she saw that she had a new admirer. "Oh no. By Praede and all that is dark, no. Find another mare to make those big brown eyes at."

"I don't know what you mean..." Torment tried to lie, but couldn't drum up much enthusiasm. "I just want to know your name."

"Odile." The mare replied with a snort, before turning to walk away.

"Odile, wait."

Torment sprang forwards to block her, but she moved quicker. The black mare lashed out with her hind feet, connecting painfully with his shoulder. Torment winced in pain, only for Odile to vanish in the distraction.

Not content with the brief meeting, Torment stalked the stream every evening. Whenever he walked, he tried to hide his limp, his shoulder bruised and aching from their last encounter.

One very wet and miserable night, Torment stood in the rain, his gold coat and silver mane bedraggled and tarnished.

There was a derisive snort from behind him, followed by a familiar voice. "You are very..."

"Persistent?" Torment turned to look for the black mare.

"Annoying." Odile corrected, as she stepped out of the shadows, her gaze still aloof, but betraying some curiosity.

Torment's ears twitched, it was not the first time he had been called such, but he did not want to be reminded of his previous life.

Odile ignored the rain that relentlessly fell, as she circled the young stallion. "I'm surprised you've survived this long with us. Are you tired of your adolescent rebellion yet? Are you ready to scurry back to the light?"

Torment followed Odile's movements, wary that she might vanish again. "Do not belittle my choice to join this herd. It is for life."

Odile flicked her tail, the black strands catching Torment's wet coat. "Don't talk to me like an entitled little lordling. Otherwise that life you speak of will be pathetically short." Odile gave a disgusted glance. "If I don't kill you, my father will."

"And who is your father?" Torment asked.

"You don't know?" Amusement laced her words. "Oh, this is too good."

"The Dark Being?"

"I am his only daughter. You are courting death itself if you dare think yourself worthy of me."

"You don't scare me." Torment replied quietly, "And neither does he."

Odile stood there, looking at him, the only sound was that of the falling rain.

"You're either very brave, or a fool." Odile finally said. "If you anger him, you will be killed. No unicorn alive can best him. Even the great Nmirr could barely match him. Does that honestly not scare you?"

Torment looked away, his sharp eyes catching the movement of the herd shifting in the rainy night. He did not feel fear, he never had. Not when his father's herd was attacked; or when faced with the mallus Siabhor; not even when an unknown world called to him.

That fearlessness was still there; in fact it was more obvious, now the softness was washed away. No, all he

141

felt now was a throbbing curiosity, and a desire to test himself. If he won Odile in the process, that was a benefit.

He turned his handsome head back to the black mare. "He has yet to fight me."

Thirteen

It was the middle of the night and Jemma must have fallen into a dreamless sleep at some point. There was a clamour in Treefort and the sound of people running and shouting.

Jemma dashed outside to see people congregating at the edge of Treefort. Jemma pulled a shawl about her shoulders and walked towards them curiously, hopefully - had they found Russit?

The trees had parted, but the crowd was too thick for Jemma to see the focus of their attention. She glanced along the border, surely all trees would part to give passage to the Gardyn and their allies?

She snuck away and moved along the border. Checking that no one was watching, she stepped closer to the huge trunks of the tightly packed trees. The leaves rustled and the trunks shuddered, then slowly drew apart, leaving a gap just wide enough for Jemma to squeeze through. The passage closed behind her with a small thud, shutting out the friendly firelight of the Gardyn camp.

Jemma made her way back along the border to a place where torchlight flickered. A strange and unexpected sight met her eyes.

A patrol stood in a large circle, swords in hand, and bows ready for use. On an inner circle, several spindly mallus crouched, hair bristling as they growled. All for a single prisoner.

A man knelt in the very centre, hands tied behind his back and a blindfold covering half of his face. He wore a black uniform with a vivid red stripe down one side. Jemma vaguely remembered the uniform from the King's men that had almost caught when she had first arrived in Enchena. Jemma squinted to try and make out his features in the bad light, but the thick blindfold hid everything but a scar that crossed the man's cheek and cut into his lip.

"This is too big for us to deal with. Get a message to the Valley immediately, we need Captain Rian."

Jemma jumped as she heard someone speak out from the shadows.

"Hey, what are you doing here?" The patrol leader moved towards her, his eyes moving up to her bright hair, "You're that oracle, aren't you? Get back inside, it's too dangerous out here."

Jemma glanced towards the prisoner, wondering how a single man could be so dangerous that he merited such a guarding. But Jemma obediently moved back to Treefort, opting to go through the already open passage and push through the crowd.

*****

Captain Rian and Lady Samantha travelled through the dark hours to arrive at Treefort at dawn. Both found the news hard to believe, but outside the border was the

144

prisoner, still in the same position as he had been all night.

Samantha took one of the soldiers aside, muttering instructions to him. The man rushed away and soon returned with Jemma, Saxton and Siarla Marsh. Siarla's eyes were red with crying and her husband looked equally terrible for his sleep-deprived nightmare of a night.

Meanwhile, Rian marched through the rings of soldiers and mallus, his sword drawn and ready in his hand. He reached down and roughly pulled away the blindfold.

The prisoner blinked in the light that now clearly showed his features, the long scar along one side of his face, cutting across the rough skin that was starting to betray his age, his eyes staring fearlessly ahead.

Eyes that Jemma had seen before. "Orion," she breathed.

"Get up!" Rian barked fiercely.

The man started to stand, but his legs were numb from hours of kneeling on hard ground, and he staggered, unable to balance himself with his hands tied behind his back. Rian grabbed his uniform at the shoulder and dragged him upright.

"Now tell me, "Rian hissed, laying the edge of his sword against the prisoner's neck. "Where is the boy, and why was Orion Losan wandering the forest alone?"

Orion Losan... A shiver went through the gathered humans and Siarla Marsh bit back a sob. None had doubted that this was Captain Orion Losan, the leader of the King's army, friend and advisor to Hrafn and the murderer of thousands of rebels. But the name had its own power and spoken aloud, made fear flicker through those present.

Losan didn't reply, but continued to stare stubbornly, fearlessly ahead.

"Co-operate an I'll make your death more pleasant than you deserve." Rian growled, more furious and darker than any had seen him, his blade now pressing harder into his enemy's neck.

Losan ignored the blood that trickled down to his collar, his eyes moved about the circle, finally settling on Samantha. When he spoke, his voice was strong and clear, "Ochata q'uen gardyn, i banyen t'Minaeri."

Only one person understood. To Samantha the words held meaning, as they had once before. *'I protect the oppressed, if Minaeri commands it.'*

"Ich behan Minaeri." She found herself saying. "Minaeri commands it."

"The boy has been taken to the King for questioning. I am here because it is time." Losan answered immediately.

Rian's eyes narrowed in suspicion, but he took a step back. "I don't understand, what is going on?"

Samantha walked slowly forward, her eyes fixed on Losan; she had not been this close to the Captain since she was Hrafn's captive in the palace. "He has come to help the Gardyn."

"I don't believe that for a moment." Rian snapped.

"H-he's been helping the Gardyn for most of his life."

At the sound of the meek voice, everyone turned to face Jemma. The attention made her cheeks flame as red as her hair, but she hesitantly continued. "He is the informer, the cloaked man at my first council. He has always been helping the Gardyn..."

Rian grunted, "I doubt that very much."

146

Losan stood tall, his gaze turning to the rebel Captain, "It was I that directed the move of the Gardyn to the forest." He began to reel off dispassionately, "I presented the map of the secret tunnels to the Deorwine boy. And I was the only one to argue against sending the Gardyn force into battle when Hrafn took the throne."

Samantha suddenly remembered something, "You helped me escape the palace, you cleared the way."

Losan nodded gently in acknowledgment and a surprised muttering went through the Gardyn soldiers.

Rian glared about the circle of soldiers, suddenly realising that this interrogation should have been conducted in private.

"Quiet." He barked at his men, then turned back to Captain Losan. "You work with the King to destroy the Gardyn, not help us. Do not think to deceive us."

Losan didn't reply, knowing that words weren't enough. He looked over his shoulder, to Treefort, then without warning he marched up to the border, passing the dazed mallus and soldiers.

"Stop him!" Rian yelled.

The humans hesitated, still fearful of Losan, but the mallus leapt forward.

The trees shook and the very ground rumbled. An opening appeared, revealing the Gardyn camp.

Knowing that the trees would instinctively crush any foe of the Gardyn, Losan stepped calmly into the gap, and turned to face them. The trees quivered violently, but held their place.

"Now will you listen?"

*****

By the horse corral, six figures gathered away from the rest of the camp.

"We should have kept him tied up." Rian muttered, refusing to sit down, and never taking his eyes from Orion Losan.

Samantha tutted, "give over, I could have him dead before he could do anything."

"Actually, I could probably kill you all and escape if I so wished." Losan said quietly. "Time is running out, and now that I am uncloaked, you must trust me still."

"Then get on and tell us what is happening." Rian snarled.

Losan looked up at him almost pitifully, "You must learn to control that temper of yours, boy."

Captain Losan then looked to Siarla and Saxton Marsh who were huddled together next to Jemma. When he spoke again, it was with surprising sympathy.

"I was with a contingent of mounted soldiers. We had been sent by Prince David to travel in the direction of your camps where we would meet one of his informants. Navigating the forest is becoming harder for enemies of the Gardyn, the tracks and trees seem to change of their own accord, but luck had it that we spotted a fresh set of tracks – four or five ridden horses – and we followed, hoping to be led to a stronghold.

"Unfortunately, we lost all tracks and signs of the group as we neared this place. We were about to retrace our steps when we saw a young boy wandering the forests alone. The lieutenant ordered my men to take him, before I could intercede. The soldiers began to ride back to the capital. I waited a few minutes then shouted, commanding my men to finish their task, then race back to the city, as were under attack. The lie worked and I was left behind. Everyone would assume that the great Captain Orion Losan had finally fallen. I let my horse loose, then waited for your scouts to find me. The boy..." Losan glanced to Russit's parents, "He will have been taken to the city for questioning."

The only sound was Siarla's crying.

"We might still be able to save him." Samantha was the first to speak, almost scared of breaking the woeful silence. She ignored the credulous look from Rian and continued, "Siarla, you have daughters, don't you? I want you to go and keep them comforted. Saxton, Jemma, you'll come to the Valley with us. I want both of you to be a part of this. Go get ready and we'll send for you when we are ready to leave."

Samantha waited for the three to walk away, then spoke to Losan. "Now, tell us what you could not in front of them."

"Hrafn will execute the boy once he has extracted all useful information."

"We could have guessed that." Rian stated.

"Really? Then you have also guessed that Hrafn expects your Lady Samantha to carry out an ill-devised rescue and plans to capture her, hopefully destroying whatever unorganised and hastily assembled army that accompanies her."

"How do you know this?" Rian asked, "Kidnapping Russit can't have been anticipated, and you have no means to contact your King."

Losan looked away, feeling torn. "You cannot be friends with a man for as long as I have, see his reactions in so many situations, without knowing his mind."

"How did Hrafn know that I was back?" Samantha asked.

A silence descended. How did the King know that the lady he had chased into another world at the edge of a sword had truly returned?

"We have an insider in your army." Losan replied calmly, "He has been feeding the King with information for many months."

"That's impossible." Rian interrupted, "No Gardyn would dare betray us. Besides, no traitor would get away undetected for long."

Losan grimaced, looking at the tall trees that made the border of this safe haven. It was an impressive bit of magic, blessings, curses, or whatever Samantha had done. "He could be undetected if he had never come to Treefort. The Valley has no such security."

"Leave it, Rian." Samantha stopped the Gardyn Captain from whatever snide comment he was about to make. "We will deal with our traitor soon enough, first we have more important things to see to. Get your captains to arrange immediate evacuation of Treefort. We plan for the worst. Get the families back to the Valley."

"Woodvale would be better, it is easier to defend. Even Treefort is more secure than the Valley, as even he pointed out." Rian argued.

"We know where Woodvale is," Losan interjected, "And have you forgotten the girl's vision of this place destroyed? The Valley is still a mystery to us... to them."

"How? You've a bloody spy nestled there!" Rian shouted.

"We cannot locate it." Losan replied quietly, his tone almost embarrassed. "The forest is impossible to navigate, every time we have a bearing or set a route it vanishes or shifts... probably thanks to your Lady Samantha."

The Captain nodded his head in recognition to Samantha's skill with the forest. But the girl sat stunned; she had done nothing of the sort. At least not knowingly. But that was a year ago, when her powers were only just awakening and none of the peculiar events had been attributed to her. Her instinct told her it was something bigger than her.

"It wasn't me. The Valley is a very old area, Autumn told me how it was once the home of Praede, the first unicorn. Between him and Minaeri, no enemy will ever find the Valley." Samantha informed them, "Now, are we going to keep arguing, or shall we get moving before Hrafn's army falls upon us?"

At that moment, Jemma came running up, out of breath and her orange hair a wild mess.

"Samantha, Rian, there's trouble at the Valley." The girl shouted, "I saw fighting. It's happening now."

"How..."

"Don't, we don't have time." Jemma flapped, "You need to go. Now!"

The Valley was usually a haven of order, but the quiet air was disrupted by the shouts of many men as the Gardyn army was suddenly and violently split into two.

Teron had done his job well and by the rising of the sun, several hundred men were armed and making their way to the edge of the Valley to join their new leader, Prince Cristan.

The prince sat upon a stolen horse, his way out of the Valley blocked by the border guards, standing shoulder to shoulder, a human barrier to stop them leaving.

"Let us pass, friends." Cristan called out, trying not to sound as frustrated as he felt.

The guards exchanged wary looks. "Sorry, your highness, we're following orders."

"You know who I am, and no doubt you have heard of what we have seen. I am leading these true Gardyn to free the oppressed. Will you join us, or are you ignorant of their torture."

"We're following orders." The guard repeated firmly.

There was an increase in noise behind him, and Prince Cristan turned to see more men running from the camp to swell the numbers crowded by the borders. He briefly hoped that they were coming to join his fledgling army, but that hope was short-lived.

"Your highness," Captain Philip called out as he ran up, "what is this madness? You must wait for Captain Rian. It would be disastrous for the Gardyn if you took half the army against King Hrafn: you would be slaughtered, and it would damn the rest of us."

"By Minaeri, my brother, listen to sense." The far-too-sensible Prince Lugal followed the Gardyn captain, his eyes betraying shock at his brother's rebellious actions.

"I can wait no longer. All brave, true Gardyn will join me in this attack." Prince Cristan replied sternly, his voice carrying out. He scanned the crowd, so far he and his faction outnumbered the soldiers and guards stopping them, but surely it wouldn't be long before reinforcements came. "Don't make us fight our way out, Captain Philip."

The men that assembled behind Cristan wavered at this threat. They were prepared to rebel against their leaders; fight and die in battle against the King, but none wanted to fight their own side.

Prince Cristan drew his sword, the action echoed by many others. "Nothing you can say will make me turn back. I will lead any that follow me against King Hrafn, or I will go alone."

Captain Philip reluctantly raised his own sword and spoke again to the fervent prince, "Your highness, I do not wish to fight you, but if you continue like this, you leave me no choice."

Cristan moved forward, ready to put the captain's convictions to the test. But it was not Philip's sword that crossed his own.

Prince Lugal stepped in, using his weight to throw Cristan back. "You must get through me first, Cristan. I *order* you to stand down."

Cristan hesitated, "I am not one of your subjects, brother. Do not make me fight you, for we both know that I am better with the sword."

The tension was broken by the sudden arrival of three riders, cantering through the crowd and forcing the men apart.

Samantha reined in her creamy-white stallion close to the centre of attention, Rian pulling up beside her on his warhorse.

As the third figure halted, those close enough to recognise him backed away, fear flooding their limbs.

"Prince Cristan, you have no authority here. Gardyn; you will stand down." Captain Rian shouted out across the gathered men and women.

The soldiers were slow to react as the news of the new arrivals passed between them. All eyes turned to Orion Losan, a wave of disbelief and panic.

One soldier in particular even felt faint at seeing Orion Losan, and he began to shrink back from his honoured place as Cristan's right hand. The man shifted to hide amongst the soldiers he had spent all night rallying after many months of whispering poison and discord.

"There he is, hold him!" The eagle-eyed Losan called.

The Gardyn were surprised by his command, and it took a repeat of it by Samantha to get a reaction. Teron was brought to the front, to face the lady and captains.

Captain Rian looked down at the man with disgust, "Soldier Teron, you are charged with entering the Gardyn army with the intention of brewing dissent in the ranks; and of betraying information to the King. Do you have anything to say?"

"Sir, lady, please." Teron stuttered, "I have done no such thing. I am a true Gardyn, I would never betray you. Are these his lies? You surely cannot believe him." Teron gestured towards the silent Losan.

"Orion Losan has proven his loyalty to myself and Captain Rian." Samantha replied in defence of the King's captain. "He has already informed us that you met frequently with the King's soldiers, with the latest meeting happening last night." Samantha turned to Prince Cristan, who appeared to finally be listening. "Did you know that, your highness? Did he tell you to delay the army 'til today so that King Hrafn could be made fully aware of your secret attack?"

"King Hrafn will have his justice, he will see your rebellion crushed to dust." Teron shouted over Lady Samantha. "And I will be honoured for the part I played. Strike me down, and Hrafn will only raise me stronger."

"Take him away." Captain Rian ordered. "Keep him under guard until we decide what to do with him. The rest of you, I suggest you lay down your weapons and return to your daily activities. There will be a time for battle and it draws ever closer. I want you all ready, and all together."

Rian watched as the soldiers began to back away, moving down the Valley, the revolt fading as quickly as it had started.

Lady Samantha released her hand from the hilt of her sword. "I think we need a council meeting," she said, shakily.

"I'll get the others immediately." Rian agreed, before hesitating, his gaze turning to Losan. "But..."

"I'll keep an eye on him." Samantha promised.

"I would never hurt your Lady Samantha," Losan looked across at Rian, until the younger captain dropped his gaze.

"Now, if you guys are quite finished... Come on, Losan, I'll give you the grand tour." Samantha offered, kicking her horse into a walk before he could answer, "Which should take all of ten minutes."

Losan gave a brief nod to Rian, then followed the young lady.

"Why do you help us?" Samantha asked as they rode over to the corrals.

Losan sighed and waited until they were away from camp, taking his time to tell his story.

"When I was a much younger man, my unit was sent to crush rebels in the city of Altair. It turned out to be soldier baiting, a trap, and most of my unit were killed. That was where I began to earn my reputation." Losan allowed a bitter smile to cross his scarred face at the memories of years ago, when his notoriety for fighting, for killing had started. "But that's a long story where I turned assassin, stalking the Gardyn and killing their leaders. I didn't get away unscathed, though. Afterwards, an old man took me in while I was recovering, he went by the name of Danu."

Samantha started at the name.

Losan noticed her reaction, "Yes, the same Danu that you met. While I was with him, he opened my eyes to Minaeri. I eventually learnt everything he knew of the goddess."

His look was so intense and meaningful, that Samantha knew that he had at least some knowledge of the dreadful truth.

"But I was young," Losan continued, "Too full of life to settle down and be a Priest of Minaeri. So, I returned to the army, and still the fire of battle floods my veins."

"So... all these years of being a feared icon and a close friend to the King... it was all an act?"

"No." The answer was blunt. A moment of silence passed, as Losan dismounted. "That is something that I will not explain to you."

Fourteen

Within the hour, the council gathered beneath the growing heat of the morning sun. Besides the usual members of the inner council, all Gardyn captains attended, crowding up to hear what was said.

Two men stood in the centre, their wrists bound, waiting for their judgement. Prince Cristan stood proud and calm, while Teron cowered, his confidence entirely drained as he stood amongst his enemies.

The shadows shifted at their feet as Siabhor growled, making them both shudder. The human guards stood back, happy to let the mallus keep the prisoners in line.

Captain Rian stood up to face them. "Prince Cristan, Soldier Teron, you are both accused of causing dissent amongst the Gardyn and rebelling against those in command. Teron, furthermore, you have admitted to being a spy for King Hrafn. Do you have anything to say in your defence?"

"You think you have any authority over me?" Teron blustered, sounding much stronger than he looked as he still trembled. "The only command comes from King Hrafn and Prince David. The rest of you are pretenders, with your false royalty, monsters and pitiful councils. You will all be swept into the obscurity of the history books by the *true-*"

Teron broke off as Siabhor snapped at his heels, obviously having heard enough from the man.

"Peace, Siabhor," Rian commanded, before looking again to the spy. "You condemn yourself with your words and blind hatred. As much as I would like to throw you to Siabhor and his pack, you are no good to us dead. You will be put in solitary confinement for a week, in which time I hope you have the sense to offer information when we meet again."

Captain Rian motioned to the Gardyn soldiers to take him away. As soon as Teron was beyond Siabhor's long claws, he began to shout and scream profanities, refusing to go quietly.

Rian waited for the noise to fade, before the council turned to the second, trickier prisoner.

"Prince Cristan, I hope that you can see that you were a tool in another man's plans. Show regret for your actions and we will move on." Rian stated carefully, offering the Prince a way out, "Or confess and we will judge your punishment."

Prince Cristan turned his calm brown eyes to the Gardyn Captain. "Whatever my regrets, I would do it again."

The comment brought a hiss from the council, followed by a buzz of dissatisfied comments.

"If I am to walk alone and unarmed into the gates of the capital, so be it. I would be doing what is morally right for the innocents, not wasting time with councils and permissions." Prince Cristan spoke out, the passion in his voice settling some of the unease.

158

"We can't act so wildly," one man spoke up, "we have to do more than win this war, we have to be seen doing it right. Otherwise you will be the king of a kingdom that has no faith in you."

"Perhaps we were too hasty in deciding to make these Princes our future monarchs," another man shouted up, "We were too desperate to believe in old legends, we blinded ourselves to their flaws."

"I never asked to be King." Cristan argued, "I never asked Minaeri to bring me back. But she did, and I will devote my new future to her people."

"No, even without a crown, you presumed to lead half the army into a trap!"

"How do we know you won't do it again?"

The council dissolved into noise and debate, which was only silenced when a female figure stepped into fray.

"Enough!" Lady Jillis commanded, a single word from her causing the crowd to obey. "Prince Cristan has a good heart. And we must always remember that each and every one of us have questioned the authority and law of the land; that is what has brought us all together and that continues to drive us. Yes, Cristan was wrong to ask the Gardyn to fight their friends and family for his cause, but I do not think we should be heavy-handed in our punishment. He is a good man, and right now we need every good man and woman united against Hrafn."

Her speech moved over every person there, quickly shifting their inner turmoil back towards peace and hope.

"If you please, Lady Jillis," one of the older captains spoke up, his voice full of deference for the young girl. "He can't escape punishment because he has a good character. Your excellent words won't persuade the whole

Gardyn army that they can trust him. There is no way to guarantee he won't do something similar again."

Jillis paused, then smiled gently. "Thank you, Captain, you are quite right. The Gardyn deserve something stronger than my recommendation. They deserve to know what Minaeri plans for him. Miss Jemma, would you be so kind?"

Jemma was standing on the edge of the crowd, with Saxton and Angrud at her side. Nobody paid them much attention when they had traipsed into the Valley, following Samantha. Now they hovered near the council – Jemma didn't know if they were permitted to be there, but no one had bothered chasing them away, so she stayed.

She had been swept along by Jillis' charm, that it took a while for Jemma to realise the lady was speaking to her.

Unable to reply, Jemma started hesitantly forward. She could feel the eyes of the large council following her, which only made her blush with embarrassment. She took a deep breath and stepped up next to Lady Jillis.

"As you all know, Miss Jemma was the oracle that foretold the return of the princes, as well as my own. She also saw this morning's incident in time for Captain Rian to stop it." Jillis paused and turned to Jemma, reaching out in support, "Can you look into Cristan's future and tell the Gardyn what you see?"

"What? I mean... I can try." Jemma replied, trying to not let her fear show. She had never had a vision on purpose, they just happened. She would never live it down if she failed in front of the whole Gardyn council.

Jemma glanced at the circles of people, all watching intently. They all believed that she could do it. All of these warriors believed a fifteen-year-old stranger could pull a magic vision out of thin air. About the future king, no less!

As a wave of panic washed over Jemma, Lady Jillis took her hand.

"Please," Jillis lowered her voice, "I know that it is a lot to ask, but I know that you can do it."

Jemma felt herself calm, the horrible red flush starting to leave her cheeks. She followed Lady Jillis to where Cristan stood, silently waiting for his fate to be confirmed.

Not knowing how to start, Jemma looked up into the soft brown eyes of the prince. Pushing aside the awkwardness that threatened to rise, Jemma felt a familiar lightness. There was a seductive pull as scenes and memories welled up, inviting her witness every inch of his interesting history. There were whispers of court life, betrayals and running, lots of running; all Jemma had to do was invite them in.

Trying to ignore her own curiosity, Jemma mentally pushed them away; she had a job to do. The images came slowly at first, then quicker, dancing along the highlights of a single man's life.

Jemma gasped and staggered backwards, surprised to see that she was holding Cristan's manacled hands, but glad for their support.

"He will be the eternal prince that never wears a crown." Jemma said with a shaky voice, "but he will follow command from now on."

There was a rush of noise and voices, but Jemma couldn't make any of it out. She met Cristan's eyes again, noting how they had lost some of their light.

Lady Jillis silenced the crowd once more. "Minaeri has shared his fate with us, I hope you are satisfied. For the safety of Prince Cristan, and the peace of mind of the

Gardyn, I recommend he take on a guard for the duration of his stay here. Captain Philip, perhaps you would be so kind."

Captain Philip, a man known for his amiability and loyalty, looked less than impressed.

"You were uncharacteristically quiet, Samantha." Rian said, sitting down beside the girl.

"It would be hypocritical of me to say anything. I've disobeyed more orders and risked more lives than he has." Samantha replied.

"To be fair, most of the time you buggered off alone, so there was only your own life at risk." Rian countered.

"You've already forgotten when Tobias tied up Lord Mgair and I led the Gardyn army to another world?"

"Ah..."

Samantha sighed and stood up, she could see Jemma standing with a worried-looking Saxton, hovering a safe distance away. "I need to go. I need to at least try to rescue that boy. If Alina and Siabhor return from seeking Sundance, I will take them with me. We'll be able to find a way in and... it doesn't have to involve anyone else."

"I should come." Rian said, without much conviction, "Or at least take Jillis, or even Lugal – he seems like a sensible ally."

"We both know that you need to stay here to deal with Losan. I might trust him, but we can't expect the whole camp to be as forgiving." Samantha reasoned, "Likewise, Jillis and Lugal will be more help here, smoothing over the Cristan problem."

"Fine, the oracle and her men go with you."

"What? She's only a kid!" Samantha argued.

"Yes, one that Minaeri sent to you. So, stop giving her the cold shoulder and use her." Rian replied sternly, "Besides, don't think you're going on a rescue without the boy's father, he has more right than anyone."

Cristan had waited for most of the gawking crowd to leave, before he set off back to his tent. The only thing he craved right now was solitude, a little time to work out what this all meant. Unfortunately, he couldn't even have that.

Captain Philip walked half a step behind him, making it clear that he was accompanying him as a professional guard and definitely not in friendship.

Furthermore, he heard running feet; Cristan did not have to look to know that his twin brother was catching up.

"Cristan, Philip." Lugal greeted them both, before falling into step beside Cristan with that annoying gait that mimicked his own. "I came to see how you fair, brother."

"I am fine, I still have my head." Cristan replied shortly.

"Do you not wish to discuss what the oracle-"

"No, I do not wish it."

Lugal walked quietly until they reached the tent that had been loaned to them. It was sparsely furnished, but comfortable enough. Captain Philip stopped outside, as the princes went in.

"I know how you must be feeling, brother." Lugal tried again. "It is alright to be disappointed. We never asked for Minaeri to spare us, or for the Gardyn of this century asking us to rule; but I know how the idea has been growing with you. The purpose it has given both our lives."

"Easy to say, when you are to be king and I your humble subject." Cristan replied bitterly, dropping into a seat.

Knowing that his brother's foul temper was not to be swayed, Lugal sat down in silence.

"Why are you here, brother? Making sure that I do not attempt something else ill-advised is beneath the future king." Cristan asked. When Lugal didn't rise to his bait, he tried a different tact. "It is a small consolation that I no longer have to contend with you for the Lady Jillis' attention."

Lugal faced his twin, waiting for him to explain. When he failed to do so, Lugal gave into his curiosity. "How so?"

"You didn't really think she was a suitable consort?"

"The Gardyn love and admire her, they already treat her like royalty." Lugal said in the lady's defence.

"And the rest of Enchena know that she is a baseborn servant, she could never be a queen." Cristan argued.

"I think the fact she has improved her standing should deserves respect, not scorn."

"And I think that you might not be so respecting if she were not so pretty." Cristan countered. "Honestly brother, is she the logical choice?"

"You sound like father." Lugal muttered. "I suppose you have a better, more suitable choice in mind?"

"You don't have far to look: she is already a leader of our people, and everyone in Enchena has heard of her."

"Lady Samantha?" Lugal asked, frowning.

Cristan smiled at how quickly his brother caught on. "She is an emissary from Minaeri, everyone says that she is an equal to their King Hrafn. And keep in mind, Enchena has already accepted that another from her land currently sits as heir to the throne."

Lugal sharply stood up. "You really expect me to believe that you are advising me from your own best intentions?"

"No, of course not, brother." Cristan replied casually, enjoying the fact that his uptight twin was getting riled. "My intentions are less than noble, but that does not make me wrong. We may have royal blood, but we are outsiders. The sooner you formalise a union with their beloved Lady Samantha, the earlier you will cement your own place."

Lugal went to speak, but decided against it. The prince turned on his heel and quickly left the tent, leaving Cristan to enjoy his peace and quiet.

Fifteen

Prince Lugal had been walking the length of the Valley, trying to clear his head of what his brother had said, but it wasn't easy. As he strolled through the Gardyn camp, people no longer regarded him with the same respect. Their awe had been dampened by suspicion.

Lugal wondered whether Cristan's rash actions had permanently damaged his chances at impressing the Gardyn. Would they ever follow his orders, if they were not visibly backed by the likes of Captain Rian or Lady Samantha?

The prince kept wandering until he saw a familiar face. Tobias Deorwine was heading towards the corral, where Jillis and Samantha were overseeing the horses being made ready for some trip.

"Lord Deorwine." Lugal called, stepping up to block his path.

"Your highness?" Tobias stopped, surprised that he should be of any interest to the prince.

"I wanted... that is to say I wished to speak with you over a, um... I'm not really sure how these things are done these days." Lugal stumbled over his words.

"Your highness?" Tobias repeated, "Is there something I can help you with? I do need to get my horse."

"Well, sir, it is a rather delicate matter. I have come to ask your permission, before I approach the lady with an offer of marriage." Lugal said sincerely, glancing down to the corrals. "I believe there are no parents? I hear that you are her only family?"

Tobias' eyes widened with shock, it was the best he could ever dream of for his sister. Jillis' beauty had attracted many would-be suitors, but none that Tobias deemed worthy, and none that Jillis even considered. "Aye, I am her only kin. If she agrees to the match, I would be honoured to have you as a brother-in-law."

Lugal took Tobias' hand and shook it enthusiastically, relieved at his answer. "Then I had best present myself, and hope the lady responds in kind."

Leaving Tobias rather dazed, Lugal headed to the corral, before his own nerve failed him.

"Lady Samantha, may I speak with you, privately?"

Samantha finished putting the bridle on her cream stallion, Legan, and turned to face the prince. "Lugal? Can it wait until I return, your highness? I'm in a rush."

"It is a somewhat... pressing and important matter. I promise I will not take much of your valuable time."

Samantha sighed, sharing a puzzled look with Jillis, before deigning to follow Prince Lugal to the edge of the corral. Hardly private, but Samantha was quite grateful that he didn't insist on traipsing further away.

"As you are aware, my lady, Cristan's actions have resulted in me being the sole King in the Gardyn's view of the future; but they have also raised doubts over... our legend, my ability to rule..." Lugal started.

167

"Does this have a point?" Samantha asked, glancing back to where her horse stood half-ready.

"I think it would strengthen the Gardyn, and provide Enchena with the best future if, when I am crowned King, you are my Queen."

"Well I think... what now?" Samantha froze as his words finally sunk in. "But that would mean that we... you and I... would be married?"

"Obviously not until after this battle, I would not want to distract you in your current role." Lugal answered logically, "But yes, we would be married. You do have marriage in your world?"

"Yes," Samantha replied in a rush, the panic evident in her voice, "but it usually has something to do with love and... and commitment."

"Love is a luxury for the common people." Lugal replied quietly, stealing a glance towards Jillis, "As leaders, we have a duty to provide strength and stability. Political marriages are common in the elite. Tobias Deorwine has already given his consent to the match, and I am sure the rest of the Gardyn will agree with him."

"Wait, he did what...?" Samantha felt her stomach sink like a dead weight.

"In the absence of your family, I assumed that he was responsible for you. Forgive me if I misjudged."

Samantha suddenly needed something to lean on, and moved over to the wooden fence for support. Today was not going how she had hoped. An enemy turning into an ally, and an ally becoming a danger, not to mention the little boy that could be getting tortured as they speak. Being sold off to the future king, by Tobias of all people, was a little too much to take right now.

"Lady Samantha?" Lugal gently prompted.

"I... I have a mission to complete. Can my answer wait until I return?" Samantha replied uncertainly.

"Of course," Lugal took her hand and pressed her fingers to his lips. "May Minaeri watch over you. I pray that you return swiftly."

Samantha attempted a smile, but feeling numb she walked the short distance back to her horse.

Jillis had finished tacking up Legan and handed the reins to Samantha, a curious look on her face. Tobias stood next to her, the young man's confusion slowly giving way to a cold realisation.

With good bloody reason; as soon as Samantha was close to him, she realised how angry she was at his damned heavy-handedness.

"How dare you?" She demanded. "Did you agree to marry me off before or after you tried to kiss me?"

Panic stabbed Tobias, "What? No, he was supposed to ask Ji-"

Before he could finish, Samantha raised her hand and slapped him sharply across the face.

Pulling her horse rougher than she should, Samantha stormed away, wanting nothing more than distance between her and Tobias.

"I'm not letting you go alone." Tobias called out, marching after her, rubbing his reddened cheek.

"I'm not going alone. Jemma and her two guards will be there." Samantha informed a stubborn-looking Tobias. "Anyway, no matter what Prince Lugal thinks, you are not my guardian."

"Then what will you let me be?"

Samantha ignored the question and swung herself into the saddle with a practised ease. Jemma and the two soldiers were already mounted and ready to go. Indeed,

169

Saxton looked like he would explode if he did not begin his son's rescue in the next few minutes.

Captain Rian came to see them off, stepping close to have a quiet word with Samantha. "You know that Hrafn is expecting you."

"Good, I haven't had a chat with Hrafn and David for ages." Samantha replied callously, as she checked her sword was firmly strapped to the saddle.

Rian grasped the horse's bridle and looked up at the young lady. "Samantha, don't try anything... like you do. Just try and get the boy back. Samantha, this is serious."

It seemed that Samantha wasn't going to reply, but then she leant down, hissing in a strained voice, "Don't you think I know that? Do you think I want to see David's dead image again? This is the beginning, and I am not looking forward to having to kill again." Samantha sat up straight again. "I said you weren't coming."

Tobias rode up to the group, apologetic smile flickering across his face, "And I'm ignoring orders. Something that comes quite naturally to the both of us."

"I would feel better if Tobias went with you," Rian said, handing up a map of the city.

"Fine, let's go or it'll be dawn before we reach the city." Samantha growled, pulling her horse round.

*****

For the rest of the day, life in the Valley went on as normally as possible.

The soldiers that weren't on scouting duties took turns on the training field. The original Gardyn, and those returned from Caelum were being inspected by Captain Rian. Curious of the rebel training, Orion Losan shadowed his movements.

"Soldier," Rian stopped to correct another Gardyn, "Either keep your shield fixed or turn and drop the shoulder to deflect the blow."

The individual took in the information with a stern nod, then turned to his designated opponent and began again. Rian waited long enough to see the improvement, then moved on.

"You're too soft in your training." Losan muttered.

Rian halted, flinching with the desire to knock this man down. "Your army may need beating into submission, but these men and women fight willingly. I shall train them how I think best."

Losan's look hardened slightly, "You are meant to be training them for a war, one in which most of them will die at this rate. How could a boy like you understand? How could you train such an important force for the Gardyn?"

The sparring pairs closest to the two captains paused in their activities, tuning into the escalating confrontation.

Rian ignored the sudden attention. "I am the best, that's why. All my life I have been groomed and trained for this position; intensity makes up for my lack of years. I am the Gardyn's answer to you."

"Ah yes... I remember being told of a programme and scheme to produce the perfect warrior." Losan sneered as he looked over Rian, "You have gone down in my estimation. The Gardyn could have easily picked someone else and you would be a nobody."

Across the field the sound of clashing swords and shields died as everyone was drawn to the confrontation.

Rian was lost for words as Losan cut close to the truth. With a lack of words, Rian went for action. In a split second his sword was in his hand, the sharp blade directed at Losan.

"Put that away, boy." Losan said, unnervingly calm. "Nobody can better me."

"I am you." Rian shouted. "Give him a sword."

The soldiers that circled them wavered at their captain's command, and did not respond.

"Now!" Rian barked.

One man moved forward quickly, handing his blade to Losan, then scuttled back to his place.

Losan held the sword up, regarding it. He glanced back to Captain Rian, but refused to attack.

Rian had no such reservations and lunged in with all his strength and skill. Losan deflected his first blow and dodged the second. He was unwilling to fight, but soon realised that this kid was better than he expected.

The two captains circled within the gathering crowd of Gardyn. They would parry, block and lunge, Rian's youthful movements opposing Losan's tact and experience. In the whole of Enchena these warriors were the closest matched and they fought on, neither wanting to step down and admit defeat.

Both were getting tired with the endless parry. Losan kept his cool, having been challenged so often; but Rian's attacks became more and more desperate as he realised with a furious anger that Captain Orion Losan really was as good as his legend.

Rian was the first to falter and Losan took full advantage, managing to give such a heavy blow. Rian lost his balance and fell to his side. The younger man was breathing hard from exertion, as Losan's shadow drifted over him, the older captain poised to strike.

"Isn't this the part," Rian said bitterly, "where the legend gives glorious testimony and strikes down the fallen man?"

Losan hesitated, then turned, throwing the sword back to its owner before walking away.

*****

Losan was sitting by one of the campfires, polishing his new sword. It was an overcast night and away from the firelight the Valley was shrouded in darkness. Losan did not need to look up to know who approached, the man unwilling to leave him alone.

"You still don't trust me." He stated in his quiet, even tones.

"The armoury obviously do." Rian answered, staring at the Gardyn-made sword.

"You still don't trust me," Losan repeated, "even though I let you live, when I could have killed you."

Rian sat down and looked at him sceptically, "You wouldn't have killed me. You knew you wouldn't have been able to escape the Gardyn camp, if you had."

"I'm Captain Orion Losan, I can do anything." Losan replied, no hint of bragging in his voice. "Anyway, you were thinking differently when you were at my mercy."

"You really think you're invincible." Rian sneered, "You actually believe that you are the legendary figure people regale."

"Why not?" Losan finally looked up and met Rian's gaze. There was no fire, no condescension, just stone cold truth. "I deserve it. Doubtless you believe in the Gardyn's view of yourself."

That left Rian speechless again. He knew that he had earned every word of praise, but it was hard to believe that one mortal man could have achieved as much as Captain Losan supposedly had.

"Who are you?" Rian asked, barely aware that he had spoken aloud.

The light from the fire showed the hint of a smile on Losan's scarred face. "I don't know. The son of a great lord. The daring and unstoppable soldier. The feared leader of the King's army. A misplaced priest. Or the Gardyn's lifeline." Losan took a deep breath, all sternness seemed to drop away for a brief moment. "By Minaeri, I've done so much, I feel that I can split it all into different people. I guess that's how I can be true to each."

"So, all this time you were pretending to be Hrafn's friend, but were really his enemy?" Rian asked.

"No. He was like a brother to me, and I never betrayed Hrafn. Until now."

Rian looked at him questioningly, and eventually Losan shrugged and continued.

"After I had met Danu, and secretly trained to serve Minaeri, I returned back to the capital as a hero. The only thing people knew about me was that I was the soldier who had single-handedly taken out a serious rebel threat. I strengthened my reputation through a few smaller missions, then during training sessions I was partnered with King Naboar's son and heir, Hrafn. I was of noble birth and had more skill than most, so I was a very suitable sparring partner and friend for the young prince. Hrafn was a few years younger than me, but he was bright and I actually enjoyed his company. I thought perhaps that was Minaeri's design for me – to help shape the future king so that Enchena might have a benevolent leader and an end to the conflict.

"It seemed to work for a few years, until Hrafn was old enough to be of interest to his father. King Naboar was a brutal man and there was no refusing him. He decided Hrafn should start to deal with the politics of the land and insisted on hardening the lad - "moulding" Naboar used to call it, so that he could excel despite the blasted prophecy that he would only have half-power.

"At that time, my services weren't needed at court, and I was sent back to protect the empire with my sword. I became very skilled in the language of violence and death, garnering respect from my peers that had nothing to do with my family name.

"After the death of Naboar, Hrafn called me back to court. He was preparing for his coronation and wanted those he could trust around him. When I returned, I found him a very changed man, the bright boy had been turned into someone dark and driven. At first I hoped that I could change him back, I thought I could still see some good in him. But then the Gardyn attack happened.

"We heard from our spies that the rebels were amassing as never before, to take advantage of the leaked prophecy. Instead of being worried, Hrafn welcomed the challenge; he confided in me that he had inherited all of his father's power, and the Gardyn would be crushed by his invincible army. After that, I tried to warn the Gardyn anonymously, but they wouldn't listen to me. After the... massacre, I decided I had best stay close to Hrafn and whilst I hoped that I could help him, I could plan to deflect most of his damage."

"Deflect his damage?" Rian echoed, "You have been the single biggest threat to the Gardyn for the last twenty years!"

175

"A threat that was exaggerated, I assure you." Losan argued. "I built my reputation for ruthlessness by fighting ruffians and extremists – they were never part of the Gardyn, although I reported that they were to help my cause. It worked, too; I started to have more control over Hrafn's army and could direct them where they would do least damage; and the fear I incited in the rebels meant that I could stop a fight without a single drop of blood spilt."

"So, you're honestly trying to tell me that you've never killed a Gardyn?"

Losan fell silent, acknowledging his guilt. "I am not proud of it. There have been many captured over the years. I have tried to give them swift deaths, to escape Hrafn's torture, and getting rid of the bodies so they did not suffer being resurrected."

"What changed?" Rian asked, "Why now?"

"Danu told me that the Gardyn would need me when Samantha returned for the final fight. I can no longer fool myself that Hrafn can be redeemed; the man that was my friend has long since vanished into his obsession for power and control. Also, David," Losan sighed, "that boy has been a nuisance, solidifying his authority as Hrafn's heir. The army acknowledge him as such, and many of the soldiers see this fresh young prince as their new hope for more glory and a stronger Enchena. The illusion is so strong that the army is fracturing, my control is not as complete as it used to be."

For a while, the only sound was the wind whispering in the night-time forest, and the crackle of the small fire.

Rian frowned at his enemy, "I will never trust you. But I think I can believe you."

Sixteen

The small party rode to the north of the city of Enchena, and camped overnight at the edge of the forest. Next to the camp was a mass of tumbled boulders that hid the entrance to a tunnel that only Samantha had visited.

They were too close to the city wall to safely light a fire, but the night was overcast and warm and all five lay down to attempt to sleep.

As the sky lightened with dawn and the sun began to show over the rooftops of the city. All five were weary but up and prepared to leave.

"Stay here, keep the horses and camp safe." Samantha instructed in a low voice to Tobias.

"Samantha, I am here to be with you – to protect you. If you think I'm staying-"

"I think you should follow orders for once, Deorwine." Samantha interrupted, marching off before he could argue further.

Jemma, Saxton and Angrud followed Samantha to the rocky tor, and into the dark cave. They held on tightly, afraid to lose the others in the darkness.

Once completely within, Samantha decided she could risk a little light. She turned her mind to the unlit torch she carried and it immediately sparked and came to life. The firelight leapt up and played on the rough, narrow walls of the tunnel.

"Come on." Samantha said gently after glancing at the map.

They walked slowly on for almost an hour, pausing every time their path branched away, putting their trust in the old map that Samantha carried.

"It's blocked." Jemma muttered, as they came up to a solid wall of packed earth, where the tunnel had collapsed.

"I can see that. Hold this, would you." Samantha spoke sharply as she passed the torch over to Jemma.

Saxton and Angrud stepped forward, ready with shovels. Samantha and the two soldiers started hacking away at the soil, but were stopped by the sheer difficulty of the task.

"It's no good. It's packed tight." Angrud complained, throwing all his weight behind the shovel and still hardly making a dent.

"Surely there are other routes." Jemma suggested.

Samantha ignored them and leant against the blockage, her eyes closed as she thought quickly. Her hand was pressed against the cool, moist earth. Her eyes flew open and she stepped back.

"Other routes may be quicker, but this is safer. It leads to an inn owned by Gardyn. They have helped us before and are one of our last contacts left in the city." Samantha gave a wary smile. "Stand back, I'll ease things up."

The others obeyed and Samantha turned, standing square to the wall. She closed her eyes again and concentrated. A strange red light played across her extended palms. An intense heat built up, making her companions shrink even further back.

There was a final blast of heat and the underground passage was filled with a bright white light that faded almost immediately to show Samantha on her knees, sweating, but otherwise unharmed in the scorched surroundings.

Saxton and Angrud walked past her and lifted their shovels to the blackened earth, which crumbled to dust and fell away.

"How – how did you do that?" Jemma asked breathlessly, "That was amazing."

"Thanks." Samantha said dismissively, shrugging her shoulders to loosen the tense muscles. It had been a while since she'd used her powers on that scale.

"We've found it." Angrud called back, knocking his shovel against the wooden slats that had been revealed in the roof of the tunnel.

There wasn't much room, but Samantha pushed forward into the little crevice, looking up at the Gardyn trap door. With a bit of effort, and some help from Angrud, they managed to shove the door open.

Samantha drew her sword and nodded to Saxton, who cupped his hands and boosted her upwards.

Samantha burst into the empty room, ready to defend herself. "I'll get us some help," she said, keeping her voice low.

She walked over to the heavy oak door of the small back room and moved into the main area of the inn. It was empty, as one would expect at an inn, so early in the day. But there seemed something odd about the stillness. The chairs were still up on the tables, the front door heavily bolted and a thick layer of undisturbed dust covering all surfaces.

Samantha walked slowly, cautiously, across the room to the bar. A heavy bell hung down, used to call for service or time, at the end of a night. Samantha reached out and gave it a sharp tug, letting its peal echo loudly through the silence.

There was a pause, then a hurried stumbling down an unseen staircase.

"Who are you? 'Ow you get in?"

A man appeared in the room, brandishing a blunt bread knife. His ragged, dirty clothes hung loose on him, as if he had lost a great deal of weight. His straggly hair was greyed with both age and stress, and his gaunt eyes balked at the sight of the girl. His gaze moved to the still-bolted door or his inn, and he did not care to hide his confusion.

"Hi, my name's Lucy," Samantha lied casually, "I'm looking for Bern's uncle."

The innkeeper was slow to reply, but his suspicion was evident at the use of the Gardyn pass-phrase. "Sorry lass, I don't know 'oo you mean."

"Really?" Samantha continued easily, "Rian will be disappointed."

The innkeeper's expression lightened, "Oh, *Bern's* uncle. I must've mis'eard you. Come upstairs an' we'll see what we can do."

Samantha nodded, "Let me just get my companions."

The innkeeper followed, mystified by the whole situation. As he stepped into the supposedly secure room, he was further amazed to see three more people in his locked inn. Two grown men, and a nervous young girl with a heavy hood shadowing her features.

They all made their way upstairs, where there were more questioning faces staring at the four intruders. Aside from the innkeeper and his wife, there were three of his grown sons, one of which was accompanied by his wife, heavy with child.

All shared the same glassy stare and taut appearance brought on by the lack of food.

The innkeeper quickly informed his family that their visitors were Gardyn, and cleared away enough clutter to let them sit down.

"Is it safe to speak?" Samantha asked.

"No place safer, Lucy." The innkeeper replied proudly.

"Well, first of all, these are for you to keep or distribute how you like." Samantha said, as Saxton and Angrud handed over four sacks. She couldn't help glancing at the pregnant woman, and how thin she looked in contrast to the tight bulge of her stomach. Suddenly the four bags of food didn't seem like a lot.

The innkeeper was more than happy to open the sacks to find fresh fruit, salted meats, flat bread and grains. "Bless Minaeri! Thank you, all of you. If there is ever anything old Billamaur can do for you, I am in your debt."

The Gardyn exchanged looks.

"Actually, we need information." Samantha began.

Old Billamaur, the innkeeper, thought that they had lost their minds. "So, let me get this right. You want t' break into the palace, get t' the prisons, get this lad an' all get out alive."

Samantha nodded, "Yep, that's about right."

Billamaur shook his head with disbelief, "I'm sorry, Miss Lucy, but that be suicide. The King, 'e been putting

181

up such an 'eavy guard, probably expectin' that Lady Samantha an' all. Surely this kid aint all that important."

"That's my son you're talking about." Saxton said coldly, speaking for the first time that day.

"Every life has its importance." Samantha interjected quietly. "And I remember that last year, Lady Samantha broke into the palace treasury and survived."

"Aye, but that's the Lady, aint it? An' she 'ad it easy, like. All the army were in the forest then, now they all be 'ere, protecting the King." Billamaur shrugged, "Besides, they underestimated Samantha before. They're prepared for her now."

Samantha frowned as Billamaur disregarded her heroics, but knew that he spoke with reason. "So, there's no way of getting to Russit." She said dejectedly.

"Now, Old Bill didn't say that. I'm thinking the King'll be 'aving an 'anging – begging your pardon, sir." Billamaur said hurriedly to Saxton, "Hoping 'e can entice the Lady. Slim chance you can get to the lad then."

Saxton seemed to be fighting with himself, he turned away, not wanting to hear how ill-fated this rescue mission could be. "We will wait then." He said roughly.

"You're more than welcome to hide 'ere." Billamaur said, "Until the lad is brought out."

Samantha nodded her thanks, "We'll bunker down, then. At nightfall, one of us can go and let Tobias know the change of plan."

"Why did you say your name was Lucy?" Jemma asked quietly.

She sat huddled in a corner with Samantha, away from the innkeeper's family, who were busy dividing up the new food rations.

182

Samantha sighed, slowly opening her eyes, Even with her training, her earlier use of power had quite exhausted her. "I've learnt to be careful. If he knew that I was this Lady Samantha, he'd either be grovelling and annoying, or would shop us in for a reward."

Jemma sat quietly, picking the dirt off her clothes. They all looked like they had been scrabbling around underground. The images replayed in her mind, of the dark, and of the sudden light and heat that Samantha managed to conjure, as though it were nothing.

"I can't get over what you did." Jemma confessed, "I mean, I've heard the stories, and seen how the trees behave at Treefort, but... to actually see you do that was awesome!"

Samantha gave her an odd look, "This coming from the girl who sees visions?"

"Anyone can see visions, mine just happen to come true," Jemma said dismissively. "I'd kill to have powers like yours."

Samantha winced at her ill-choice of words.

"What?" Jemma asked, sensing she'd made an error.

"That's how it all works, the powers are gained by killing the previous owner." Samantha explained, "Apart from me, the powers of fire and death were always connected to my soul, and manifested when I came to Enchena. So, each king has to murder his own father to inherit the powers of life and water that everyone is afraid of. No wonder they've all been tyrants."

"So... that's why Lugal and Cristan are normal?" Jemma asked about the two-hundred-year-old princes and frowned, "Relatively normal?"

Samantha nodded, "Their older brother, Brandon, killed their father to continue the line of kings. I wonder if they even know…"

"OK, I take it back, I don't think I could kill someone. Not even to get amazing powers." Jemma replied. Her own ability still seemed pretty shoddy compared to the things Samantha could do. She was trying to follow Samantha's advice to embrace this new part of her, and it was starting to get easier. Her only worry was, what if her effort was all too late?

Jemma glanced over at Saxton, who stood next to the window, in stony silence and detached from the rest of the group.

"When we rode to see the capital, there was a moment when I felt an oncoming vision. I hated the sensation and pushed it away." Jemma confessed, before the guilt became too much, "What if I was going to see Russit's capture? What if I could have stopped it?"

"Asking 'what if' can drive you mad." Samantha said softly, "Minaeri works in strange ways, you've done nothing wrong."

A niggling thought arose in Samantha's mind – how could Minaeri guide any of them, when King Ragoul the First had killed her? Samantha pushed the thought away, as she felt a phantom pain through her gut.

*****

As the day passed into afternoon, the blistering midday heat remained, scorching in the rancid streets of the neglected city. From the luxury of his palace, the King of Enchena looked down on the few busy folk, his suspicion raised at their need to scurry about his city. Hrafn didn't trust the commoners, small people living small lives, all too eager to turn on the King that allowed them to live in his fine city. As removed as they were, in the royal palace, Hrafn could sense the tension mounting. It would not take much for it to ignite.

Despite this, Hrafn felt powerful. True, his natural heir had been murdered, and his beautiful wife, the Queen Arianne, now wasted away with grief. But they were just mortal lives and Hrafn belonged with the gods.

Footsteps made the King turn from the window, to face his son-in-law and new heir. David continued to grow stronger and sharper. He was now taller and broader in the shoulder than Hrafn, and the young man had become increasingly sure of himself.

Hrafn knew that David was a dangerous ally – as much as he gave support to his King, he also sapped strength from Hrafn's claim to the throne. But with the disappearance of Captain Losan, and the fact that his army was no longer invincible, Hrafn had no one to turn to.

There was one small relief, that the Princess Helena had only given David a daughter. The secret tradition of Kings was to hand over the crown when a grandson had been born to secure the line. Luckily, a girl was useless.

"The boy has been broken." David reported. "We have a rough idea where the stronghold is."

Hrafn nodded. "Then we shall have him hanged tomorrow. Such a waste of young life."

David bit back a smile, he knew that Hrafn was thinking of his dead son, Prince Tagor, who had been the same age as this Gardyn lad, when he was murdered. The rumours had been that Lady Samantha had committed this sinful crime, but how many rightfully suspected David?

"Samantha is back." David was pleased to see a hint of fear in the King's reaction to this revelation. "Unfortunately our informant has been discovered, before he was able to instigate a premature uprising. The Gardyn have captured Losan, he'll persuade them to rescue the boy and everything will carry on as planned. I'll set the hanging for tomorrow afternoon, give Samantha time to sneak into the city."

King Hrafn waved David away, not trusting his voice to stay steady. Samantha – Lady Samantha, the rebels called her – she was the only aspect that made him falter. He remembered her as a silly, unsure girl, but she had thwarted him many a time, and now... how powerful had she become since they last clashed?

Seventeen

For the past few hours, the main town square had been filling with citizens of the capital, where they were herded by heavy-handed guards. Samantha grasped Jemma's hand as they pushed through, closely followed by Saxton and Angrud.

In the centre, a platform had been raised and a noose hung in readiness. There was a murmur of excitement and nerves running through the crowd.

Jemma squeezed Samantha's hand, "There are archers placed on top of the houses, and soldiers are hidden in the crowd."

Samantha felt her skin prick and glanced around. "I don't see anything." She murmured.

Jemma looked to the older girl, but the heavy hood that hid her flaming hair also hid most of her face. "I see more than you." She nodded softly, "The crowd will listen to you."

Samantha frowned at the irrelevant information, "I'm proud that you're accepting your role, Jemma, but can't you tell me how this will all happen?"

The crowd suddenly started shouting, jeering and cheering, and as one, they all turned to face the platform.

"It's not my place."

Samantha only just heard Jemma over the din.

Surrounded by armed guards, King Hrafn and Prince David stepped up onto the platform. Samantha caught her breath as they both scanned the crowd, obviously looking for her.

Amidst another group of guards, Russit was forced up next to them. The shouts and jeers of the people of Enchena died away as this young boy was lifted onto a stool and the noose shoved roughly about his neck. The crowd had all been expecting an adult Gardyn spy, and they were disgusted to see a child up there.

Russit wavered on the stool, his limbs shaking with pain and fear. His bloodshot eyes roved the crown desperately, and his unfocussed gaze found his father, Saxton's presence calming the lad.

"They say that the Gardyn are compassionate and live by their hearts," Hrafn addressed his people, "But they will forsake their own sons when it suits them. Their heroes are false, and their lies seep into the cracks of this good city. I will ensure that every last one of them is destroyed; I will put an end to their deceitfulness."

Hrafn paused, waiting to see if any hidden Gardyn moved forward. Disappointed, he gave the signal.

The hangman stepped up. The crowd screamed as one, as the stool was kicked from under Russit's feet. Jemma also cried out in pain, as Samantha's hand burnt her own.

The rope became taut, then snapped, the frayed ends burnt through.

Saxton took a single step towards his son, but staggered to a halt. There was the zip of a flying arrow which embedded its sharp point in Russit's chest. The boy fell as a dead weight onto the platform.

"She's here! Hold them in." David suddenly took charge, shouting across the square to the waiting soldiers.

"Find her." King Hrafn demanded, his eyes already searching the crowd.

Panic was setting into the gathered crowd, and Samantha struggled to stand strong against the pushing and shoving. She turned to a distraught Saxton, "Take Jemma, get back to the inn. Go!"

When he failed to respond, or even show that he had heard her, Samantha turned pleadingly to Angrud. The young man was visibly upset, but he seemed to have his wits about him. "Angrud, get them to safety. If I don't return within the hour, leave without me. I need you to promise."

"Aye, my lady." Angrud said quietly, his resolve growing.

Samantha watched as the Gardyn soldier obeyed and with the help of Jemma, they dragged Saxton away, the three of them disappearing into the masses.

Samantha paused, trying to think. In her hand, she tightly grasped the old map of the city, each of its secret underground routes scrutinised and memorised last night. She hoped she knew what she was doing. She lifted her head to the platform and saw David; a flickering smile told her that he also saw her.

There was no need to hide now. Samantha flicked back her cloak, putting on clear display Minaeri's sword. She kept David's gaze as she slowly walked forward.

The crowd parted, staring at the dangerous young lady.

"Samantha, so good to see you again." The King greeted with false warmth.

"Save your lies, Hrafn. The only thing I want to hear from you is your abdication."

"Then I assume you are not going to come quietly." He said, resigned. He signalled to his guards.

Samantha drew her sword - Minaeri's sword - grasping the black hilt, its curving, antler-like pattern surrounding her hand. The dark blade was flickered with a fire of her control, held ready for any attack from the King's soldiers that encircled her. Samantha had changed so much since the first time she had been taught to hold a sword; instead of it being a heavy and clumsy weapon, her muscled arms and torso balanced it in preparation to wield it with precision, whilst her once terrified eyes gazed undaunted at each and every man that threatened her.

The crowd backed away, but did not leave, mesmerised by the flame-wielding young woman.

But the soldiers did not attack. Instead, another figure entered the ring.

"Why do you continue to fight us, Sammy?" David asked lightly, "It's not too late to join the rightful King."

"You're a murderer and a ghost, David." As strong as she appeared, her voice still shook, "How many times do I have to turn you down before you understand? I am Gardyn, and if need be, I will die for my people."

"Can't you see the inevitability of it all? Sure, you're going to die either way, but all of this stubbornness and bravado... the more you fight it, the more Gardyn get

190

killed along the way." David sighed, knowing that it was futile to continue.

The prince turned away, and leapt back up onto the platform. He leant down and when he stood back up again, Samantha could see that he was holding up the body of poor Russit.

David smirked as he saw a look of horror on Samantha's face. "Tell you what, join us and the King will bring him back to life. A fair deal, don't you think?"

Samantha glanced at Hrafn, who hung back as a shadow, more than happy to allow his heir to deal with her.

"An evil shell will hurt his family a lot more than a dead body." Samantha replied.

"Fine, just one more dead rebel." David said with a shrug and threw Russit's body from the platform, so that it landed with a thud and a snap as the fatal arrow shaft broke away. "That reminds me, you did say goodbye to all your friends before you left – what's it called? Treefort? Such a shame, I would've liked to have seen that pretty maid Jillis again."

If David was expecting some sort of reaction from Samantha, he was to be disappointed. The young lady kept a stern expression, as she crouched down beside Russit, gently lifting his lifeless body. Samantha turned, and looking past the ring of armed guards she witnessed the sea of gaunt faces of those that had become prisoners in their own city. They had all been silent, listening to the battle of the two young people that would control their future.

Samantha took two steps forward, trusting the senses that made her different.

"People of Enchena," Her voice rang out, "I will return, and I will free you from this tyranny."

Samantha heard David start some bitter comment on impossible escape, but ignored him. Fire flooded her veins and her skin prickled with the enormity of what she was about to attempt.

With the grief of Russit's death, her power came more readily, and she was surrounded with intense heat that she forced downwards. With such sudden intensity, anything would crumble to nothingness.

Suddenly the ground fell away and Samantha dropped, deep down through the crumbling stone. Her feet hit solid ground again and she stumbled and recovered,

Looking up, she gasped at the daylight coming through the hole that continued nearly two metres above her. Adrenaline was rushing through her veins, and she turned and ran down the secret tunnel she had hit, still carrying the dead weight of Russit.

Samantha paused only to send a wall of fire behind her to hinder any pursuers. She prayed to Minaeri that her route would not be blocked, and continued to run through the darkness.

The tunnel began to rise, and the roof was so low that Samantha had to stoop. She could feel the beginning of exhaustion as her legs felt unsteady and she couldn't tell if it was her heart that pounded so noisily, or the running feet of soldiers behind her.

Ahead, shafts of sunlight pierced the darkness of the tunnel and Samantha gently lowered Russit's body. She lifted her hands up to feel the slats of wood, they creaked and gave way as she shoved harder.

Still inside the city, she came up in a tiny backyard that wasn't far from Billamaur's inn.

Samantha couldn't remember the last time she had been so thankful to see the sky, even though it swirled with heavy grey rain clouds.

Back at Billamaur's inn, the atmosphere had changed from nervous anticipation, fear and hope to a sad and depressing silence. Old Bill's family had quickly vacated the small room where Saxton Marsh sat, his head in his hands. He had not moved since he returned and made no sound other than an occasional deep sigh as he tried to order his thoughts and emotions.

Jemma stayed in the room with him. Although inside and safe from attracting attention, she kept her hood up, letting it hide away the tears that refused to stop and her reddened eyes. She had never known anyone die before, and to have dear little Russit murdered so cruelly before her was more than she could bear.

Angrud stood at the doorway, ready to protect them, or to stop them running away if necessary. The young man refused to meet anyone's eye, and was being uncharacteristically professional.

There was the sharp noise of someone coming through the main door of the inn below. Everybody jumped to their feet, grabbing the closest weapons, as footsteps raced up the stairs. There was a sigh of relief when Samantha appeared.

"Mr Marsh, sir." Samantha cradled the lad against her chest as she crossed the room, before setting him down carefully next to his father. "I am so sorry. I brought him to you. I couldn't let Hrafn bring him back, making a brave young Gardyn into a slave for his army."

193

Saxton lifted his head and gazed unseeingly at his son.

"He shall be wrapped and prepared to travel with you, so you may bury him properly." Billamaur spoke quietly and respectfully, then left to fetch some cloth.

Samantha followed the innkeeper and touched his elbow gently. "There is something else... I doubt the fact that I fled here will stay quiet for long. I have put you all in danger. You and your family must leave with us at once."

Billamaur shook his head, "Bein' Gardyn – every day means danger. Look, 'ow many 'osses you 'ave anyway?"

"Five, but..."

"An' with that poor bairn to carry too. Take me sons an' daughter-in-law. Us old 'uns will stay. We aint afeared of death no more." He held his hand up to her arguments. "That's that. Just get yerself back to the forests. You 'ave given Enchena hope, now see it through."

Samantha shook his hand, and went back to find her companions. She caught sight of Jemma, huddled in a corner, hiding in the shadows.

"Jemma, are you alright?" Samantha asked softly, realising this might be the young girl's first taste of this terrible reality.

"I warned you." Jemma sobbed. The younger girl lifted her head and shrieked, "I said there were archers. Why didn't you stop them?"

Jemma stood up, the movement causing her hood to fall back, her face and hair showing similar shades of red. "Why?" She shouted.

It hit Samantha that maybe... with that warning the outcome should have been different. "Oh, Jemma..." She murmured quietly, more to herself than the crying girl.

194

Jemma was fighting with herself, her muscles tensed, wanting to expel the fire of grief. Exerting control over her sudden flare of anger, Jemma turned to the wall and slouched down again in sullen silence.

The journey back through the tunnel was slow and silent. Samantha and her team had failed; even though they led Billamaur's family to freedom, everyone knew that freedom had a price.

When they reached the end, Samantha clambered desperately over the boulders and collapsed into Tobias' arms, taking comfort in his presence and forgetting all the anger she had felt towards him.

With hardly a word, Tobias' camp was hurriedly dismantled, and they all mounted, doubling up on the horses.

Tobias climbed up onto the white stallion Legan, then pulled Samantha up behind him. Samantha was too exhausted to argue, and wrapped her arms around his waist. They set off at a steady pace, and Samantha leant against Tobias' back, allowing the motion of the horse to soothe her ragged nerves.

She could see Jemma and Angrud riding together; Billamaur's family sharing two horses; their depression tangible. Saddest of all was Saxton, who cradled his dead son, wrapped in a pale cream cloth.

No one spoke.

The first gasp of pain was heard by all.

Samantha and Tobias stopped and turned their horse back to the group, to see Jemma slumped in Angrud's arms.

"What's wrong?"

"I don't know," Angrud said, panic in his voice, "She was fine, and then she just..."

Jemma was vaguely aware of the voices around her, but she couldn't really understand them. She was standing at the edge of a pool, its waters the darkest blue and peaceful. There was the now-familiar background of trees, as the forest stretched away from this idyllic place. Jemma knew this was a vision and looked around, waiting for something important to happen. But nothing came. Growing slightly impatient with this vision that Minaeri had sent her, Jemma began to walk the length of the pool, finding her footing on the wet rocks and mud.

She eventually came up against a rocky tor that blocked her path.

"Look."

Jemma thought she heard a voice, and froze. What was she supposed to look at?

Not sure what on earth she hoped to achieve, Jemma started to climb the rocks in front of her, the rough surface cutting into her soft fingers, and the minimal footholds causing her to slip. But she climbed upwards, until she came to the very top, where a solitary tree clung to a rocky ledge.

The view was incredible, Jemma could see the Great Forest roll out before her like a roiling green sea, as the trees followed the contours of the land. Bringing her gaze closer, Jemma looked down. Once she had gotten over the dizzy height, she noticed movement to the right. Where the rocks had stopped her access, there was obviously some way in, as several creatures moved beneath the canopy. Jemma glimpsed a pearly horn and realised that these were unicorns! She had only ever seen Alina and Sundance when they first came back from Caelum, and it was a shock to see the many brown, chestnut and black coats that were well-camouflaged in the forest.

Watching the majestic animals, Jemma noticed a dark shadow on the horizon, moving steadily closer. It was oil, it was poison, and it seeped through the trees and the rocks until it was within the unicorn's sanctuary. From her high perch, Jemma could see the calm break, and the unicorns started to panic, fighting the black cloud. Their screams drifted up high, making her shudder, and one-by-one they fell.

Jemma willed herself to wake up, unable to watch any more of the horror, and with a great struggle she jerked upwards.

Jemma noticed that she was curled up like a child in Angrud's lap. Trying to hide her embarrassment over that fact, Jemma looked around at the ring of worried faces.

"Sorry." She muttered, "I still can't always control it."

"Never mind that, did you have a vision?" Samantha asked.

"Yes, it was about unicorns." Jemma replied, taking a moment to recall what had happened. "There was a herd of them, and they were attacked by something dark, something evil."

Samantha exchanged a quick look with Tobias, before questioning the girl again. "Was there a fine chestnut stallion in the herd? Where were they?"

Jemma closed her eyes to concentrate on the fading images, "It was hard to see through the trees, but yes, there was definitely a unicorn that had a fiery coat. I didn't recognise where they were, but I had the feeling that it was safe. They never expected that danger could find them."

"Wentra." Samantha muttered to Tobias, then turned to Jemma, "Do you know what attacked them?"

"No, it was just darkness and death seeping through the rocks." Jemma said, shuddering at the very real memory.

"I have to warn them." Samantha said. "Angrud, get these people back to the Valley, they are your responsibility now. Tobias-"

"I'm coming with you." Tobias countered before she had a chance to argue. "Legan can carry two."

"Fine, let's go." Samantha snapped, desperate to find Autumn before Jemma's vision came to pass.

Eighteen

Deep within the Great Forest there was the unicorn sanctuary of Wentra.

Autumn paced about his herd, his graceful movements hiding the fact that he was anxious. He couldn't pinpoint why he was worried, and tried to logically dismiss it – they had never been away from the Valley this long, and it was natural to feel nervous. Since the humans had wrestled their way in, and gradually taken over, Autumn had decided that enough was enough. He had to stand up for the rights of his herd, before they were treated as nothing more than glorified packhorses.

Moving to Wentra had been a sacrifice, but it was a necessary one. The only problem they had now, was that Wentra was not designed as a permanent residence for the unicorns. A lot of the younger herd-members felt cooped up; but constant travel to and fro only risked the secrecy of their hideout. Plus, the cold weather was only a few months away, and Autumn didn't know if Wentra could adequately feed his herd for another winter.

Autumn moved between the unicorns, noting that the herd had an edge of nerves to everything they said and did. It was obvious that it wasn't just their leader who was worried as another evening descended.

Autumn was surprised to see the young human Samantha running through the secret passage, her male companion leading a familiar white stallion behind her.

"Samantha, Alina had told me that you returned from the other land. We appreciate your visit, but shouldn't you be with the other humans?" Autumns words were civil, but the meaning clear. She no longer belonged with his kind.

"I've come to warn you... about danger..." Samantha stopped and caught her breath, leaning against the nearest tree until she could get her words out in the right order. "We have an oracle, one that can see the future. She saw darkness and death invading Wentra."

"Impossible." Autumn stated, "There is nowhere safer, only those trusted to know the way can enter. We can stay here and wait for whatever danger you've invoked to wash over us and fade."

"Autumn... I don't know what is coming; but I do know that Jemma has seen the death of your herd. You need to get them to safety, then we can argue over whose fault it is." Samantha snapped, before the tension drained from her. "I'm sorry, Autumn, it's been a rough day. I don't want to lose you, too."

The chestnut stallion snorted, lowering his head a little, but his ears still back and showing his displeasure at her presence. "Some in my herd would say that you are trying to draw us into your battles again. How am I to calm their suspicions?"

"Some? You mean Tân and his friends?" Samantha remembered the stubborn bay stallion, and shrugged. "Nothing I can say will persuade him to trust me. Just... see if the herd is willing to move out of Wentra for a few days. It might save their lives, and if nothing bad happens, you don't have anything to lose."

Autumn was about to reply, but paused. He raised his head, ears pricked. Behind him, the rest of the herd were suddenly on alert too.

"What's wrong?" Samantha asked quietly, not wanting to startle the great stallion.

"Hush, young one. Can't you sense the stillness?"

Samantha looked around, not a single unicorn moved. Beyond that, the birds and small creatures were silent, the forest eerily quiet without their rustling.

"Only mallus, and unicorns belonging to the Dark Being have this effect. Danger must be near." Autumn's thoughts tumbled out, as he strained to hear or scent anything that could tell him more.

"We need to leave now."

"And walk straight into the monsters that wait for us?" Autumn snorted. "We will be safer here."

"Autumn, please, I am begging you to trust me once more. I swear by Minaeri and Praede that Wentra will not protect you now; but I will. Whatever is out there, I will do everything in my power to protect your herd."

Autumn met Samantha's eye, uncertainty still hovering in his thoughts. But he lowered his horned head in assent. The stallion gave a low whinny to his herd, and with a river of thought too intense for Samantha to follow, the unicorns started to move towards the way out.

"You're a stubborn bugger when you want to be." Tobias commented, as he led their horse back through the rocky passage.

Samantha didn't spare him any notice, and jogged along, until she was back out in the forest. Night was starting to roll in, and the shadows lengthened and merged into one. There was no evening chorus from the birds, it's absence now very noticeable.

Samantha peered between the trees, not sure if she could see movement, or not.

Autumn emerged, leading his herd from their safe haven. He stepped up beside Samantha, his eyes locking onto the darkness.

An unearthly scream split the air, and the shadows started to move.

Samantha's breath caught as she saw a familiar black stallion approach, his horned head scything wildly. She had only had the misfortune of meeting the Dark Being once, but she quickly felt a stab of fear at seeing him again.

The black stallion wasn't alone, behind him his dark herd shifted, forming limbs and hooves and sharp teeth from the shadows. They had come for the sole purpose of destroying Autumn and the other unicorns. Nothing could persuade them to stop.

Autumn ordered his herd to head towards the Valley, but a few hung back, stepping up to protect their leader.

Autumn's ears flattened as he noticed Tân hovering at his haunches. "Go to the herd, Tân. You're not fit enough for this fight."

The bay unicorn narrowed his eyes and his thoughts were very clear on the matter. His leg had never fully recovered from the filthy mallus' attack, and his limp affected everything. Grudgingly, he backed away, and disappeared after his herdmates.

Autumn turned to face the Dark Being and his kind. The bright chestnut unicorn rushed forward, a single flame against the darkness; beside him were two brown shadows, as Billan and his mate galloped towards the enemy.

Samantha watched the unicorn's brave actions, but for all their bravery they were outnumbered. The unicorns probably knew the sacrifice they were making for the rest of the herd, but it was a price that Samantha didn't want to pay.

Samantha tried to find the trigger for fire, but despite the fact that Russit's death was still painfully fresh, she felt empty. At the sickening sound of hooves against flesh, she looked up. Autumn was dodging the Dark Being, but Billan was surrounded by the dark herd, being attacked from every angle.

Billan's mate screamed and, forcing a dark grey unicorn to back down from her vicious hooves, she raced to her mate's side. The two of them fought side by side, and held their own to begin with, but began to falter. They disappeared in the crowd of unknown unicorns, who soon moved back from their unmoving victims.

Samantha forced away the panic that threatened her, and focussed on the grief that fuelled the fire that finally sparked and sputtered into life. Samantha looked in the direction of their enemies, and set the forest ablaze. The fire spread quickly across the dry leaves and bushes, forming a searing barrier between Autumn's retreating herd and the dark ones.

"Let's get out of here!" Tobias yelled to Autumn, as he leant down and pulled Samantha up onto their white horse.

"Wait, I can stop him!" Samantha protested, but she could already feel her power starting to slip and fade after using too much earlier.

Autumn span away from the Dark Being, lashing out with his powerful hindlegs, catching the unicorn one last time. He raced for the last clear path to safety, the fire licking at his heels. The fire continued to take hold and spread, even without Samantha's magical assistance. The unicorn gave them a brief glance to make sure his old friends were alright, then cantered close by, heading away from Wentra.

Gripping onto Tobias with all the strength she had left, Samantha looked behind them. The fire lit up the black stallion and his followers. For a fleeting moment, Samantha swore she could see Sundance's golden coat...

The night had fully descended, when the Valley was flooded with unicorns for the first time in months. Some, like Captain Philip, were thrilled to greet their old friends; but many of the Gardyn had only ever seen glimpses of Alina. Now, they came out of their camp to witness the whole herd.

Autumn came trotting in last, alongside Samantha and Tobias. The chestnut stallion snorted, his ears twitching back as he saw how the humans had taken over so much of his old home.

Alina rushed over, taking time to breathe in Autumn's scent and take comfort in his presence. Her soft muzzle moved over the new, deep cuts that adorned his fine coat. "It is good to see you safe."

"I am, but we lost Billan and Niamh today, they sacrificed their lives so we could escape." Autumn nuzzled the grey mare, before his wise brown eyes fixed on Samantha. "I am still unconvinced that it was a necessary price to pay. I should never have put my herd in such danger. In all his long years, the Dark Being has never known the way into Wentra."

"Sundance." Samantha said quietly. "Sundance was with him."

A wave of panic flooded from Alina.

"Relax, dear one." Autumn's thoughts came across warm and comforting. "We will discover what this means, and save your nephew."

Samantha said her farewells and went back to the camp with Tobias, glad she could hide her doubts. Something in Sundance had been bubbling up during their stay in Caelum, and her last memory of him was his violent actions in the Valley. Had he gone with the dark herd willingly?

*****

Dawn had barely broken when Samantha was awoken by someone rummaging around in her tent. She hardly recalled last night, her head had hit the pillow and she had gone into a deep, exhausted sleep. As she struggled to open her eyes, her body screamed that it needed a good few hours more.

"Jillis?" She mumbled.

"Samantha, I didn't mean to wake you." The younger girl said quietly, without looking her way. She was dressed in a grey-green tunic and brown breeches, and sturdy boots, looking ready to leave.

"Where y'going?"

"We noticed smoke to the north. Rian is sending a scouting party to Treefort, to see if Miss Jemma's vision came true." Jillis explained, sitting on the end of Samantha's bed and deftly plaiting her long black hair into something manageable.

"You don't have to go, do you?" Samantha asked.

"I can provide them help, as an archer. Besides, I could do with getting away from the Valley." Jillis looked towards Samantha, "Lugal... told me about his proposal."

Samantha sat bolt upright, "Jillis, I'm so sorry, I should have said something, but I was so mad with Tobias at the time. It definitely wasn't my idea, I still don't know what to think about it. Are you alright?"

"I'm fine. It's true that I liked him, but I agree with Lugal – he needs to think of the future of Enchena. I cannot blame him for choosing you." Jillis said with a sigh. The girl went to say more, but thought better of it, and pushed herself off the bed.

Samantha felt a pang of guilt as she watched Jillis leave the tent.

*****

Alina left the Valley as soon as it was light to seek the dark herd and find the truth about Sundance. Sneaking away from Autumn's side had been a hard decision, but she didn't want to risk him trying to stop her, nor did she want to put him in any further danger. Instead, she took an old friend.

Siabhor was the logical choice, he could track better than any unicorn, and Alina had seen that even the Dark Being feared him. But if she was honest, Alina had missed him when they were in Caelum, and it was satisfying to have an excuse to spend time with him.

They still made a very odd and unnatural pair, but Alina no longer shivered whenever the mallus was near.

They made their way to Wentra, the fire had died down, the area a mess of black and grey. Siabhor picked up the tracks of the dark herd, which they followed across the charred ground. They travelled until the sun was high in the sky, and at midday they came to an area that bore signs of use by unicorns. The grass was trimmed low, and the ground rutted from numerous hooves.

Alina moved forward with more caution, her silver coat forever gleaming in the forest, she found no natural camouflage. She raised her head to the breeze, and noticed the familiar scent of her nephew mixed with that of unknown unicorns. Alina tried to hear Sundance's thoughts, but couldn't even sense a whisper. The unicorn glanced at the Siabhor, who jumped nimbly up into the nearest tree, giving the predator the best vantage point.

With a nervous twitch of her ears, Alina walked on, alert for any sound or movement.

The peace was suddenly broken by a stallion's cry, which rang out through the trees. A unicorn moved towards her, his coat as black as night, his once fine form covered in the scars of his vicious life. His thoughts dripped like oil, poisonous and lingering.

"I remember you: sister of Nmirr," The Dark Being eyed the beautiful mare, "Have you realised that your Autumn is a coward? Do you seek someone stronger and more worthy of you?"

Alina's ears flattened to her skull and her teeth bared at his comments. Her gaze moved nervously, noting the movement in the trees and hoping it was only Siabhor. "I seek my nephew, nothing more."

The black stallion walked closer, his very presence a threat. "What if he does not want to be found? Perhaps we should ask him." He threw back his head and called, confident that every member of his herd was paying attention to their master.

A lithe golden unicorn came obediently forward, the palomino a stark contrast against the forest and shadowy herd-members.

"Sundance-" A whinny left Alina, and her eyes moved over her nephew, looking for any sign of damage.

The palomino came and stood at the Dark Being's flank, refusing to move any closer.

"Sundance, I'm so glad I found you. You can come home now."

"I am home." He replied shortly, his once-lively thoughts rolling out with a new monotone.

"You see, Torment has rather had enough with being the human's slave. He no longer follows the staid rules that are set for the benefit of others." The Dark Being shared, his eyes fixed on Alina.

"Torment?" The mare snorted at the name. "You will always be Sundance, son of Nmirr-"

"Don't mention my father." Torment thoughts screamed, as he jumped forward, his horned head lowered.

Alina skirted aside, and only just missed getting gored. She noticed that more unicorns had appeared behind her, blocking her exit, every one of them ready to attack at their master's command. Alina felt torn, her desire to flee this danger was overwhelming her, but she couldn't leave her nephew.

"Leave now, Aunt. Run back to your humans-"

Torment's bitter words were cut off by a sign from the Dark Being. "Oh, she's not leaving this time, not when she comes so willingly to the dark herd."

Alina shuddered as she felt the broad shoulder of an unknown unicorn pressing against her flank, pushing her deeper into the herd's territory. The mare lashed out with her back legs and caught them hard enough to make them squeal with pain.

There was a press of bodies, and confusion.

A moment later, Siabhor had tackled a bay unicorn to the ground. The enemy struggled beneath the mallus' teeth and claws, and gave one last dying scream.

The rest of the herd backed away, unable to overcome their fear of the predator.

"Home. Now." Siabhor hissed, detangling himself from the dead unicorn's limbs.

Alina gave her nephew a lingering look, before reluctantly turning and running, Siabhor close on her heels.

The Dark Being lowered his head to his fallen herd member, snorting at the swift death of the bay unicorn. He turned away, his furious gaze fixing on Torment. "If you want to stay in this herd, and if you want any chance with Odile; the price is Alina. Bring her to me. And if you manage to kill her tame dog, I will even give you my blessing."

Torment stared down the path his aunt had taken, then looked to where Odile hovered in the shadows. The young stallion slowly nodded his horned head.

Nineteen

The Valley was in a sombre mood. The day after they had returned from the capital, the funeral rites were held for Russit, and many in the camp helped build his pyre. He looked so tiny, dwarfed by the wooden lattice.

Jemma's eyes were red from crying, but she was beyond caring that people saw her tears. She had been wanting to speak to Siarla all day, and finally found a moment when she was not surrounded by friends.

"Siarla," Jemma said nervously, "I wanted to say how sorry I am about R-Russit. I wish there was something more that I could have done."

When Siarla looked at her, Jemma could see the doubt – was there something that she should have done differently? The moment of weakness passed, and Siarla pulled up the mask of calm that she had been living behind since Russit's kidnapping. "I don't blame you, Jemma." She stated wearily.

Jemma stared at the ground. "I'll move out. I can... ask them to relocate me. It just feels wrong that I'm allowed to sleep with the family, when he can't."

Siarla took Jemma's hands in hers. "No, stay. My daughters have been through so much, now they've lost their brother and Saxton... hasn't spoken a word since he returned. They can't lose anyone else; I don't want to try to explain why you've left them."

Jemma burst out crying again, she opened her mouth to speak, but before she could Siarla had pulled her into a fierce hug.

Later that evening, when the sun started to set, the pyre was lit. The Gardyn gathered and stood respectfully, there were many more than Jemma had remembered. The families from Treefort only made up a small portion; as another force of Gardyn had made their way to the Valley.

More noticeably, Autumn's herd spread across the remaining open space, over fifty unicorns making a striking scene.

As the fire died down, everyone drifted quietly away.

Jemma followed the Marsh family to their tent, and as she lay down she felt a familiar lightening sensation. For once, she welcomed the vision openly, eager to escape the pain of grief that threatened to overwhelm her.

Jemma was stalking through the forest, her movements slow and precise. It was getting dark, and there was the smell of burning wood on the breeze. There was a handful of other Gardyn, following her lead.

She carried a bow and arrow, a full quiver on her back. She tensed as she heard a rustling ahead, and raised her bow to aim at the newcomer.

When the young man rushed towards her, she sighed and lowered her bow, recognising the Gardyn.

"Lady Jillis, I can confirm that Treefort is on fire." The man reported, "Just like the Oracle predicted."

She nodded, "It is a relief to know that everybody is safe in the Valley. Was there any sign of Hrafn's men?"

The scout shook his head. "The blaze looks like it has been going for a while, it makes sense that they headed back to the city when they found Treefort empty."

"Still, it wouldn't harm to make a sweep of the area." She reasoned, "I don't imagine Hrafn would leave the place without a patrol. With any luck, they might betray some useful information."

"Or we could just, y'know, kill them." An older chap spoke up, making the group chuckle.

Giving a rueful shake of her head, she turned on the guy with a bright smile, "Thank you for volunteering to take point, Conor."

The group smirked at the interaction, but quickly became professional again, moving in sync through the darkening forest.

The closer they got to Treefort, the stronger the smell of burning, and a strange orange light flooded the surrounding forest. It was horrible to see, the great walls crackling with the fierce flame. It was a miracle it didn't spread any further.

There was the snap of a branch behind them, the noise half-hidden by the fire.

"Archer!" One of the Gardyn shouted, firing an arrow into the leaves.

Alerted by the shout, she spun round. In a practised move, she aimed and let her arrow fly, just as she felt a deep pain in her thigh. She gasped as she looked down, hardly understanding why an arrow shaft stuck out of her leg.

She was vaguely aware that her own arrow had hit the hidden assailant square in the chest, and he had fallen from his perch in the tree. As she went to give orders to the Gardyn, she *felt her balance shift, her vision beginning to swim, and she collapsed unceremoniously on the grass.*

After Jemma awoke and alerted the Gardyn, a large party swiftly assembled to rescue their Lady Jillis and her men from whatever had befallen them. By dawn they had all returned, hurrying Jillis to the healer's tent. People milled outside, waiting for news.

Tobias and Samantha stood up quickly as the healer came out to meet them.

"Lady Jillis still lives," he began quietly, "She drifts in and out of consciousness. The injury puzzles me, she is not badly hurt and one as strong as Lady Jillis would not react to such an affliction. I have done what I can, if she makes it to morning, she will be on the road to a full recovery."

Tobias gave the healer permission to retire, then he and Samantha went inside.

It was not much later that Prince Lugal entered the tent, a worried expression clouding his face. "How is she?" He asked quietly.

"Still sleeping." Tobias replied, "We have no idea what is wrong. Where is your brother?"

"He could not resist meeting the unicorns. I would have accompanied him, but... Captain Philip is with him, all is well." Lugal knelt beside Jillis and hesitantly took her limp hand, his touch was gentle and caring, and betrayed his feelings. "Is there anything that can be done?"

"The arrowhead was tipped with poison."

Everyone turned to see Jemma hovering in the doorway, she looked very pale, her eyes red from tears that threatened to fall again.

213

"After the vision last night, it was difficult to separate from Jillis. Mixed with grieving over R-Russit, it hid what I should have realised sooner. It is a slow-working poison, designed to draw out the death of the victim. It has no cure."

Moments of silence passed, as they took in this news.

"Is Hrafn trying to delay us?" Lugal asked, "Poisoning the most-loved Gardyn, they make us stay in the forest trying to save her?"

"I don't think Hraf-" Samantha broke off, a thought occurring to her. "Hrafn could save her."

Tobias gave her a sceptical look, "I really don't think we can persuade him-"

"I meant specifically his power to restore life." Samantha snapped, "If I got close enough to kill him, I can claim his powers as my own. As long as Jillis is alive, I will be able to cure her with no risk to her soul."

"Samantha..."

"The prophecy that brought me here said that my powers would combine with Hrafn's. It doesn't actually state who gets to keep them."

"Samantha, you're talking about killing a king." Lugal cautioned.

"He has to die, and I have to be the one that does it." Samantha argued.

"And Hrafn will already know all this." Tobias said, holding Samantha's arm, as though scared she'd go on her suicide mission immediately. "The King will be waiting for you. Whether you go alone, or with an army at your back; Billamaur told you that the King's troops have all been recalled to protect the capital."

"Samantha, I agree with Tobias." Jemma said in a small voice, "I have a bad feeling about you rushing in."

214

"I didn't ask your opinion, Miss Jemma." Samantha snapped, "More reinforcements came yesterday, we can't assume that the Gardyn army will get any bigger than it currently is. Now is the time to act, along with anyone that will follow me."

Lugal and Tobias shared a look, neither approved of rushing to battle, but both loved Jillis in their own way, and knew they would follow Samantha.

"Shut up, shut up, shut up!" Jemma squealed, her fists clenched against her ears, her whole face scrunched with pain.

"What?!" All three people turned to her, surprised by the show.

"Not you, them!" Jemma said with a jerk of her head. She blinked away tears and relaxed. "Wow, that was a new experience, one that I do not want to repeat."

"Jemma, what are you talking about?" Samantha asked wearily.

"Hm, oh the dr-" She broke off, looking to Lugal and Tobias, not sure how much they knew. "Leukos and Caminus started speaking in my head – they are really loud."

"And what did they have to say?"

"They don't want you to fight Hrafn now, they say you will be outnumbered. They say..." She broke off, nervously trying to put the dragons' warning into the right words, "that in the bigger picture, Jillis is just one life to sacrifice."

Samantha tensed and turned away, marching out of the tent.

Samantha wasted no time at all, and after a rather rousing speech to the Gardyn, she had her army. It came

215

as no surprise that the rebels were ready to fight Hrafn and claim their freedom and revenge; but it was endearing how many wanted to save their beloved Lady Jillis.

Jemma grit her teeth, as she heard them make plans to leave that very evening. She'd hated speaking against Samantha, hated that she had to voice that they were going to have to choose between losing the war, or losing Jillis.

Now that she had given her advice, she didn't know what part she was supposed to play. Everyone was readying for war, and Jemma was no fighter. She drifted back to the Marsh family tent, only to find Siarla alone and crying over Russit's old jumper. It was the first time that Jemma had witnessed the woman's strong emotional wall crack, and she wasn't sure what to do.

"Siarla, are you alright? Would you like me to make some tea?" Jemma asked.

Siarla wiped her eyes, and set her son's clothing down, her fingers caressing the material. "I'm fine, I'll be fine. I just... heard that they are off to war, and I fear for Saxton."

Jemma automatically started to fuss, getting the mugs and tea leaves ready. "Saxton will be fine, he's been training for this."

Siarla shook her head, "He's not himself, he hasn't spoken a word since Russit... He can't fight if he's in a daze."

Jemma fidgeted with the empty kettle, a thought occurring. "I need to go heat some water, I will be back shortly."

Before Siarla could reply, Jemma hurried out. She ran over towards a group of familiar soldiers, who pointed her in the right direction.

She found the person she was looking for, cosying up to one of the girls from Treefort. Angrud was gently brushing aside a lock of the girl's dark brown hair, as they quietly spoke.

Jemma gave a dramatic cough, before it could get any more embarrassing. "Can I have a word, Angrud?"

The young man looked less than happy at the interruption, and stared at Jemma, willing her to go away. The girl that was with him blushed, and pulled away, suddenly nervous. She made her excuses and left.

"What?" Angrud barked. "By Minaeri, what is so important?"

"Sorry, I didn't mean to interrupt your... canoodling." Jemma apologised, gesturing towards the girl, before she realised she still had a kettle in her hand. "Who was she?"

"I want to say... Emelia? She came to confess her feelings before I went to war." Angrud said dismissively, "So why are you ruining it?"

Jemma took a deep breath and explained about Saxton. "Do you think there's a way you can stop him fighting?"

Angrud looked down at Jemma with honest pity. "Jemma, I wish I could; but short of tying him up against his will... He's already lost his son, do you want him to lose his honour, too?"

"I just... I can't bear the thought of Siarla and the girls losing him. They are such good people, and they don't deserve any of this." Jemma blinked back the tears that were always threatening to fall these days.

Angrud looked uncomfortable at her sign of emotion, and crossed his arms before he was tempted to give her a hug. "They're the best, which is why we are fighting against Hrafn's rule. He and his heir are responsible for the Marsh family's pain, and hundreds of others, too. Saxton will want to be a part of that fight."

Jemma bit her lip, none of it seemed very fair. "Can you... can you promise to stay with him? To protect him? And bring him home?"

Angrud gave a crooked smile, "Yes, yes, and I will do my damnedest."

"You know, I'm starting to think that you might actually be a good person, Angrud."

"And you are still a pain in the arse, Jemma." Angrud teased, "Now bugger off, so I can find Saxton."

Jemma grinned and hurried away, nearly swinging her kettle into a group of approaching soldiers.

*****

"This is the most dangerous thing we've ever attempted." Tobias muttered quietly to Samantha as they walked through the assembling ranks, each person kitted out with their new armour and weapons.

"Isn't every battle we've fought been dangerous?" She questioned, before answering herself, "But you're right, these brave men and women face their biggest challenge, all to get me close enough to kill Hrafn."

"You admit I'm right? Are you feeling unwell?" Tobias teased.

Samantha ignored his comment and looked directly at Tobias, "I don't want you to fight. I mean it, I'm on the verge of losing your sister; I can't bear to lose you too."

"All my friends march to war and this is my last chance to be with you." Tobias replied with a shake of his head. He quickly glanced up, the familiar figures of the princes were coming towards them.

"You don't understand," Tobias continued hastily, "If we fail, we all die. If we win this war I still lose you - you become Queen Samantha and I go back to being nobody."

"Samantha." Lugal greeted, "I was hoping to find you, I thought it would benefit the troops' morale to see us together."

Prince Cristan coughed, to get their attention. "Well, Captain Rian was looking for you, Samantha. So, I would recommend the royal couple go find him."

"Ah yes, quite right. Shall we?" Lugal offered his arm to Samantha, and nodded to Tobias, "Lord Deorwine, we will see you later."

Tobias watched solidly as Samantha walked away with the man that may become king.

Captain Rian was surrounded by Gardyn, preparing for the mass exodus of the army. When he glanced up and noticed that Losan and Samantha were heading towards him, Rian made his excuses and left the group.

"It looks like we're all going to get our moment of glory." The Captain said, as he led to the armoury. "And I have to show you something that may help."

"I don't want glory, I just want to save Jillis." Samantha replied, "Although I admit that I am looking forward to finally ending this thing."

"Siabhor and his pack have already agreed to fight alongside us." Rian said, "Have you spoken with the unicorns?"

Samantha sighed, the unicorns could help to drive their victory, but the alliance was weaker than ever before. "Alina will be there. Autumn feels indebted to us for saving his herd, so he will fight. I guess we'll find out how many of his herd join him when we head out; half of them are still convinced that I orchestrated the attack from the Dark Being."

Rian didn't push the subject, knowing they couldn't ask the unicorns to risk their lives. He stepped into the armoury, and led to a curtain that divided them from a section that Samantha didn't even know existed. In the shade of the canvas, row upon row of gleaming armour lay prepared. Losan followed close on her heels, curious what the modern Gardyn had created.

"When you returned from Caelum, I had the smithies work non-stop to fulfil the requirement. They finished the final two last night." Rian lifted up two identical helmets, passing one to Lugal. It had a deep russet base with a silver metal crown encircling it, and the looping symbol of Minaeri engraved over the brow. "For your highness and Prince Cristan."

"What about the others?" Samantha started to move down the rows, inspecting some rather peculiar designs.

"Each Gardyn has armour to protect the torso, and the arm pieces are designed in honour of the mallus."

Samantha picked up the gauntlet and slipped it onto her own arm, she tightened the leather straps and inspected the russet-coloured metal that reached from just below her elbow to her knuckles. Four silver spikes ran along her hand, reminiscent of the mallus' claws. She flexed her wrist and fingers and the spikes remained straight and strong. A smile crossed her face.

"I'll take that as approval." Rian added as he continued. "As for helmets, they represent the three sectors the army will be split into: the royal tined stag that will be led by their highnesses."

He picked up a helmet close to him. Out of the basic, russet-coloured cap rose light, yet strong silver antlers that reared up with presence.

Rian spoke again as he walked down the rows, "Secondly, the majestic unicorn, led by our own Lady Samantha and Lady Ji-" He halted in his words, looking worried.

Rian lifted the helmet to fill the silence. The base looked more flared than the stag's and had the decoration of a single silver horn that shone brightly. Rian said nothing more until he had reached the furthest region of the tent and picked up the third style. It matched the colouring of the others, but this one spiked and bristled, the silver metal picking out slitted shapes that could be eyes, and a row of spiked teeth than ran across the brow and down the extended cheeks.

"And this is my sector. It was supposed to be the strength of the bear, but Siabhor saw it and was so proud to have his kind immortalised and honoured that I couldn't disappoint him. So... the mallus it is.

Samantha still gripped the unicorn helmet in her hands, but looked steadily out across the red and silver gleam of armour. "We will be demons at dawn."

221

Twenty

It was the darkest hour before dawn when thirty mallus clambered silently up the wall of the capital city, each carrying a lightweight man clad in black. Each mallus made several climbs, so that a hundred Gardyn fighters crept along the high path with stealth and silence. The Gardyn blended into the clinging night with their black clothes, and the mallus were natural creatures of shadow.

Each of the King's watchmen was dispatched without a sound, as the rebels moved swiftly along the wall, heading for the gatehouse and other watch towers. After a slight scuffle the Gardyn had control and their presence was still unknown.

The signal was lit and the golden gates were pulled slowly open. Several thousand armed individuals entered, their silver horns, antlers and teeth gleaming as the sky lightened. The only sound was that of hooves and pounding feet, as the soldiers marched with grim determination. Amongst the horses, unicorns threaded their way over the rough roads.

They flooded the streets of the city, overcoming any in their path.

Finally, the shout went out, warning bells rang and horns sounded. The King's army was sluggish at assembling, and the Gardyn was deep within the city before they met any real force.

The first ray of dawn pierced the pastel sky, as the battle cry rang out from the rebels. The Gardyn warriors met their enemy with such fire that the first line of the King's soldiers wavered, fearing these demons that had broken into their strong city.

Chaos went through the ranks, as they discovered their Captain Orion Losan, clad in Gardyn armour and fighting for the rebels. The soldiers' loyalty torn between their commanding officer, and their King.

The fray pushed steadily towards the palace, but the King's soldiers kept coming, the weak lines getting denser and denser. The army might have many young and untrained soldiers, but sheer volume started to press the Gardyn and tilt the advantage.

Towards the front of the rebel force, Lady Samantha urged her white stallion to move forwards, her sword rimmed with fire, slashing down on the opponents that dared face her. She looked up as she heard another horn sound, and she could make out drumming that accompanied more feet marching in time. She could see the left flank of the rebels struggling to keep their position, and tried to move her horse to go help them.

Before she had chance to act, dark shadows raced between their legs, and the mallus set the enemy screaming.

Samantha took a deep breath, then joined the fight again, her arms tiring from holding the sword, her every muscle aching, she couldn't go on like this. The Gardyn couldn't go on... they needed a miracle.

"Minaeri, please..."

Her words were swept away as another press of soldiers surged in, knocking her from her horse. The fight became a blur, and Samantha noticed fewer and fewer Gardyn surrounding her. Her allies were steadily falling, human, mallus and unicorn alike.

Eventually her own sword was knocked flying from her aching hand, and Samantha felt herself being wrenched up unkindly.

"Kill the rest."

She recognised the commanding voice, and looked up to see David holding her, before he dragged her away to the palace.

Jemma snapped out of the vision, her limbs shaking and a sudden wave of nausea washed over her.

Like most of the camp, Jemma hadn't been able to sleep after the Gardyn army marched off to war, and in her restlessness, she had made her way into the healer's tent. Nobody had tried to stop her, those left behind in the Valley had their own concerns, and paid little notice to their oracle.

Jillis lay as though sleeping, the only person that looked peaceful and unworried. Jemma had slouched down at the foot of the bed, and quickly sought a vision of what the day would bring, desperate for some hope. Any at all.

Unfortunately, it was not to be. She idly played with her silver necklace as she tried to settle her mind after the horrific scene of the battle. Samantha had ridden to war

224

knowing this would happen, just as the dragons had said. The dra-

A thought hit Jemma so hard she stopped breathing.

She closed her eyes and tried to calm her excited pulse, focusing on the dragons. They were so rude to terrorise her in visions, it was time she returned the favour.

Jemma opened her eyes to find herself somewhere dark and warm. A red light flared, revealing stone walls and a rubble floor. Jemma staggered towards the light source, and blinking, stepped into an enormous cavern. It must have been a mile wide; and the ceiling disappeared into darkness.

As Jemma stepped forward, she heard the great clack of leathery wings overhead, and a flash of blue scales. With a few mighty beats of its wings, Leukos hovered 20ft above the girl, his frame huge and imposing. Even at this height, Jemma could feel the cold air washing over him, causing frost to form on the ground around her.

"Why-"

"Are you here?" The sentence was ended by Caminus, who came lumbering out of the darkness, counteracting the coldness.

"I decided it was my turn to have a say." Jemma said, crossing her arms and not being intimidated by the beasts. "And by the way, next time you jump in my head, can you please talk *quietly*? I thought I was gonna explode!"

Leukos dropped out of the air, and made the cavern floor rumble violently. He clicked his sharp-looking teeth in thought. "We will try," his voice like thunder.

Caminus walked closer, his reptilian body swaying with each powerful stride. "Why are you here?" He repeated.

"I want to change the outcome of the battle," Jemma replied casually.

"You are-"

"The oracle. Your duty is to watch,"

"As it is ours. We watch, we-"

"Relay Minaeri's plans and-"

"Warnings. You cannot change what is set."

"I refuse to believe that. Every person can change their destiny." Jemma argued. "Every dragon, too."

Having caught their attention, Caminus and Leukos both fixed their glassy eyes on the small girl, a curious hum rumbling up their throats.

"You need to help the Gardyn, and I'm not talking about visions. You need to physically support them." Jemma stated.

"We have not-

"Left this mountain for-

"A thousand years."

"Then it's about time you did." Jemma huffed, "Aren't you bored? Don't you want to see the sun, to fly through the sky again?"

"We have-"

"Our visions." Caminus snapped his teeth at her impudence. "A thousand-"

"Years is a long time, and we have learnt many-"

"Ways of experiencing the world." Leukos' tail slammed the floor in frustration, sending shockwaves through the ground. "We are the greatest lords-"

"That ever lived in Enchena. It is-"

"Only right the world comes to us."

"Sure it does; by Minaeri, don't you want to actually experience these sensations, instead of existing in a dream world? Don't you wish you could interact with these

people? You spend so much time watching and guiding them from a distance; don't you want to be a part of the history they make?" Jemma asked.

The dragons growled, their fierce claws scraping up loose rock and dirt in their agitation.

"Alright, clearly not." Jemma shrugged. "Fine, forget about what you want. You have the ability to see what will happen if someone makes a certain choice – you got Samantha to stop the war and take the Gardyn the Caelum. Tell me, *O mighty ones*, what would happen if you left for the capital this very moment?"

The dragons backed away from her, and Jemma thought they were about to ignore her, when Caminus let out a mighty blast of fire into the air above them.

Leukos raised his head and wrapped it in ice, forming a golden sphere.

The spectacle was brief, and the dragons soon had their answer.

"We can overturn-"

"The inevitable."

Jemma smiled, "Of course, knowing that you are the only ones that can save the people you have invested so much in... I guess the only question is: can those rusty wings get you to the capital in time?"

Jemma jumped back as one Caminus thrust open his massive wings and roared his disapproval. The girl grinned at the reaction she'd caused. She could feel the numb sensation in her fingers and limbs that meant her vision was coming to a natural end.

"You only have a few hours before dawn, fly fast, my friends..."

Twenty-One

"Minaeri, please..."

Samantha saw another wave of soldiers moving towards them, when everyone froze. A terrible, guttural roar ripped through the air, and many looked skyward.

"It can't be..." Samantha muttered, recognising the sound. To her delight, she saw the two dragons fly overhead, and she cheered.

Both armies seemed stunned at their appearance, not knowing what threat they posed, or to whom.

An almighty cheer went up from the Gardyn, as Caminus swooped down and engulfed the approaching reinforcements in flame, sending the surviving enemy running for their lives.

Leukos landed, his claws digging into the roof and wall of a large building, sending blocks and mortar tumbling into the ground. His icy breath froze the enemy in place, and sent others howling in pain.

"Those are... dragons." Prince Lugal appeared beside Samantha, trying to stem a cut on her arm. "How are there dragons? They are naught but myth."

"Aye, they are dragons. It's alright, they're on our side." Samantha replied. "Order out troops to attack."

The Gardyn captains rallied their forces, and pushed the enemy back, driving them towards the palace.

The dragons took to the air with a mighty crack of their wings, and swooped down, attacking where the King's soldiers were heaviest. Everywhere they looked, men were laying down their arms and surrendering to the rebels and their allies.

The remaining fray pushed steadily towards the palace, and the palace gates were flung open. The familiar figure of Prince David strode out, sword in hand. Behind him there surged a flood of soldiers, some fresh-faced and full of energy; and others that bore signs of wear.

King Hrafn must have been pushing himself to the limit, as every fallen soldier twitched and stirred, as Prince David passed them. Many got unsteadily to their feet, the dead joining the living, to sweep away the rebels, at their master's command.

They crashed down upon the Gardyn, and the area became a chaotic mix of black uniforms, and red-plated demons.

Caminus was the first to note the new attack, and he banked sharply, blasting their flank with fire. The soldiers screamed, and Prince David dived out of the destructive path. Once the fire died away, there was a grotesque scene of bodies rising, their flesh still burning, but ready to fight again.

Samantha pushed towards the melee on foot, and found Captain Losan making his way towards her, his already-scarred face bearing a fresh cut.

"I thought Hrafn's powers weren't working properly!" Samantha shouted.

229

"They're not!" Losan shouted back, gesturing at the stumbling, inept bodies. What they lacked in skill, they made up for in numbers, and perseverance. Even with the dragon's help, they could only hold them back. "Hrafn needs stopping. Go, I'll deal with Prince David."

Samantha allowed herself one brief glance towards David, then nodded. The young woman sprinted away to the palace entrance.

Captain Losan, adjusted his grip on his sword, and after a quick prayer to Minaeri, he headed straight for David.

The young man looked wild, his armour spattered with the blood of his enemies; his blond hair flying, and his blue eyes bright with battle. When he spotted Captain Losan, he paused, taking in the telling appearance of the King's closest advisor.

"Traitor!" He yelled.

One of David's loyal followers jumped forward to attack Losan, but David grabbed the man by the scruff of his neck and threw him aside, the soldier landing with a sickening thud.

"Losan is mine!" David commanded, his blue eyes fixed on his old mentor.

The surrounding battle seemed to hush, as Losan focussed solely on the young man that had destroyed everything.

"I rejoiced when I heard you had been killed by the enemy," David said, stepping towards Losan. "But this... seeing you alive and well, and one of them. This is an even better end to your story; the legend becomes the traitor."

"Minaeri works in strange ways." Losan replied, stalling for time, to gather his strength.

David snorted, "There is no Minaeri. No gods, only us mere mortals."

The young man circled Losan, trying to find some weakness in the Gardyn-made armour. With little warning, he swung his sword towards Losan's torso, and aimed for his neck on the back-swing.

Losan deflected the first with his shield, and barely dodged the latter. The Captain struck back, following blow after blow, to try and create a weak spot; but David was defended with the quickness of youth.

"Not up to your usual standard, old man."

Losan didn't rise to the prince's goading, and years of experience allowed him to keep level-headed amidst the chaos. He held back until he was ready, then attacked.

The two warriors fought on, Losan steadily gaining ground with his greater skill. It was suddenly over, when his sword got through David's defences and struck true.

Prince David slumped to the ground, silent and undignified, as the battle carried on around them.

Losan couldn't feel any joy in the victory over the poisonous young man, and he turned and re-joined the fight, aware that he had to defend the Gardyn until Samantha removed Hrafn's ability to raise the dead...

A thought struck him, just as a dagger was driven in his back.

Losan turned, the pain spreading, and his vision already starting to blur. He could still see Prince David, hovering behind him.

As Losan dropped to his knees, David grinned, "You didn't think Hrafn would let his heir die? Goodbye, old man."

*****

Samantha hesitated as she glanced up at the pale building that was once her gilded prison, then ran up the steps and burst in. The halls were deserted, the soldiers having been sent to fight, the servants cowering in hiding places. Lady Samantha was unhindered as she ran through the vaguely remembered corridors, her heart thudding with the enormity that... it was all about to end.

The first place she hunted for the King was his quarters. It was empty, except for the lifeless form of Queen Arianne, who lay as though asleep on her bed, even paler in death, yet retaining the icy beauty that had made her queen. Samantha stopped just long enough to say a quiet prayer for the deceased, before moving on again.

Her running feet took her to the throne room, a grand hall where the King took visitors and commanded his court. Samantha threw open the huge double doors and stopped in her tracks, King Hrafn sat on his high-backed throne, a rich cloak wrapped about him and his sword drawn and placed on his knee.

"I knew you would come, Samantha, but not this soon." The King spoke with self-confidence, though there was a shake in his hand that betrayed how frayed his nerves were.

"I have my reasons." Samantha retorted, stepping warily closer. She held her shield defensively before her body, feeling so frail in front of this man, despite her training. The round shield of hide and wood seeming so useless, her sword arm hanging by her side, hand sweating on the leather bound hilt.

Hrafn took a deep breath, but Samantha cut him off, "Don't call your guards, they can't kill me, you won't let them. We both know that you need to do that."

"You speak as though you come to surrender or barter," Hrafn sneered, "But that is so unlike the famous Lady Samantha."

"Why would I surrender? Your troops have fallen; your city flooded with rebels and mallus and unicorns; hell there are even dragons in the sky. You have lost." Samantha shouted.

"Death of men is nothing, it is reversed in a blink." Hrafn answered, "And once I have the powers intended for me, not even your assembly of monsters will stop me. So stop wasting time girl, and do what you came to do. Fight; die; and know that the last hope of the Gardyn dies with you."

The King rose from his throne, casting off his cloak. The shake in his hand had vanished, and he fought with a manic fervour. Another enemy he might have humoured and drawn out the humiliation of defeat and death; but Hrafn wanted Samantha gone, unable to cause him any more problems.

Samantha parried the first few strikes, and moved away to give herself time to breathe. He was good, very good. Samantha may have been trained by a great Gardyn warrior, and she had grown stronger and swifter after a year of intensive training; but Hrafn had been taught by history's best fighter, the famous Captain Orion Losan, and his age gave him greater strength and skill.

They would fight, parry, lunge and break, each testing the other and trying to break through to no avail, like some grotesque dance. Samantha began to feel the fatigue of battle course through her veins. How long had she been fighting now? Hours? Days?

Hrafn must have noticed her weariness, because he began to rain down blows so heavy and constant that Samantha felt that her arm must break from blocking them as her shield gave way, the thick wood shattering as though it were made of glass.

Samantha felt herself stagger back, but seemed strangely detached from her body, everything seemed to slow, everything seemed to grow chilly and she was afraid of dying here, alone and far from her allies.

Not alone, never alone.

Jillis interrupted her thoughts suddenly, her life hanging on this wild gamble. So many others depended on her, her journey as the Lost Soul wasn't going to end here.

Samantha gave a sharp scream as she felt her tired limbs rejuvenated, the sweat that soaked into her clothes no longer testament to her weariness. Her legs found strength and pushed forward, forcing the King to retreat as she continued blow after blow against his shield, both hands gripping her sword, the remnants of her own shield hanging forgotten from her left arm.

Fear crept into Hrafn's eyes, feeding Samantha's own strength, but increasing the King's desperation as he now fought to survive. He began to fight back, but his shield arm seemed weakened so that some of Samantha's strikes cut across his arms or rang across his armoured torso, cuts that were mirrored on Samantha's young flesh.

Samantha followed through the movements almost automatically, feeling increasingly distanced from the fight. Then she stopped, her breath catching. Glancing down she did not understand, did not understand the pain coursing through her body, nor the sword thrust through her gut. She could hear screaming, her own? Someone else's?

Hrafn let his sword slip from his grasp as he felt her blood run warm over his hands, felt her own weight drag Samantha down to her knees. The King was breathing heavily, a wretched smile crossing his lips, interrupted by gasping breaths.

But this was wrong, all wrong. What had been the point of her adventures if this was how it ended, the point of all those lost lives. The dismal thoughts filled her confused mind as her hands, slicked in her own blood, fumbled at the hilt, desperate to pull out the blade with her waning strength.

So she was to die, all alone. Warmth enveloped her, and Samantha felt herself to be drifting, away from pain. But no, never alone. A strong, female presence came to her, *'it is time to give in to me,'* words whispered in her mind and Samantha readily fell into that warmth.

Hrafn had staggered back a step from Samantha, watching her as a small, helpless girl, her life slowly draining away. Finally, *finally*, he was going to receive all that he had craved for nearly forty years.

He did not understand the stabbing pain as the four mallus spikes were driven into his thigh, and as his leg gave way, the sudden thrust of his own sword up, under his armour, driving through his gut and up. Samantha knelt before him, her hands pushing the sword up to the hilt, an inhuman snarl on her lips and a distant light flaring in her eyes.

"Only our own weapons can kill us." Samantha said in a deep resounding voice that was not hers.

The King collapsed to the blood-stained palace floor, his own breathing laboured.

235

"An ancient wrong is finally righted." Samantha whispered as she sensed the life leave Hrafn's body.

The strength that had been granted her was swiftly taken away and the pain of her injuries lanced through her again and Samantha fell to the floor, her own blood pooling about her, mingling with that of the dead King's, 'How bright the colour', came her hazy thoughts. A light seemed to hover, then descended and sank to her flesh. Samantha took a deep, gasping breath as her vision sharpened and the pain of her injuries faded to an ache.

Samantha struggled to roll herself over and scramble up. Her hand reached out to grasp Minaeri's sword - her sword - and her other bloodied hand reached up to pull off her helmet.

She stayed on her knees, trying to understand what had just happened. Her clothes were torn and soaked with still warm, still wet blood, but the wound by her waist had become nothing more than a fresh pink scar, painful to the touch. Her senses were going wild and she was utterly aware of everything about her and even further afield.

Samantha didn't waste a moment, she raced back through the corridors of the palace. When she burst out of the doors, a cheer erupted from the Gardyn. The battle was over, and they all worked to relieve the surrendered enemy of their weapons.

"The King is dead!" She shouted, as many expectant faces turned her way. "Hrafn is dead! Let there be no more killing!"

Samantha saw a familiar figure push through the crowd towards her, the grey unicorn's beauty and majesty a harsh comparison to the battle scene.

As she drew close, Samantha leapt onto her friend's broad back, begging her to carry her swiftly back to Jillis. They paused momentarily, to pull Tobias up behind her; then they set off with all the speed Alina could muster.

*****

The Valley was deadly quiet, all were subdued with the thoughts of battle and whether their loved ones survived.

The tent where Jillis lay was small and dark, Samantha and Tobias ducked inside, leaving the tent flap open for Alina's sake. Jillis lay pale and unmoving, her eyes closed and lips slightly parted. Jemma sat with her back against the bed, her knees brought up and arms wrapped around them as though holding herself together.

"Is she...?" Tobias' voice shook and he dare not finish his question.

"I could resuscitate her the first time, bu..." Jemma choked.

Samantha felt hot tears begin to fall. She could not believe that the beautiful and kind Jillis, who had always been there, was truly gone. Samantha tentatively reached out and touched her hand.

"She's so warm." She murmured.

"Lady Jillis left us just before you arrived." Jemma informed them, with a sob. Jemma faced Samantha, a bold look in her eye. "You can do something, Samantha. It if wasn't for her – for me – you might be dead. You owe her. Besides, the whole point of the fight was to get Hrafn's power to bring life."

"No, it wasn't." Samantha snapped, ignoring the guilt that bloomed, "The point of the war was to defeat Hrafn and to free Enchena, that's done. Jillis gave us heart, and now she's gone... And don't you dare lecture me girl, you

237

don't know Jillis, you have no idea what she means to me."

Tobias glanced to Jemma with a silent apology for Samantha's harshness, but was yet to come to terms with it himself. "Samantha, you have the power now to bring back the dead, to give life again."

Samantha looked at him with disgust, "I have the power to make the body live, but I cannot bring back the Jillis we love. I can't believe you'd be willing to settle for a shell without a soul."

Jemma lifted her head slightly, a thought striking her. "Perhaps... there might just be a chance..."

Jemma fumbled at her neck, pulling out the chain that she had been wearing so constantly she almost forgot its importance. The initiatus crystal allowed a person travelling through a portal to retain their soul. It had been Gran, the one who started her journey, who now provided the answer.

"Samantha, trust me, Jillis is not lost yet." Jemma said calmly. She placed the necklace over Jillis' head, so that the crystal lay above her breast. "Trust me. I refuse to believe this is the end of her story, Jillis is too important to the Gardyn."

When Samantha didn't reply, Tobias put his arm around her.

"Please," he murmured, "I don't want to lose my sister, and our new world will be a better place with her in it."

Samantha shrugged away from his touch, "What about the hundreds that have died? I have no right to decide to give one life and deny it to the rest."

"For Minaeri's sake!" Jemma shouted, suddenly flipping. The younger girl grabbed Samantha's arms.

"This is not your decision. So get over yourself and do your duty!"

Samantha's eyes narrowed at the insult, and she pulled back from the girl. "I will do this, but only on the account that if this goes wrong, you, Miss Jemma, will put the soulless person out of their misery."

Jemma nodded slowly, before stepping back to give Samantha any room she needed.

Samantha closed her eyes and delved into the darkness, not sure what she was looking for, but there was a faint silver thread laid before her, straining to hold the essence of the soul to the fading hope of life.

Tobias and Jemma moved back as a silver light descended and encompassed the two ladies...

Twenty-Two

Almost all fighting had stopped in the city, leaderless without their King, many more had lain down their arms.

The crowd parted to let a single unicorn through, as she carried Samantha and Jillis swiftly back to the scene of their victory. The Gardyn cheered as they passed, two mere mortals and their unicorn ally that had been elevated and held with love over the past two years, and now controlled the future of an empire.

They rode to the very centre of the city, and there was a glorious reunion between the heroes and Lady Jillis. No one had been unscathed by the fight, but it was a welcome relief to see the faces of their friends.

"No!"

A cry above all others made them turn to the palace where Prince David stood at the top of the stone steps, his furious gaze focussed on Samantha.

"It is not over yet. All loyal soldiers to me!" The heir cried, "You have my gifts Sammy, they belong to me and I will take them back."

He lifted a bow and arrow, pulling the string taut.

Soldiers were suddenly pushing towards David, to join him or to kill him. Out of the masses, one man leapt up. David's deadly aim was knocked askew, as Captain Rian took the feet from under him.

"Stay back!" Rian's firm voice warned the soldiers, "He does not deserve your loyalty."

Samantha pushed through, her eyes widening at the sight of David. He was ghastly pale, and gasped for breath, not even making the effort to rise, as he glared up defiantly.

"I'll finish him for you, Lady Samantha." Rian stated quietly.

Samantha shook her head, lost for words, forcing herself to look upon the fallen version of the one she had risked her life for, had loved, and had fought against.

"Give me what is mine, Sammy, I am Hrafn's successor." David demanded. "Give it to me, and I will live, isn't that what you want?"

She sighed, choking back tears, and knelt beside him. "I'm sorry. But I promise it will be painless this time."

Samantha reached within and sent forth the wings of death, the first power revealed to her on her long journey, but one she had refused to use. Up 'til now.

David froze, feeling fear for the first time since he had been shot down in the forest. But he could fight this death no more than the first, and slipped into eternal sleep.

He looked peaceful, as though he really were just asleep. The black, twisted version of David dissipated and Samantha was left kneeling over the body of a lad she knew, the popular boy from school. She wiped away a sorrowful tear and looked up into the pale face of Captain Rian.

"I have long known that I would be the one to kill him."

"He would have died anyway, without Hrafn's powers sustaining him, as will many soldiers here, brought back from death to bring hell into the living world." He spoke with a hint of bitterness. Rian looked away to the crowd, who waited in anticipation. "It is time to lead your people."

Samantha stood up obediently and walked back to the masses, aware that all eyes were on her. As she passed those she was close to, she reached out and briefly held them, drawing on their courage and belief.

She climbed onto an overturned cart that was still reasonably stable, then hesitated.

"The tyranny is over." She shouted out. "Accept the Gardyn and we will not hold ourselves above you. We have fought long to bring freedom to all, and to overcome the blindness held to the suffering about you. It is done now."

She paused, regaining her thoughts, and in the silence another voice shouted out, "Long live Queen Samantha!" The shout was taken up by the crowd, but Samantha held her hand up against it.

"I am no queen. I was brought here to free you, not to lead you. From this day, the empire Enchena holds will no longer exist. Each country shall find their true monarch and make their own choices. As for Enchena, the rightful heir will be crowned. The son of King Gearalt, the Royal Prince Lugal"

Lugal took his cue and stepped awkwardly up onto the cart. He otherwise made an impressive figure, with his tall stature and a metal crown already circling his helmet.

Samantha stepped up to him and hugged him close, "I cannot be your queen." She whispered.

Lugal was taken aback by this, but with so many people looking on, he forced himself to appear unfazed. He said nothing, but let go of her and turned to his people. "People of Enchena, in due course I will prove in every way, that I am worthy of the crown, but for now, many have died and many more are injured. Let us tend to them first."

Samantha started to head for the main gate of the city, but it was slow work. Every few strides, people stopped her to express their gratitude; to bow; or to just touch the shoulder of their saviour.

As much as she understood their desire to meet her; she was relieved when she finally caught sight of her horse. Legan pricked his ears and walked towards her. The gentle cream stallion looked to have gotten away unscathed. Not caring who was watching, Samantha threw her arms around his neck; he had been such solid companion, and she was glad he had made it to the end of their journey. Samantha pulled herself together and jumped into the saddle, there was one more ally she had to meet.

As she rode down the main street, drawing close to the golden gates, Samantha spotted Tobias, riding in on a bay horse, with Jemma behind him. It had taken so much longer to travel back on a normal horse, than when Alina had travelled with all the speed of Praede.

"All is well?" Tobias asked.

"Aye, everything is over." Samantha replied, "Jillis is at the palace, along with the princes and Rian, if you are looking for them."

Tobias' face fell a little. "And... has it been announced? Do I have to bow and call you 'your majesty' now?"

"Now is hardly the time." Samantha huffed, "Especially as I rejected the throne in front of half of Enchena. I turned down Lugal's proposal."

"Really?" Tobias sat straighter, finding the news more than he could have hoped.

Further words were halted by Jemma suddenly making herself known, jabbing her finger into an unarmoured section of Tobias' torso. "If you two are gonna start spouting stuff that's gonna make me uncomfortable, can you please wait 'til I'm off the horse and have the ability to run away?"

Samantha laughed, "Sorry Jemma. Don't worry, I'm leaving, I need to get on and see a couple of old friends."

Feeling somewhat lighter, Samantha kicked her horse on and rode out of the gate.

The friends that she intended to meet were not hard to find. Caminus and Leukos were in the grassy plains to the south of the city. Samantha was relieved that they had not tried to stay within the city walls; as grateful as they were for the dragons help, the capital wasn't built for anything their size.

The two dragons turned to face Samantha, and even Legan seemed to falter in his stride.

"My lords, I came to thank you, on behalf of the Gardyn. We couldn't have won without you." Samantha shouted up to them.

"No, you-"

"Could not." The dragons answered.

"I didn't know you were going to come." Samantha said, still processing the fact that they were actually here.

244

"It was not supposed to be."

"We were never supposed to be a part of it."

"I don't understand." Samantha admitted.

"The oracle came to us. She-"

"Forced us to create a new future." Caminus ended with a snort, flames flickering in his nostrils.

Leukos bared his teeth. "We do not-"

"Like her. She insulted us."

Samantha paused, Jemma had insulted the dragons? The girl was certainly brave, or foolish. Samantha smiled, "She insulted me, also. Instead of telling me what I wanted to hear, she told me what I needed to hear in a moment of stubbornness."

"Dragons are not stubborn, we-"

"Are merely experienced and know-"

"What is best." Caminus finished with a stamp of his clawed foot, sending dirt flying.

"Except for this time. Wasn't Jemma right?" Samantha asked, then realising it was likely a sore topic, she changed the subject. "What will you do now, return to your mountain?"

The dragons exchanged a look. "We have been in that mountain-"

"For so long. We forgot-"

"What the world felt like."

"We think it is time,"

"To experience it again."

Samantha bowed her head, "Then I wish you well on your adventures, dragon lords. I hope we will meet again."

The dragons lowered their torsos in an odd bow, then turned away. They both opened their wings and, with a short run, they were airborne.

Samantha watched as they circled overhead, their might cry echoing over the city. They dipped their wings towards Samantha in farewell, then flew away to the horizon.

Samantha smiled, she had a feeling that Enchena would be abuzz with stories of the dragons, now.

*****

The death toll was great and terrible. The healing of the injured, even with Samantha's magical influence, was a slow and steady process; but gradually the city began to stir and work toward their beautiful new world.

The Gardyn dead were carried out of the city and back to their home towns for funeral rites to be carried out by loved ones. As the pallets were drawn through the streets, flowers were thrown over them so they were adorned in bright colour.

Samantha mourned the friends she had lost. Captain Philip had died in the first attack, a sorry fate for such a good and kind man. Half of the mallus had been killed, as they pushed through the legs of the enemy lines, relishing in the attack, and many falling. Luckily Autumn had not lost any more of his kin, but there was hardly a unicorn that didn't carry some injury from the battle.

Then there was Captain Losan. Witnesses had reported that Losan had been stabbed in the back by Prince David. Despite her mixed feelings for the enemy-turned-ally, Samantha was sorry that his legend should end in such a way, and swore that she would see his funeral carried out with respect.

A great pyre was built outside the city's wall and it burnt throughout the night. But even with the warmth of the flames, Samantha felt cold. She had dealt death to so many, she hardly deserved to be here. She kept glancing to the Great Forest, something strong was drawing her, and she knew that she had to go.

Strong arms wrapped about her supportively and she finally found some comfort; but even Tobias' embrace couldn't distract her from the call of the night-time forest. When everybody else had settled down to sleep, Samantha crept away into the welcome shadows of the trees...

Twenty-Three

Creatures of the forest felt the subtle shifts, they were aware of the mass human departure, and they were tuned into the sudden darkening in the future of the unicorns.

Alina felt a sense of foreboding, knowing that she had to find Sundance; and equally knowing that she wouldn't like what she found. It pained her to travel to Nmirr's old herdlands. She was accompanied by Samantha, who felt the restlessness of the forest and insisted on coming.

Torment had waited alone in his father's clearing for nearly a day, weighing up his options. He had tried to find the Valley, to offer the Dark Being something of value; but he couldn't find his old home. The trees and trails twisted him, until he was fully lost.

He remembered being told that the Valley had once belonged to Praede, and would always protect those within from their enemies. Torment had always thought that Autumn was boasting and exaggerating, but it turned out the dull stick-in-the-mud had been telling the truth.

Now he had to come to terms with the fact that he had failed the Dark Being. The master would punish him; and the rest of the herd would take it as proof that he didn't belong, deserving nothing but pain. Worst of all, he was further away from being able to claim Odile.

He could run, and get hunted down; but Torment had a much better idea...

The forest always became eerily quiet when the Dark Being was close, the creatures fearing the one unicorn that broke nature's law at every turn. On his heels, the herd followed him, keen to see the punishment of the upstart intruder, who dared to call himself Torment.

The black unicorn moved ahead, appearing beside Torment with a grace that defied his age. "Where is Alina?"

"I tried, sir, but I could not find the Valley." Torment replied.

"Could not find..." The Dark Being's thoughts curled and teased, "It is not a hard task, to find your old home. If you are really this incompetent, I'm afraid I can't ignore this-"

There was a hum of excitement from the unicorns that encircled them, all waiting to finally break the son of Nmirr.

Torment raised his head and met the Dark Being square in the eye. He didn't hide his intentions, his thoughts clear. He was going to kill him, and take his place.

The Dark Being read Torment's plan with patronising disinterest. He had lost count of how many young stallions had come of age, and thought they could defeat him.

Before Torment could make a move, the Dark Being lowered his horned head and charged. The palomino leapt out of the way, delivering a stinging kick as he did.

The two began to circle, assessing the other for weakness, then attacked. It was a blur of hooves, horn and teeth, black coat against gold.

Finding his opponent stronger than he had expected, the Dark Being gave an equine scream of fury and lunged forward with horn lowered. Torment hung back, dodging again at the last moment and placing an infuriating kick in the ribs. The black stallion reared and turned, his forelegs cutting down on golden hide.

The fight drew on through the night as the two stallions circled again and tested each other, or came together in cruel grips and struggled for dominance. The thud of hoof against ground and flesh echoed through the forest. In the darkness, the Dark Being faded to nothingness, but Torment's white mane and tail attracted any existing light.

Those gathered to witness the battle noticed the Dark Being slowly becoming less willing to start an attack, waiting instead for the younger stallion to make all the moves. The young Torment was still moving lightly on his hooves, possessing the stamina of Praede.

Perhaps he was ensuring that the Dark Being was truly tiring, or perhaps he was enjoying the prolonged torture the old stallion must be enduring. By the time the sky was lightening, Torment had still not ended it.

Torment paused as the first ray of sunlight crept into the forest, throwing away the memories of a better time when he would dance to welcome the sun. Now he would kill instead.

"A new day, a new leader." Torment projected his thoughts to the Dark Being alone, before lashing out.

The old stallion crumpled to the churned ground. Torment looked away from the black heap and glared at the gathered herd.

"By our lore, you are all mine." He stated solidly. "Any who think they can flee will be hunted down and killed."

The palomino stallion stood in his powerful glory in his father's clearing as the sun became stronger. As one body, the herd members dropped their head in deference to their new leader. Only one black mare stood tall, brazenly walking up to Torment's side.

"Odile." Torment greeted.

"My lord." She replied in amusement.

Torment snorted, for the briefest moment, he thought he saw his aunt hiding in the trees. She had seen what he had become. Good.

He called to the herd, and led his unicorns back to the shadows where they belonged.

*****

Alina couldn't stop the shiver that ran down her spine, as she witnessed her nephew fight the most feared unicorn in the Great Forest. Every strike and grunt of pain pierced her heart, and she was glad that Samantha kept her company.

"No." Alina argued, "You cannot interfere. This is Sundance's fight, he will never forgive us if we help."

"I can't stand by and watch my friend-"

"Samantha, if you ever loved him, you will." Alina's thoughts were hard, the closest she ever got to angry.

251

"This is the way of unicorns, you have to stop humanising us."

Shamed into silence, Samantha hung back and waited.

When dawn finally broke, Alina felt a swell of pride as she saw that her nephew had beaten the Dark Being, which surely proved that he would be greater than even Nmirr. Hope flared up for Alina, surely now that her nephew had removed the threat of the Dark Being, and shown the world that he would bow to no one; now he could find his way back to being the old Sundance.

The hope was short-lived. As soon as her nephew chose to kill the defeated black stallion, Alina knew he had changed. She barely breathed as she watched her nephew turn and claim the dark herd as his own, cementing his new place.

The brief moment their eyes met was almost enough to shatter her. Alina's gaze followed her nephew's departure, and stayed locked on the disappearing herd. She was vaguely aware of someone calling her name, and eventually snapped her attention back to her human friend.

Samantha placed a hand on her quivering grey coat, the silver mare unusually tense. "Alina, it will be alright, we'll get him back." Samantha said, unconvincingly.

Alina looked around her brother's old herdland, the area still depressing and deserted. "We need to leave. Come, Samantha, it will be quicker if I carry you."

Samantha obediently jumped onto Alina's broad back, a feat that was now so familiar and easy. They travelled through the forest in an uncomfortable silence, and it was almost a relief to reach the forest edge, the capital city sitting ahead in glorious sunshine.

Samantha dismounted, not wanting to weigh Alina down longer than necessary. She took a couple of strides towards the city, before noticing that the unicorn wasn't coming with her.

Alina stood firmly in the shade of the forest, her silver tail swishing in frustration.

"Alina? What is it?"

The silver mare tossed her fine head, glancing back into the forest. "I have to go back to the Valley, warn Autumn and the others."

"Alright, will you be back for Lugal's coronation?" Samantha asked.

"I won't be returning." She answered.

"What?"

"Your war is ending, but I feel that ours is just starting." Alina replied. "At least with the Dark Being, we knew his tricks, and we knew his reign was coming to an end. The fact that the dark herd has been taken over by a young stallion with fresh ambitions... every unicorn needs to be warned. Old alliances have to be reformed."

"I'm sorry, I didn't realise." Samantha apologised. "Once things are settled here, I'll come help you."

Alina's grey ears flicked nervously, and she lowered her head sadly, "You will only make it worse, Samantha. Autumn's herd are the most open-minded unicorns in the forest, and even they barely tolerate you. If you were present, we would be accused of being tame and pandering to human needs."

Samantha wanted nothing more than to wrap her arms around Alina's neck, as she had done so many times before; but she felt a new distance growing between them. "Will I see you again?" She asked quietly.

"I hope so." Alina replied warmly. "It has been an honour, Lady Samantha."

The grey unicorn turned and sprinted silently back into the forest, her flashing silver hide fading from sight.

Samantha backed away, heading towards the city, and blinking away the tears that threatened to fall.

Starting the slow walk back down the grassy slope that led to the capital, Samantha was surprised to see another unexpected friend,

A mass of dark shadows moved across the ground, the brown shapes easily distinguished as mallus, loping across the grass.

"Siabhor!" Samantha shouted, glad for a chance to see her steady companion.

The mallus in question skid to a halt, sitting on his haunches, letting the rest of his pack pass him by.

"Siabhor, I'm so glad to see you, I've just spent the night with Alina..."

After Samantha had finished filling him in, Siabhor cocked his head aside, curiously. "Annoying Sundance controls evil unicorns now?"

"Yes, it was awful. Alina has gone to warn the other herds, I don't think she'll be coming back." Samantha looked away to the forest, and noticed Siabhor's pack disappearing into the trees. "I'm sorry, were you going hunting?"

"No. We be going home. Human war is over."

Samantha felt like the bottom of her heart had fallen out. "But you could stay, you helped us, you're heroes!"

Siabhor grunted, "Samantha be stupid, we be mallus, nothing more. We not belong in stone walls, on stone ground. We belong in forest, where free to hunt; to run; to climb."

"You could-" Samantha started to say something, but stopped herself. "You weren't even going to say good bye?"

"Silly humans waste words, when result is same." Siabhor grumbled.

Before Samantha could say anything else, the mallus dug his claws into the earth and shot off, after his pack.

Samantha could just about hear the clicking of nails against wood, that had once driven fear into her heart, and she smiled.

Twenty-Four

The streets milled with activity, the war was over, but now began the very long task of recovery.

The new king had ordered that tents would be erected in every town square, to cater for the injured; making every healer in high demand. Volunteers were welcomed readily.

One such volunteer was the Lady Jillis. She had finished reassuring her friends that she had recovered, and thanked them for their belief in her, then tried to make herself useful in the aftermath. The hours flew by, as she carried water and fresh linen, helped to bandage and generally keep spirits up.

"Shouldn't you be resting?"

Jillis looked up at the familiar voice, to find Prince Lugal hovering behind her.

"Your majesty." She greeted, curtseying briefly, before turning back to the sling she was tying around a blushing soldier's neck. "I've rested long enough."

Lugal gave a small smile, "I've not been crowned yet, and I would rather you call me by my name."

Jillis finished with her patient, and with a few kind words, moved on to deal with the pile of used bandages. Her brown eyes flicked up to the future king, bemused to find him here of all places. "Aren't you needed at the palace? Doing... kingly things?"

"I've written missives, formalising my claim and inviting the regional governors and gentry to the coronation. There is an interim council in place, while we shape the proposal for a government. There are no needs more pressing, than those of the injured and displaced people." Lugal answered. "Besides, everywhere I walk in the palace, nobles are coming out of the woodwork, vying for favour. One can hardly believe their previous liege is not yet cold in his grave."

"Well, Lugal. If you insist on helping, grab the other side of this basket and help me cart it outside." Jillis said, quite happy to order around royalty.

Lugal chuckled at her audacity, but obediently lifted the basket, heavy with blood-stained bandages. "I'm glad our paths crossed, Lady Jillis, I wanted the chance to express my... relief that you are well. I feared... we all feared for you."

Jillis was glad to focus on shuffling past the makeshift beds, as a blush spread across her cheeks. "I owe my life to Samantha, and everyone that joined the battle. If we're going to be friends, ought you not call me Jillis?"

Distracted by her big brown eyes, Lugal hit a table and stumbled, the picture of awkwardness. Across the tent, there was a tutting from one of the healers, but Lugal did his best to ignore them.

"I also wanted to apologise, Jillis. The engagement to Lady Samantha was poorly done, and I had not considered how it would damage our... friendship, and I am deeply sorry for any pain I caused you." Lugal rattled off, while he still had the confidence to do so. "The arrangement we had has been ended. I mean, Samantha ended it, I mean-"

"I already know." Jillis said quietly, saving him from further embarrassment.

They sat the basket down outside, next to a vat of boiling water.

"I can take it from here, your maj- I mean, Lugal." Jillis said, knowing that her history as a maid was better suited to washing, than his royal princeliness.

Lugal saw the judgement in her eyes, and smiled, rolling up his shirt sleeves and getting started. "You forget that Cristan and I were without luxuries after our father died, we are no stranger to manual work."

They worked in silence, washing the bandages, then hanging them to dry. After that, the healer in charge, set them tasks with various patients, most of whom were surprised to find their future king helping them. They were so busy, they hardly had time to speak to each other; and as the day wore on into evening, their energy began to flag.

When most of the work was done, the healer shooed them away to the palace, demanding they get some good food and sleep, and he didn't want to see either of them until tomorrow.

They walked through the streets of the city, tired and blood-stained, hardly looking the part of nobility.

When the shadow of the palace loomed ahead, Losan stopped, wanting to say something now, before things became formal again.

"Jillis..."

Jillis paused, looking back to the prince, his normally rich brown hair was dishevelled, and his eyes betraying his exhaustion.

"I have to say something, now, before life threatens to interfere. I know I have no right saying it, and this is hardly a fitting time and place, but..." Lugal gently took Jillis' slender hand in his own. "Jillis Deorwine, I want nothing more than to marry you."

Jillis froze, both thrilled and mortified by the declaration. She slowly pulled her hand away. "I believe you, Lugal; but what you want might not be what the King needs. Every person of privilege will try to dissuade you from marrying a *servant girl*; they will throw every eligible lady in your path. Regardless of your feelings towards me, I will always be waiting for the day you set me aside again, for the sake of a political marriage."

"Jillis, I am so very sorry for the choice I made. I knew it was wrong from the start, I should have never listened to anyone other than myself." Lugal said, his hand reaching for her waist, wanting to keep her here for a moment longer. "I have loved you from the moment I met you. You are beautiful, the kindest and most honest person that I know. I know that you will be more than a wife to me, you will be a friend, and an advisor. When I thought I was going to lose you, I realised that no princess, or nobleman's daughter could ever compare. So please, say you will be my wife."

"Oh, I don't think it's quite that simple." Jillis replied with a smile, brushing past his hold and heading back to the palace, "I think you need to prove yourself worthy of me."

"Worthy?" Lugal was speechless, after a moment collecting his thoughts, he jogged to catch up with Jillis.

259

"I am to be the King of Enchena, the highest position in the land."

"I can't love a crown – cold, hard, inanimate object." She mused aloud. "I want to know that Lugal is worthy of Jillis."

"Very well." Lugal struggled to find a suitable affirmation. "And... how do I prove myself to you?"

"Oh, I'm sure I'll think of something." She replied with amusement, her gaze teasing as she ducked within the palace walls.

*****

The following week, the capital was abuzz with excitement, Enchena was due to crown its first benevolent king, a fact that brought both joy and scepticism.

The commoners filled the streets, and there were parties, music and celebrations that their city had been freed.

The nobles filed in with a wariness, not sure how they fit into the new court, but hiding it behind perfect smiles.

At the centre of it all, the Gardyn were jubilant, and not letting anything cloud their day.

The throne room was filled with rich colours and flowers, casting off the dark and imposing nature it had beneath King Hrafn.

In front of the rows of Gardyn heroes, and Enchenian nobles, the soon-to-be-king walked out of the antechamber, and stepped up onto the dais, his twin brother a few strides behind him. Lugal looked magnificent, he had the dark look of the royal line, and his handsome face was confident and calm. He wore a splendid gold tunic, with the black and red insignia of his house; his rich, red cloak swept the ground.

260

As Lugal took his place on the throne, Cristan stood to his right, acknowledged as his brother's heir, until a son was born.

A priest of Minaeri stepped forward, raising the crown for all to witness.

"In the name of Minaeri, we name you Lugal, King of Enchena, and lord of the empire." The man's voice rang out clear and strong.

With that, the priest placed the crown on Lugal's head; then stepped back and bowed to his King.

The amassed crowd rose to their feet and cheered, the nobles remaining sophisticated, but the Gardyn broke decorum by expressing themselves through noise. Lugal rose from his throne and made his way down the throne room, his gaze meeting Jillis' as he passed her, a small smile cracking through his cool composure.

The cheer was picked up outside the palace, and carried through the streets, as the coronation was officially announced, the new king stepping out onto the balcony, and waving to his subjects.

*****

A grand feast followed, with music and dancing.

Prince Cristan moved away from the crowd of nobles congratulating King Lugal. He found his new friends congregating half-way down the hall, sharing drinks and laughter.

Cristan paused to let a servant refill his wine glass, then pushed in between Samantha and Captain Rinar.

"Cristan! How does it feel to be brother to the king?" Samantha asked loudly, her gaze a little hazy after the flowing wine.

261

"King Brandon, or King Lugal?" Cristan grinned at her well-meaning question. "I wonder if there will be many differences from the crowning of my elder brother, Brandon. I suppose there are two hundred years between them, and I don't think Lugal plans to hunt down and kill me."

"Oh…" Samantha blushed, "You get to be the king's heir, Lugal obviously trusts and respects you."

"Ah, we both know that is a temporary position. Lugal will have a son, as soon as he secures his bride." Cristan replied, chancing a look towards Jillis, who hovered at the edge of the group, her eyes constantly moving to the new king.

Jillis turned back to her friends, noticing Cristan for the first time. "Cristan, for shame, you have left your brother to fend off the nobles alone?"

"Aye, m'lady, I'm trying to gently ease him into dealing with them on his own."

Jillis looked up to the mass of people surrounding Lugal. "That hardly looks gentle. This is supposed to be a celebration, perhaps I shall venture forth and rescue him."

Jillis smiled and walked up towards the king, her dark hair and red dress making a striking appearance, and causing many to pause and look her way as she passed. She walked up to the group around the king, and was quickly greeted and drawn into discussions. The men vied for the attention and opinion of the beautiful young woman, and Jillis replied as politely as possible. She met Lugal's eyes, and hinted towards the floor where couples danced.

Relief shot through Lugal's schooled expression. "Lady Jillis, would you honour me with a dance?"

The crowd watched as they stepped out, moving gracefully, drawing all eyes. Lugal leaned in and said something private that made Jillis laugh.

Cristan forced himself to look away. "Why should my brother have all the fun? Lady Samantha, would you care to dance?"

Samantha smiled, handing her empty glass to a passing servant. "I would love to, Cristan. I look forward to a dance partner that doesn't have two left feet." She replied, looking pointedly at Tobias.

The prince led out the young lady, her new silver dress sparkling in the candlelight.

*****

Later that night someone knocked on Jemma's bedroom door. Jemma was still wide awake and giddy from the party. She kicked away the silken sheets and dashed across the large, luxurious room.

After the war, her temporary family had been reunited – thanks to Angrud, Saxton had survived, and assuaged some of his grief through battle. It only followed that the Marsh family had headed back south to their old village, to try and move forward with their lives. They had invited Jemma to go with them; but Lady Samantha had stepped in and insisted that she stay in the capital.

Jemma had been given a room in the palace; she had never experienced such luxury, and she rather hoped the stay would be permanent. At the same time, she hoped that she'd have the freedom to visit Saxton, Siarla and the girls on a regular basis.

Now, she opened the door to Samantha, and stood aside to let her in. "Hi, I wasn't expecting anyone so late. Did you enjoy the party?"

"Yes, yes." Samantha said distractedly, stepping into the room and fumbling a little as she took a seat by the darkened window.

This was the first time she had witnessed Samantha being drunk, and Jemma smirked a little.

"What's up?" Jemma asked, then realised she already knew, "I had been wondering whether I'd ever get to go home, and now I don't know if I want to."

"Well, it's all set. Now that the war is over, and a good king placed on the throne, our roles are over. It is time to go home. We will have an escort to Saviour's Gate in the morning, where I will open a portal to England, so I can send you home." Samantha replied quietly, her calm voice almost reluctant.

"Aren't you coming?" Jemma asked, "But why?"

Samantha shrugged helplessly, "I haven't decided yet. It's hard to explain, but I don't know where home is anymore."

Suddenly, something dawned on Jemma, "Samantha, I can't tell you what choice you make, because an individual's choices are not predestined."

She half-smiled, "I know, and I'm sorry. I tried to talk to Tobias about it but... he doesn't understand. I want to go back, but I can't imagine leaving."

The two girls sat quietly in the room. The darkness gave a sense of peace, with only flickering candles as a source of gentle light.

"My mum, she'd practically drag me out of bed every morning," Samantha broke the silence suddenly, her voice sad and a reminiscent smile touching her lips. "It was so easy to stay in bed when there was only school to get up for. My friends - Lucy, Sally, Rachel... they'll have finished high school now, I wonder what they're doing. Oh, the things we used to think important.

"Then every evening at home, crowding round the telly, waiting for my big sis to call. My baby brother, he-he'll be four years old now... By Minaeri, all the things I miss; even the arguments with my mum and stepdad. My mum had an annoying habit of throwing my shoes out into the garden if I didn't put them away..."

As Samantha calmly poured out her misery, Jemma sat listening silently. The young girl didn't want to confess how much it pained her thinking of her mum, home alone.

Samantha broke off suddenly, but she appeared much more content. She jumped up from her seat, "Sorry, I'm boring you. I only came to let you know about tomorrow." Lady Samantha stood up and moved back to the door, "I'll see you in the morning, Jemma."

Twenty-Five

It was an unusual affair the following day, many of the city's inhabitants paraded all the way to the forest edge to see off the famous Lady Samantha and the young oracle, Jemma. But many city folk still feared the forest, and it was a much reduced number that rode the overgrown path to Saviour's Gate.

It was normal for Samantha to be in the company of the Deorwines, Rian and the other Gardyn captains, and even Prince Cristan and King Lugal; but where they had gone camouflaged and soundless in the forest, they were now all dressed in the best that Enchena had to offer. They laughed and spoke freely, their noise hiding their sadness at a final parting.

Saviour's Gate was hardly a clearing, but a place where the trees thinned enough for the party to crowd into the area. Jemma looked about, wanting to save her memories – this was the place that she had first entered Enchena; where she had first met Saxton and Angrud and started the adventure of her life.

Samantha regarded the area with her own sadness. Messengers had gone out into the forest yesterday to let

266

Alina and Siabhor know that their human friend was leaving, but neither had been found, nor had they left any trace of their whereabouts. Samantha felt like a part of her was missing, knowing that the unusual friendships they had struck up were finally over.

The last farewells were drawn out, but it still ended with Samantha and Jemma clasping each other's hands and staring into a seemingly empty forest.

Jemma glanced about uncertainly, looking for the vivid swirl of purple and black of the portal she had stepped through before.

"Don't worry," Samantha explained, "It is just more discreet on this side."

She lifted her free hand to wave it slowly in mid-air, which thickened and rippled at her touch. Samantha made to step forward, but Jemma hesitated, gripping her hand tightly.

"I promise it won't hurt this time." Samantha said.

The two girls took a final look behind them, then stepped through the portal.

Samantha felt a comforting warmth wash over her and a peculiar sensation of not being alone.

"Whither to now, Lady Samantha?" A thousand voices asked in unison, *"You have refused the crown of a great mortal empire, what else can you aspire to?"*

Samantha knew who spoke to her, the immortal guardians, the divine beings.

"You have done too much to return to the life you once led. Yet your actions have proven your worth, you may join us and take Minaeri's place."

Samantha's thoughts wavered and she thought of her friends she had left behind and the world to which she had to return, a grey life in comparison that threatened to

267

consume her and shroud everything she had become. Samantha felt as though she would never feel happy again. "All I want is a mortal life where I can be myself."

The voices fell quiet and Samantha felt herself to be of solid form again.

Jemma was completely unaware of any other beings. She became one with the mists of space and time and almost instantly stepped out to find herself in a small, familiar kitchen. Samantha stood beside her, and behind them was the black and purple vortex, still maintained.

An old woman was standing before them, leaning heavily on a gnarled walking stick. She was dressed in her best and smiled at the two girls, Gran then bowed her head respectfully.

"Gran." Samantha wrapped her arms about the frail old woman, but quickly let go, embarrassed. "I'm sorry."

"Don't be sorry, Lady Samantha," Gran croaked, "I'm relieved to see you both return, relatively unharmed."

The three women stood together in silence in the kitchen, their surroundings so normal that it amplified the surreal life they had led.

"Well, it is over now." Gran was the first to speak. "To think Minaeri's retribution would come within my lifetime. At least now my family can all rest in peace."

Jemma remembered Gran's sad story, of how she had no family left, and she felt compelled to give the old woman a hug.

"Oh, don't pity me, dear." Gran hugged her back. "Now, my only wish is to see the land we have protected before my time is up, I have spent years dreaming of seeing Enchena."

"Then it shall be so." Samantha stated, "And I shall accompany you."

"But... I thought you were home now." Jemma stuttered.

Samantha glanced about the dingy kitchen with a stony look, as though loving and hating everything she saw. "It's hard to explain, Jemma." She began, "But I feel more at home in Enchena than I have ever done here. I have been gone for so long and done so much, how can I return to a normal life? To do so, I would have to shun everything I have become, because people here would not understand."

Samantha looked down at her own hands. "These hands have healed, and killed. I have brought as much destruction as hope. I have no place here, but there is still much to do in Enchena, perhaps I can help Lugal create a good and strong land. It won't be easy, and there will be many challenges along the way."

"Then I will come back with you." Jemma felt torn, she finally had a chance to return home, but how could she when Enchena called so strongly.

"I am sorry, Jemma." Samantha said quietly.

Gran looked at the flame-haired girl with understanding, "You are still part of this world, Jemma, and we are not. You must return home because you are all that your mother has, and it is not yet too late for you."

"If that's so important, I could always bring my mum. She'd... well, she'd probably hate it."

Samantha chuckled at her comment.

Gran sighed, "You and your mother have to stay here. I have transferred the deeds of the house to you two."

"You've what?" Jemma asked, trying to work out what she meant.

"Oh yes, I have negotiated a deal with the developers. After they finish the project next year, the house that sits in this plot will belong to you. You will be the new guardian of the portal."

Jemma blanched, nobody had ever done as much for her, never. "You're giving us a *house*? We won't have to rent anymore?" That meant a huge financial burden off her mother's shoulders, and the freedom to go to university when the time came…

"I think she's happy." Samantha murmured, "She's quite hard to silence. Come on, we should go, I'm not sure how long I can hold the portal open."

Jemma snapped out of her daze. "Will I see you again? Will I see Enchena again?"

"My dear, to be a lady of the Gardyn, you will always be part of Enchena." Gran said, her grey eyes crinkling.

The old woman and Samantha moved to stand beside the portal, both smiling sadly.

"Lady Jemma, I'm honoured to have known you." Samantha said with all honesty, then she and Gran stepped back through the portal.

The smoky visage faded completely and Jemma was left alone in an empty house. There was a feather-soft touch on her cheek, and she knew that it would not be the last she saw of Samantha, or Enchena.

Other books by K.S. Marsden:

Witch-Hunter:
The Shadow Rises
The Shadow Reigns
The Shadow Falls

Enchena:
The Lost Soul
The Oracle

The Northern Witch:
Winter Trials

Did you enjoy The Oracle? Why not try:

Wave Singers (Equilibria Collection #1)
By Echo Fox

At the dawn of time, the harmonious land of Pangaea was split asunder. Cracks rent the ground and the fabric of reality was torn in two. New, separate lands were created and the peoples that had once lived together found themselves alone in strange new worlds...

The only future that eighteen year old Merry Malone sees for herself is one involving music. She needs to win a music scholarship or all her dreams will come to nothing.

However, the discovery of a mysterious locket leads Merry to a faraway land, with strange customs and an even stranger people, the Mer. Music plays a magical role here and Merry finds herself warming to this alternate reality.

In an epic battle to free the Mer from their tyrant king, should Merry trust Leander, her childhood best friend or Dylan, a man of the Mer?

Winter Trials (The Northern Witch #1)
By K.S. Marsden

With Midwinter just around the corner, Mark's Nanna decides that it is time he learnt more about his family heritage. Learning witchcraft shouldn't be too difficult, right?

Balancing school, magic, and the distractions of the gorgeous new guy, should make this a very interesting winter.

273

69407189R00152

Made in the USA
Columbia, SC
21 April 2017